— PRAISE FOR —
# ELAINE FLINN
*Barry Award-Winner*
*of the*
*Molly Doyle Mysteries*

"Lively fun, laced with sharp writing and obvious knowledge, make this a series worth bidding on."

—*Chicago Tribune*

"Superior storytelling... Flinn smoothly combines details of the antiques business and the varied personalities that the trade attracts into a solidly plotted amateur-sleuth mystery."

—*Ft. Lauderdale Sun-Sentinel*

"A crackerjack mystery novel from beginning to end."

—*Carmel Pine Cone*

"The cast of characters that winds through this and the previous mysteries is among the most appealing going. The fascination emanating from the relics of yesterday shines through Flinn's style.... You'll have a fine old time. Guaranteed."

—*Maine Antiques Digest*

"Flinn knows Carmel like the back of her hand, and this familiarity allows her to create an instantly recognizable sense of place.... But what really carries the book is the strength of Molly's voice.... The plot clips along as Molly charges into danger in the search for justice. Flinn's wit and sense of story make *Deadly Collection* one of the best cozies I've read in a while."

—*ReviewingTheEvidence.com*

"As always, Flinn's sly wit, skillful plotting, and gift for character raise her work above the norm."

—*Chicago Sun-Times*

# DEADLY VINTAGE

# DEADLY VINTAGE

## *a Molly Doyle Mystery*

*Elaine Flinn*

PERSEVERANCE PRESS · JOHN DANIEL & COMPANY
PALO ALTO · MCKINLEYVILLE
2007

Copyright © 2007 by Elaine Flinn
All rights reserved
Printed in the United States of America

A PERSEVERANCE PRESS BOOK
Published by John Daniel & Company
A division of Daniel & Daniel, Publishers, Inc.
Post Office Box 2790
McKinleyville, California 95519
www.danielpublishing.com/perseverance

Distributed by SCB Distributors (800) 729-6423

Book design by Eric Larson, Studio E Books, Santa Barbara
www.studio-e-books.com

Cover painting by Cie Goulet

2 4 6 8 10 9 7 5 3 1

LIBRARY OF CONGRESS CATALOGING-IN-PUBLICATION DATA
Flinn, Elaine.
Deadly vintage : a Molly Doyle mystery / by Elaine Flinn.
p. cm.
ISBN-13: 978-1-880284-87-2 (pbk. : alk. paper)
ISBN-10: 1-880284-87-1 (pbk. : alk. paper)
1. Doyle, Molly (Fictitious character)—Fiction.
2. Antique dealers—Fiction.
3. Wineries—Fiction.
4. Carmel (Calif.)—Fiction.
I. Title.
PS3606.L565D45 2007
813'.6—dc22
2006101553

*For Donna Kalafatis,*
*a wonderful friend of forty years,*

*and for Max, my beloved Siamese cat.*

*I miss you both.*

# ACKNOWLEDGMENTS

As always, my thanks to my family for putting up with the perils of living with a writer. A special thank you to my husband, Joe, for becoming such a terrific cook. And to my daughters, Sharon and Kelly, and daughter-in-law, Karen—the real models for Molly Doyle: were I as bold and courageous! To my son, Pat, for telling his mom to keep rockin', and to my grandson, Dymund, whose wit and maturity I've borrowed for Emma.

Thank you to Meredith Phillips for welcoming Molly and me with open and generous arms. Not just an editor, but a wonderful friend, and a true lady who offers her expertise with grace, humor, and a light touch. My appreciation to John and Susan Daniel for their enthusiasm, which I hope they will not find misplaced.

To my mystery community friends—just knowing all of you has been worth the trip. A special thanks to Maili Montgomery for allowing me to use her name as a continuing character. Maili's appearance this time was brief—but that was only because she was busy elsewhere. And to my delectable lap dancing volunteers from DorothyL: Coco Ihle, P.J. Coldren, Alma Faye, and the inimitable Del Tinsley (madam extraordinaire)—thanks for offering to appear. You were stunning, ladies!

And last, but certainly not least: I am indebted to the many readers who have embraced Molly and Emma—and whose e-mails, letters, cards, and greetings at conventions and signings have made the hundreds of hours in front of the computer worth every single moment. Many, many thanks!

# DEADLY VINTAGE

# Chapter 1

MOLLY DOYLE was placing a lot of faith in the power of positive thinking as she set the CLOSED sign in the front window. She was afraid she was going to need it when Carla Jessop arrived in a half hour. When Carla had called earlier to say there were some problems, Molly'd bet it had to do with Carla's husband's objection to hiring her. Molly had hoped they would be finalizing the commission to redecorate and refurbish the wine-tasting room of Carla Jessop's family winery in Carmel Valley, but now she had her doubts. Add that to the bad day she'd had so far, and Molly was ready for Murphy's Law to rear its ugly head. She crossed her fingers that Todd Jessop wasn't coming.

The first meeting last week had been a disaster. Jessop had made it clear he was against hiring her. He'd not been subtle when he'd insinuated she was a small-town dealer hardly up to handling so large a project. With her Irish under control, Molly prepared a list of former New York clients to present to him when they'd met again at the Jessops' home the following evening. Having to hold back a smug smile when Jessop had read the list and recognized two names from the Fortune 500 hadn't been easy. His silence confirmed she'd made her point. Jessop was a newly rich dot-com dropout. Desperate to mix with the big boys, he maintained a small office and assistant to keep the illusion he was still a serious player. He should have been duly impressed.

Todd Jessop, while not a part of the family business was, Molly quickly determined, a control freak and was against his wife's vision of a Mediterranean mood in the tasting room. He was campaigning for the sleek, modern look he'd had in his Silicon Valley offices and insisted on using his former designer. But Molly knew Carla Jessop had strong will and wasn't a wilting flower. Holding that thought as hope for the future, she made a last check of the portfolio she'd prepared. The photos of several Italian and French antique tables, chairs, sideboards, and vintage wine accoutrements she'd gathered were neatly stacked. Price, measurements, provenance, and availability were noted on the back of each photo. And now, after Carla's telephone call, Molly feared all her hours of work might be ready for the wastebasket.

Her Saturday had actually started out well. For once, she had managed to open Treasures, the antiques shop she managed in Carmel, at ten and had found a group of five tourists at the door. For almost an hour they'd kept her busy answering questions and writing up sales. Molly's good fortune was brief. Sometime during the day, a lovely set of alabaster bookends, two Royal Doulton figurines, and a small brass coach-style clock had been stolen. Molly had thought of asking Emma, her young niece, to come down from their apartment upstairs to help keep an eye out, but she hadn't wanted to interrupt her homework. And with Bitsy Morgan off to Palm Springs and Molly's part-time clerk also out of town, Molly needed four sets of eyes and six pairs of hands just to stay on top of things.

The loss from the stolen merchandise was particularly annoying because it was Molly's own merch and had set her back seven hundred bucks. Not a great way to start the weekend. Max Roman, the owner of the shop, and Molly's early mentor, had encouraged her to offer her own buys. It was a generous gesture, and meant to help Molly build a nest egg. Besides, Max knew Molly's eye was unerring and anything she might add to the inventory could only enhance his stock.

Setting the portfolio aside, Molly checked her watch. She still had time to tidy up her desk and to send Max an e-mail asking for a price sheet for the two truckloads of new merchandise he'd sent from San Francisco yesterday. Moving aside the stack of today's mail, her eye fell on a postcard peeking out from between two envelopes. Molly picked it up and smiled. The photo of London's Big Ben brought back memories of buying trips to England when she and Derek

Porter, her runaway husband, were still together. Molly quickly dismissed thoughts of Derek. That chapter in her life, when her husband and his girlfriend had been caught selling fake antiques, was not a memory she wanted to relive. They were still fugitives from the law, and the day they were caught would be one of celebration. Turning the postcard over, Molly was surprised to find it blank. It was addressed to the shop on one of those computer-printed mailing labels. But the message section was blank. Strange, she thought, but then she had made that same mistake herself once or twice. On a trip, in a hurry, trying to keep promises of postcards to friends was often a pain in the neck. Setting the card aside to ponder its mysterious sender another time, Molly put the mail in the desk drawer, then headed for the small storage room off the main floor to freshen up before her meeting with Carla Jessop.

Satisfied her lipstick was on straight and her hair was neat, Molly stepped into a cloudy mist of perfume, stole another glance in the mirror, and made a mental note to add some highlights to her hair soon. She would be forty this year and was pleased to note she didn't look a day over thirty-nine. She'd been weaning herself off cigarettes and was down to four a day. But her weight was going up, and she wondered if she had the fortitude to control both of those demons at once. Now that summer was on the horizon, it was time to get back to a regime of beach walks. The twice-weekly dinners at Daria's restaurant in her private back room with the gang weren't helping her waistline either. But Daria DeMarco, whose heart was immense, insisted, and the family atmosphere for Molly and Emma was more important than a few pounds. Well, maybe ten?

Molly returned to the salesroom with a small Imari charger stacked with lemon cookies she'd bought at Tosca's, the tiny coffee bar in the courtyard behind the shop. She set the plate on a lovely Edwardian center table. She wondered if placing a pricey set of eight Stourbridge wineglasses engraved with a grape-and-vine decoration on a nearby chest was a bit too obvious. She knew she was showing off for Todd Jessop, but the need to flaunt her expertise was too compelling. What the hell, she thought. They would stay out. It would be a pleasure to shove *something* in that arrogant face. Molly cautioned herself not to get carried away with her distaste for Carla's husband. She wanted this job. And she wanted it badly. This would be her first venture into interior design, and creating another niche in the local market was her dream. Sales had been good the past few months, but as in any luxury business—and that was exactly what a first-rate antiques business was—one had to keep a cool head when dealing with the pompous *nouveau riche* such as Todd Jessop.

When Molly heard the bell over the door, she sucked in her stomach, mentally promised to mind her tongue, then turned with a smile. "Oh, it's you."

Kenneth Randall, Carmel's chief of police, gave Molly one of his lopsided grins. "Yeah. Me. Got a problem with that?"

"Don't get snarky, okay? I wasn't expecting you until later."

"So, I'm an hour early. Beat me up."

Molly laughed. "I'm sorry. I thought it was Carla Jessop."

Towering over Molly's five-foot-ten, Randall had a presence that made body builders back off. Walking like a cat, he silently headed for the table Molly had set. After careful examination, he picked up a cookie, plopped it in his mouth and chewed, then said, "I know. That's why I'm early."

Molly brushed away a crumb from the gleaming table. "Uh, care to explain that? And how did you know she was coming?"

Reaching for another cookie, he said, "Guess you forgot you told me this morning at Tosca's. Jessop was a problem last night at the banquet, remember? I want to make sure he's over it. I wasn't crazy about having to ask him to cool it, and I don't want to have to do it again." Tossing his hands in the air, he quickly added, "And don't get huffy on me, okay? I know you're a big girl and all that, but guys like Jessop are addicted to throwing their weight around."

As much as she'd wanted to, Molly hadn't forgotten Todd Jessop's outrageous antics last night at the Highlands Inn. He'd insulted just about every grower in the region at the vintner's banquet. "I'm touched. Really."

"Yeah, sure." Randall grinned, then pulled up a chair. "We've got a few minutes before they show up. Take a seat, Ms. Doyle, and let me fill you in on this guy."

Molly pulled out a small footstool. "He may not be coming with Carla. She called earlier and said there was a problem."

"He's a problem, all right! Look, Molly, I know this is a big job, but you'd better know what you're getting into."

"I've done some homework. Carla Jessop is highly regarded around here. Her family has been in the Valley for two generations. The family winery, Bello Lago, is well established."

Reaching for another cookie, Randall said, "I'm talking about the husband. He has a nasty rep. That dot-com business he ran into the ground up in San Jose lost a lot of stockholder dough, but he walked out with a big bundle. I hear her family isn't too crazy about him either. Second husband, not Italian, not local, and he knows zilch about wine."

Molly sighed. "I know. But I'm not working for him. I was sorry to see Carla take the brunt of his temper last night about market strategy. I couldn't believe he'd talk to her like that in public. And when some of the other vintners got involved, it was a miracle you managed to cool them down." Molly smiled. "I loved the way you stepped in front of Todd Jessop when he was inching toward Louis Valdotta from Château Monterey."

Randall studied another cookie. "Chalk it up to experience. Most blowhards don't like to have my big face in theirs. Anyway, I just thought I'd drop by and maybe browse around when they show up."

"If I've learned anything about you, it's not to argue with your logic. But how about maybe staying upstairs with Emma? No point in being too obvious. Seeing you here might set him off."

"That could work. But leave the door open, okay?"

"Deal. You any good at math? She's studying for a test."

"As in all that I do, I'm a genius."

Molly smiled as she watched Randall climb the stairs. She marveled again at how much difference Emma's presence had made in all their lives. It had taken only a few days after her sister Carrie dumped the bright, engaging twelve-year-old on her doorstep last year to witness Randall's seemingly gruff façade melt when Emma was around. Daria DeMarco's maternal instincts, sadly buried since children were no longer an option, revived in full bloom. Bitsy

Morgan, the doyenne of busybodies and Molly's self-appointed fairy godmother, was putty in Emma's hands. Even Dan Lucero, the district attorney, and Bevin Loomis, Randall's former Homicide partner from Los Angeles, had become doting surrogate uncles.

Thankful that Randall had agreed to make himself scarce, Molly was genuinely touched that he'd been concerned for her and had gone to the trouble to do a background check on Todd Jessop. But Molly had done her homework as well. Bitsy, a walking dictionary of local gossip, had bent her ear. But it was Daria who really knew the Mattucci family and its rise from ranchers to producers of a premier boutique winery.

Molly made a quick tour of the shop, fluffing decorative pillows with lush fringes and pinching off dead blossoms from the fresh flower arrangements on tables and chests. She reached for the small crucifix under her sweater, gave it a good-luck pat, and promised to behave if Carla's husband showed up. She also promised to keep a smile on her face. No matter what. Whether she ended up with the job or not, Emma had at least made a new friend in Carla Jessop's daughter, Michelle Giordano.

They had met at Santa Catalina, the private girl's school in Monterey, and clicked right away. Emma had been having a problem making friends when she had started there a few months ago. Both girls were string-bean skinny and taller than most girls a year older. Worse, Emma's counselor had reported she was considered too brainy to be popular. And, she'd told Molly that some of the girls resented Emma's near-perfect recall of what she read. The counselor had laughed when she'd added that their major problem, however, was they were not boy-crazy yet.

The ringing of the telephone broke into Molly's reverie. She rushed to her desk just as she saw Carla Jessop pass the display window facing Ocean Avenue. Molly waved her in, then quickly told Daria on the phone that Carla had arrived and she would talk to her at dinner. She felt like doing a happy dance when she saw Carla was alone. When Molly turned to greet her, she caught her breath when she saw the flaming welt on Carla's cheek. "Oh, my God! What happened?"

Not quite as tall as Molly and smaller-boned, Carla Jessop was almost ethereally thin. Her short blond hair flared back from a prominent widow's peak, and her eyes were the smokiest gray Molly had ever seen. Carla looked at Molly, paused briefly, then said, "Todd hit me."

"Oh, my God!" Molly sputtered again.

"You said that already."

Molly touched Carla's arm, then gently led her to the chair Randall had recently vacated. "I've got some Jack Daniel's in the storage room. I'll be right back."

"Don't bother, but thanks. Coffee is fine. I'm not ready to hit the bottle yet. I need to keep my mind clear."

Molly hesitated, then sat with her. "Look, we can do this another time. You've obviously got some issues that are more important."

"Screw Todd. My personal problems can wait. Nothing is more important now than getting the tasting room done. My father is living on borrowed time. His latest stroke was devastating. He's confined to a wheelchair now, and it's just killing him to lose his mobility. I want him to leave this world knowing I can handle the winery."

Molly poured their coffee, then said, "We can still do this later. Why don't you take the portfolio home and look it over? We can get together tomorrow night after I close."

"I've already seen most of what you've put together, Molly. I'm sold. I may not be good at picking husbands, but I know a good woman when I meet her. Todd will get his when the time is right."

Sitting with their backs to the staircase, Molly and Carla hadn't heard Randall come down. "You sound like a devoted daughter, but a foolish wife," Randall said. Standing before them, he looked at Carla's face. "That looks nasty."

Carla smiled. "Isn't, though."

"If your husband did that, I'm obliged to arrest him. Domestic violence laws are very clear these days."

Carla darted a look at Molly. "I ran into a door."

"Not very creative," Randall said. "I saw his act last night. Remember?"

Carla's laugh was grim. "Hell, that was nothing. You should have seen him this morning."

Randall's eyes tightened. "Like I said, I can have him arrested right now, and I can get you protective services. What's it going to be?"

Carla rose. "I'll call you when and if I need you."

Molly rose, too, and placed her hand on Carla's shoulder. "Maybe you should stay at the ranch tonight?"

"And let my father see my face?" Carla shook her head. "No way. He'd kill Todd."

Before Molly could say more, Todd Jessop stormed into the shop. Not much taller than Carla, he was lean and built for speed. His custom sport coat failed to hide a wiry body just aching to jump the starting gun. His longish hair, almost too black to be real, was artfully styled to allow the sides to casually rustle each time he moved his head. Molly was convinced his too-green eyes were contact lenses and would bet he was a tanning salon addict with weekly facials. Halting in front of his wife, he said, "What the hell is going on here? I thought we agreed that—"

"We agreed to nothing. I'm here to hire Molly. It's my decision, so stay out of it."

Molly held her breath. She decided the best thing to do was keep her trap shut. Her instincts were on the mark. Todd Jessop exploded. "Goddammit, Carla!" He grabbed his wife's arm. "I don't want her! I told you that!"

"That's about it, pal," Randall cautioned. "Let her go."

"Stay out of this," Jessop shot back as he shoved Carla away. "I'm talking to my wife."

Molly gestured to Carla to step back. Jessop was out of his mind in taking Randall on, and she wasn't surprised when Randall said, "I'm gonna say this just once, so listen up. Back off, or I'll be forced to arrest you."

"For what? Yelling at my wife? Since when is that a crime?"

"You're manhandling her. You just bodily forced her against her will. That's a misdemeanor. Will that do?"

"That's bullshit," Jessop snarled.

"Where have you been lately? It's the law."

"Screw you," Jessop said. "You can't make that stick. I barely touched her."

Randall's laugh was hardly audible. "I have a low tolerance for men who get tough with women. Don't push me too far. You might not see daylight tomorrow."

While Molly had discovered Todd Jessop to be aggressive and arrogant, she didn't think he was foolhardy enough to push Randall much further. As she moved out of the line of fire towards Carla, she saw that two women had entered the shop and were standing near the door. *Damn it!* That was all they needed, an audience. She hadn't heard the bell over the door, and realized Carla must have left the door open when she arrived. No wonder her husband managed to surprise them. She had little doubt the women heard the angry exchange between Randall and Jessop. Molly quickly moved to them and said, "I'm so sorry, but we're closed."

One of the women asked, "Is there a problem? I see our chief is here and he's not smiling."

Molly forced a laugh. "Everything is just dandy. You must have misunderstood. We're just about to leave for dinner. Would you mind coming back tomorrow?"

The woman who had been doing the talking looked at her friend, then shrugged. "Sure. I'm looking for ruby glass. Do you have any?"

"Not at the moment," Molly replied. "But I know a collector in Nashville who has a large collection and is downsizing." Gently herding them closer to the door, she added, "Stop by tomorrow, and I'll give her a call."

"I'm not paying for a long-distance call."

Anxious to get them out of the way, Molly said, "Of course not. I wouldn't think of it."

"Well, sure she wouldn't," the second woman said to her friend. "She's gonna make money on the deal, so what's a telephone call?"

It was hard, but Molly gave them both a smile. Anything to get them out. Closing the door behind them, she turned the deadbolt and prayed they hadn't heard too much. When she returned, she saw Randall casually leaning against the staircase staring at Jessop, who stood defiantly with his arms crossed. Carla was at Molly's desk. The portfolio Molly had spent hours preparing was in her hands. "Is this what you put together for me?" Carla asked.

With both men dangerously silent, Molly merely nodded. Her faith in Randall's ability to handle almost any situation gave her some relief, but she was still worried Jessop wasn't going to leave quietly. "Maybe you'd like to take it home. Look, I'm here anytime, okay?"

Todd Jessop turned and stared at Molly. Those green eyes that Molly swore were not his true color seemed to shoot right through her. It was all she could do not to shudder. Without a word, he gave his wife an even more withering look, then left.

Molly waited until he was out the door. "I mean that, Carla. Day or night…just call me."

Carla Jessop lifted her chin defiantly. "Thanks, Molly. But don't worry. He won't get away with this. I'm Italian, remember?"

# *Chapter 2*

THEIR SHORT WALK to Daria's for dinner was unusually subdued. Molly was lost in her own sense of déjà vu. The bruise on Carla's face brought back memories of her own nasty tussle when her marriage ended. Her bruises and fractured ribs had healed quickly, but the memories lingered on. Randall, too, was unusually quiet. Thankfully, Emma didn't seem to notice and chattered about school.

By the time they reached the restaurant and headed for the private back room, Molly had managed to shake off her melancholy. Daria DeMarco was setting the table as they entered, and when her warm smile did little to chase away the expression on Randall's tightly set face, she said, "Okay, what's the problem? Too many cats up in trees today? No, that was yesterday, right? Maybe an unruly tourist?"

Randall took off his sport coat and blew Daria a kiss. "Cute, Ms. DeMarco. Very cute."

Molly shook her head. "Todd Jessop showed up. That tell you something?"

"I think Mrs. Jessop should just divorce that macho jerk. Michelle wouldn't mind at all," Emma said.

Shocked, Molly said, "Emma! What made you even say that?"

"I heard everything. I was at the top of the stairs. Anyway, it's true. He's mean and talks terrible to Mrs. Jessop all the time. Michelle told me he's a bully, too."

Molly sighed. "I don't want you to tell Michelle what happened, Emma. I'm sorry you heard it, but it's best not to worry her, okay?" Molly gave Randall a look. "Right?"

"Right. Just between us, okay, Emma?"

"You should have arrested him," Emma said.

Daria set down the last dish with a bang. "What the hell happened?"

Randall ignored her and told Emma, "It was Mrs. Jessop's call."

"But I heard you tell him he was manhandling her!"

"A figure of speech. He got the message. That's what's important."

"Will someone please tell me what happened?" Daria asked.

Molly jerked her head towards the door. "Can I help you bring dinner in?"

Daria nodded. "Good idea."

Molly filled Daria in as they picked up two trays with salads and French bread. "That Todd Jessop is a real piece of work," Daria said. "I don't know why Carla is still with him."

Back inside the room, Molly helped Daria set out the food, then said, "I just realized you only set four places. Where's Dan tonight? And Loomis?"

"Loomis," Randall said, "is in San Jose meeting up with an old fishing buddy. He'll be back later in the week. Our intrepid district attorney, Daniel Lucero, is in Sacramento hobnobbing with his political buddies to drum up support for a few new laws."

"It's like part of the family is missing," Emma said. "Maybe sometime I could ask Michelle to join us? She told me that you and her mother used to be school friends."

Daria grinned. "That was centuries ago. Carla and I were laughing about old times last week when she came in for lunch. You can ask Michelle anytime."

Halfway through her salad, Emma said, "Michelle told me her real father died in a helicopter accident and her grandfather can't stand her mother's new husband."

Molly almost choked on a tomato. "You shouldn't be repeating things like that."

"Well it's true. I mean, Michelle told me it was. And she said her grandfather on her father's side blames her grandfather on her mother's side for it, and that it wasn't an accident, and—"

"Whoa. Stop right there," Molly said.

Randall looked at Daria. "What's all this? Something here I should know?"

Daria passed the bottle of wine to him, then waved him off. "Gossip. That's all it is. Typical Italian male gossip. Testino Giordano has been blaming Domenico Mattucci, Carla's father, for years. The old man sees conspiracies in every corner. You'd never know he's second generation. He acts like he's back in the old country with *vendetta* a daily slice of life." Passing the platter of eggplant parmigiana, she added, "Since you're a half-breed, you know the type."

Randall grinned. He always got a kick out of Daria referring to his half-Italian heritage that way. "Seriously, what are the accusations and why?"

Molly was all ears. It was bad enough to have to be around Todd Jessop, but now to hear there might be a real-life family feud going on was more than she'd bargained for. "Uh, maybe I should forget doing the tasting room?" she joked.

"Don't worry, Molly," Daria said. "Testino Giordano wouldn't step on Mattucci land for all the grapes in the world. But then, that's what started the feud. Well, mostly, anyway. It was all hugs and kisses in the beginning when Carla and Tony Giordano got married. With a joining of two of the biggest ranches in Monterey County, a dynasty was in the works. But then, after ten years or so, Tony got—" Daria paused when she saw Emma was all ears and wide-eyed behind her Harry Potter glasses. They'd all become accustomed to Emma's seeming maturity. Sometimes they forgot her true age and that some topics of conversation needed to be edited. "Uh, when Tony got adventurous, things started to unravel."

"Adventurous? Did he go on dangerous hunting trips, or something?" Emma asked.

Randall covered a grin. "Yeah, that's probably what Daria means."

"The veal is delicious, Daria," Molly said.

Emma laughed. "Okay, I get it. Change the subject. The kid's in the room."

Molly gave Daria a warning look and said, "I've got a lead on a few antique corkscrews for Carla, but now I'm wondering if maybe I should just forget them and the whole thing." She reached for her wine and sighed. "I'd really love to do this job, but if it's going to be a daily diet of butting heads with Todd Jessop, I'd just as soon bow out now."

"We don't really need the job, do we, Aunt Molly? The shop is doing great now and with Bitsy paying my school tuition, we can get by okay, can't we?"

"We're fine, honey. It's just that doing the tasting room could help me start branching out."

"I don't think Jessop is going to give you much heat after tonight," Randall said. "Let's not forget that he doesn't have any stake in Bello Lago. It's her family operation, not his."

"Yeah? Tell *him* that," Daria said. "Reggie Sullivan, Bello Lago's marketing director, and Dino Horne, their master winemaker, were here for lunch last week and they gave me an earful. Todd is wreaking havoc all over the place. Dino is ready to punch him out next time he interferes with his crew. And Reggie said Todd's badgering him to back his ideas of redesigning the bottle labels. He wants them to ditch the established style of elegant script and romantic vineyards-under-the-Tuscan-sun thing and switch to the new trend of offbeat labels with scantily dressed women and abstract animals. He thinks it will attract a younger crowd of buyers."

Helping himself to a large serving of *pasta con pesto*, Randall said, "Sounds like he wants to attract the football-and-beer crowd with those ideas."

"Reggie also told me Jessop was snubbed by the Napa–Sonoma clique and is determined to show them up with his cutting-edge expertise," Daria added.

"Well, that sure goes along with the stark, minimalist look he wants for the tasting room," Molly said. "That may be cool for computers but not for wine. But why does he get away with all this? Because he's family?"

Daria shook her head. "No. And he's hardly considered a member in good standing. Carla's father, Domenico, was furious when she married him. The bad blood there is explosive."

"What happened up north?" Randall asked.

"He tried to buy his way into one of the wineries up there. Lost out on a bid to take over the DeFalco vineyards. Word is, three or four of the St. Helena guys formed a syndicate and outbid him."

"Why?" Molly asked. "I mean, why should they care?"

"He's an ass, that's why," Daria said. "Besides being an arrogant jerk, he's a bigot to boot. When you tell people that California wines are made by men who are two steps away from being illiterate peasants, it doesn't take a rocket scientist to know his mindset."

Molly wondered how on earth Carla Jessop could stand the man. Passing the grated cheese to Emma, Molly was startled to hear her cell phone ring. She reached into her large tote under the table and finally fished it out after the fourth ring.

"Molly? Todd Jessop here. I, ah, owe you an apology. I was out of line. You've really done a super job. I hope there's no hard feelings. Your portfolio looks great, and I won't butt in again."

Molly's eyebrows shot up. She waved her hand for quiet, and said, "That's very gracious of you, Todd. Apology accepted. No hard feelings. That's wonderful. I'm glad you've decided to go along with Carla's plans."

"I'd like to make amends," Todd said, "and I need your help. I assume you're familiar with Blue Moon Auction house in Maine?"

"Yes. In fact, I have their new catalog. Isn't the next auction in a few days?"

"It's Monday, and that's another reason for my call. I'm going to be out of town and I'd like you to bid on a few items for me. Well, not for me. For Carla. It's a surprise. I think they would work with the look you two are after. I realize this is last-minute, and I could do the bidding myself, but I'm afraid I might get carried away."

Still in semi-shock from Jessop's apology, Molly said, "I'd be happy to help, but I'm out for dinner now. Can I call you when I get home?"

"Perfect. Don't worry about the time. I'll be up late."

Molly closed her cell and set it on the table. "I need more wine after that."

Randall filled Molly's glass. He winked at Emma. "Okay, *share*. Isn't that the operative word these days?"

"You're goofy sometimes, Chief," Emma said laughing. "*Dish* is more *au courant.*"

Molly relayed the content of Todd Jessop's call, then said, "I don't know what he has in mind until I call him, but I'm not sure this is a good idea. I'm not crazy about blind bidding on merch I haven't examined. Photographs hide too many secrets. With furniture, you can't see patina fading, heat blisters, repairs, evidence of infestation, or if the piece is a 'marriage.' Or simply a damn good reproduction." Molly took a sip of her wine, then added, "And not to forget, a total refinish job, which makes a piece worth much, much less."

"Sounds like a 'Let's make up, I'm sorry I smacked you' gift, " Randall said.

"Expensive way to say 'I'm sorry.' Blue Moon offers only high-priced stuff. Unique items not easily found, and mostly imported from Europe. Thus, the name: 'We only offer items you'll find once in a blue moon.' "

"Catchy name. Never heard of them," Randall said.

"They're fairly new and competing with Red Baron in Atlanta," Molly explained.

"Oh, I love Red Baron's catalogues," Emma said. "Really cool stuff." She threw her arms wide. "Huge stained glass windows from old churches and big tiered fountains you'd find at a palace. They even have bronze doors and fancy showcases from old jewelry stores." Giving Randall a mischievous glance, she added, "They have trains sometimes, too."

"I've got all the trains I need, thank you," Randall said.

"Boys never have enough of their toys," Daria said with a laugh as she began clearing the table.

Randall watched Molly help Daria, then asked, "So, what are you going to do?"

"Call him, as I promised. A lot is going to depend on what he's interested in. I'm going to make it clear, though, that I can't guarantee condition. If I'm lucky, I might not be able to sign up as a telephone bidder this late."

Daria winked. "Ah, luck. Don't count on it."

# Chapter 3

MOLLY FINALLY got Emma off to bed after she promised to let her have first look at the Blue Moon catalog. "Okay. Enough drooling. This stuff is too rich for us. We don't have the clientele who'd want this kind of merch, or the money."

Emma sighed. "Too bad. They really have some sweet stuff."

"Sweet?" Molly laughed as she hugged her. "Is that another new *in* word these days?"

"Michelle and I are trying to stay on top of the lingo. Some of it is pretty stupid, but it's an occupational hazard of being a pre-teen."

Molly moved down the steps to the shop at a snail's pace. It had been a long day, and she was beginning to feel a fair measure of fatigue. Weekends in Carmel were always busy. Tourists poured in like salt spilling from a broken container. Minding the shop alone on a Saturday during tourist season was challenge enough. Add to that the thefts, and then the scene with the Jessops. Molly wasn't in the mood to pore over an auction catalog that would most likely prove to be a waste of time.

Turning on the desk lamp, she spent the next fifteen minutes looking for possible pieces that would work in the tasting room. She shook her head in dismay. The man must be nuts, or wealthier than she'd thought. The low estimates on most of the lots were way past a "make-up gift." But, she thought, what price guilt?

Only three pieces seemed plausible for the tasting room. One was a good-sized pub-style bar and the other two were tall, Country French–style, matching display cabinets. If these were the lots Jessop was interested in, and if by some miracle they took them for mid-estimate, they were talking about thirty-four grand, not counting the buyer's premium of fifteen percent. Molly was surprised the fifteen percent the auction house tacked on as their fee was so low. Most auction houses now were charging up to twenty-percent premiums on each lot sold. Well, there was only one way to find out, and that was to make the call. Jessop picked up on the second ring.

"Are you thinking about the pub-style bar and the two French cabinets?" Molly asked.

"Ah, you are good. I underestimated you, didn't I?" Jessop laughed. When Molly didn't reply, he quickly said, "I won't make that mistake again. Okay, got a pencil ready? Here are my bids."

"Wait," Molly said. Hoping to sound gracious, but not rolling over, she put a lilt in her voice. "Let's just see if I deserve the compliment. You'll go mid-estimate, right? The pub is listed at fifteen to twenty-five thousand. The display cabinets are being sold individually, and at six to eight thousand each."

Jessop's laugh was so loud, Molly had to pull the phone away from her ear. "Give the lady the brass ring. Right again. Think we've got a chance?"

"Auctions are a crapshoot, Todd. Depends on the crowd, depends on the desire. I'll do the best I can. Are we firm on your bids, or do you want to add a little wiggle room?"

"No. Stick to the middle."

"Okay. Just one thing. I have no idea what condition these pieces are in. Photos can hide a million sins. I'm not even sure of the age on any of the pieces, or if the pub is a marriage."

"Marriage?" Todd asked. "What the hell is that?"

"Sorry. That means two different pieces of furniture have been joined as one. Say, for instance, a footed base belonging to an Edwardian chest added to a Regency chest whose base was either damaged or missing. Different periods, but the wood is the same, so it's hard to tell unless you can physically examine the piece. The other problem with furniture is the risk of infestation, heat blisters a photo won't show, repairs, and replaced hardware. What I'm saying is, without seeing them in person, I wouldn't put too much stock in what the catalog says. Not that the auction house would knowingly misrepresent anything; it's just that mistakes can happen. As long as you're willing to take the chance, I'll bid for you. Something else you need to know: My standard fee for client bidding at auction is five percent of the total hammer prices."

"I'll take those chances, and your fee is fair," he said.

Molly wished she had thought to record the conversation just in case, but it was too late to worry about that now. "Okay. I'll fax our intentions right away. I've never dealt with this house, so I don't know if we're too late to get into the phone bidding queue. Keep in mind there will be a fifteen percent buyer's premium on the hammer price, and then the shipping costs as well."

"I understand. I've got out-of-town meetings most of Monday, so I won't be able to get back to you until later in the day. Hope you'll have good news for me."

"Oh, wait. You've got to contact the auction house and set up payment information. They'll want a credit card, or a bank letter if you plan to use a personal check. Also that you're authorizing me to bid on your behalf. They can suggest a shipper as well."

"No problem. I'll have my assistant handle all that first thing Monday morning."

Molly laughed. "I don't think she'd like getting up before dawn. It would be better if you faxed them your information tonight."

When Jessop didn't answer, Molly said, "Todd? You still there?"

"Yes, yes…I was making a note to myself. I'll take care of it."

Molly hung up, rubbed her eyes, and wondered if she was out of her mind. Bidding blind was for idiots, and no matter what Jessop agreed to, she had a bad feeling about this. But then, what could really go wrong? The chances of them taking even one of the lots was remote. The three lots he wanted were up early in the sale. That meant she'd have to be ready by five A.M. on Monday. She turned on the computer, pulled up a fax form, introduced herself and the client on whose behalf she would be bidding, listed the lot items and the rest of the pertinent information, then sent the puppy off.

Tempted to crawl up the stairs, Molly took each step slowly. She thought about the pieces Jessop wanted. The pub was too English-looking and way too big. With a mid-estimate of twenty thousand, it would be a waste of money and look like a stepchild. Or worse, something they'd grabbed out of desperation that reeked of bad taste. She paused on the last step. That could kill her reputation in an instant. Besides, the shipping costs for the twelve-foot enclosed setup would be enormous. She could always back out of the bidding on the pub before it reached mid-estimate. Jessop wouldn't know. Worst case scenario, if he decided to follow the auction on-line, she could always claim a misunderstanding. But then, would he even do that?

And the low estimate of six thousand each for the cabinets was just as crazy. But then, Molly reminded herself, newly rich tycoons, at least those she'd had as clients, frequently assumed that if something cost a bundle, it had to be quality. As Max Roman often said, "You gotta hurt them, or they won't think it's worth having."

Molly awoke the next morning to the sound of rain pounding against the French doors. It was the first of June, but Carmel's weather paid little heed to the calendar. Rain, fog, and overcast skies were normal companions until August, when summer finally arrived. And then it was glorious until early October. Molly pitied the tourists who arrived in shorts in July. Sunny California was a myth. The state had so many different micro-climates, it was almost impossible to standardize a season.

She opened her eyes and looked at the clock on the night table. It was six A.M. She had another hour before her alarm was to go off. It was tempting to just snuggle deeper into the down comforter and to close her eyes, but once awake, she was done for. At the foot of the bed, two of Tiger's offspring, Killer and Toastie, were cuddled together. She nudged them with her toe and smiled as they unwound themselves, gave her annoyed looks, then promptly closed their eyes and ignored her. Molly was still trying to adjust to having three cats in her life. But she hadn't the heart to deny Emma's plea to keep two kittens from Tiger's litter. Randall and Daria had taken the other two, and now it seemed they were all bound by even more than a close friendship.

In the small kitchen off the living room, Molly pulled a package of croissants from the freezer, turned on the oven, set them inside, then hit the start button on the coffeemaker. After talking to Todd Jessop last night, she'd noticed several pages had arrived on the fax. The price sheets she'd been waiting for from Max for the new merch he'd sent down from the City had finally arrived. If the rain kept shop traffic low today, she might be able to get some of the new smalls tagged and onto the floor. And if Emma had finished her homework, she could help out for an hour or two. The new shipments were in the garage, and it would be impossible to be in two places at once.

Emma was itching to get into the boxes of smalls. Molly smiled. What a natural Emma had become. She'd taken to the antiques trade almost immediately. Her gift for near-instant recall had produced a walking encyclopedia. Not complete yet, naturally, but with enough knowledge to keep Molly on her toes. Emma would need years of hands-on experience, but she was acquiring enough lingo, facts, and trivia to sit down and talk the talk with seasoned dealers. Give her a few more years, and she could hold her own with the best.

Molly set a new record for opening on time. Today marked the sixth day in a row she'd unlocked the door to Treasures exactly at ten A.M. sharp. She was filled with a sense of power and euphoria. Emma applauded from the stairs. "Don't forget to call Mrs. Jessop," she said. Molly waved a salute, opened the door with a flourish, and filled her lungs once again with the sweet scent of rain-washed air. She'd kept the window of the El Camino pickup truck open all the way to the Carmel Mission for Mass earlier until Emma begged her to roll it up.

"There's just something about the air here after it rains," Molly said.

Emma pretended to shiver. "Maybe it's the zillions of pine trees? I don't really care. I just want to live here forever."

Molly thought about Emma's comment as she turned on the small CD player in the storage room and searched for the pine-scented air freshener. "Out of the mouths of babes" came immediately to mind. Could it only be three years, she wondered, since she'd left New York in shame and brokenhearted? So much had happened since then, it fairly made her head spin just to think about it. Was it simply fate that had plopped her into three murder investigations in a village that hadn't experienced a homicide in years? And what were the odds of her estranged sister showing up after so many years, and with a niece she didn't know existed? If this was her karma, then she was at least thankful for the good fortune to meet so many wonderful people who now made her life so full. Emma was right, she mused. She just wanted to live here forever, too.

At her desk, she called Carla Jessop to ask if she still wanted to meet this evening. When the recorder came on, Molly left a message. As she hung up, Randall walked in. "I'm going over to Tosca's. You want me to bring you back something?" he asked.

"No. I had croissants earlier. But thanks. I didn't see you at Mass this morning."

"Had a law enforcement meeting in Salinas. I stopped at St. Joseph's in Spreckels on my way back." Randall leaned against the door frame and grinned. "You keeping tabs on me now?"

"In your dreams. Emma was looking for you. She's having trouble with her new cell phone. Something about texting. That's what she called it. She thought you could help her figure it out."

"What a way to bruise an ego. Here I thought maybe you'd missed me."

Molly pulled out a box of sales tags from her desk, then laughed. "I think of you constantly. Feel better now?"

"Yeah. I'm buoyed with happiness. Okay, tell the squirt I'll stop back after I've had my espresso fix."

"I'll come with you," Emma said, as she skipped down the stairs. She waved her cell phone in the air. "This dumb thing is goofing up again. Michelle and I were in the middle of an important conversation and it went nuts on me." Linking her arm with Randall's, she said to Molly, "Michelle said to tell you that her mother will stop by after lunch."

"Great. I tried to get her a few minutes ago. Homework done?"

"Yep. I'll be able to help you mark the new merch now. Okay if I go with the chief first?"

"Be my guest. He seems to need attention today."

Molly stepped outside for a moment. Carmel's streets were un-usually quiet for Sunday. The typically crowded sidewalks were actually passable, and traffic seemed light. No doubt once the sky had cleared earlier, the crisp air had lured the tourists down to Carmel Beach. She could imagine the grumbling going on in many of the shops. She couldn't blame the tourists, though. It was a glorious day, and she, too, would prefer to be strolling on those pristine white sands than stuck in a shop. If she didn't have to do the telephone bidding for Todd Jessop tomorrow morning, she and Emma could get back to their morning walk routine. For sure, they would begin on Tuesday.

Molly checked the fax machine to see if Blue Moon had sent confirmation of her intent to bid. The tray was empty. No doubt the auction office was busy and would get back to her sometime today. Auction houses worked around the clock, including weekends, when they had an auction on the horizon. Molly just hoped Todd Jessop didn't forget to forward the payment information. And, she quickly thought, she'd better hide the catalog. She didn't want Carla to see it. She might eyeball the same lots and ask Molly to bid for her. That marriage was volatile enough. She sure as hell didn't want to add fuel to the fire.

# Chapter 4

BUSINESS THAT DAY, as Molly expected, was slow. By two in the afternoon, she'd only made two sales: a small brass Art Deco letter holder and a pricey ivory Mah Jongg set in a handsome walnut case with brass fittings. She knew Emma would be disappointed to see the set gone. Loomis was teaching her to play, but business was business, and the customer who'd bought the set hadn't tried to haggle on the price of six hundred dollars. Considering the tiles were ivory, and not one was missing, her price was fair. She'd made her profit. It was time to move on.

Molly checked her watch. It was way past lunch time. She wondered if Carla Jessop was going to show up. Scooting into the storage room, she opened the door to the garage. She'd only discovered the door last month. It had been covered by storage shelves and hadn't been used for years. When Max had exterminators spray the building for ants, they had found it. It certainly made moving stored merch into the shop much easier. "How's the tagging coming, Number One Assistant?"

Seated at a card table, Emma was using her newly created "posh script" to transfer data from Max's list to their fancy new parchment sales tags. "Almost done, Honorable Slave Driver. Randall thinks you should pay me more now that my elegant writing is making Treasures tags look so toney. He said ten bucks a week was a pittance for my artistry."

Molly laughed. "Randall is a troublemaker. Stay clear of him. Ten bucks a week is pretty good for someone your age."

"Hey, I'll be thirteen in a few months."

Molly heard the bell over the door. "I'll take it under consideration. Got a customer coming in."

Molly was relieved to see it was Carla Jessop. Even though Todd wanted her to bid for him, she nevertheless worried that something could go wrong, and she'd lose this great opportunity. Waving her over to a handsome camel-back sofa, she said, "Have a seat. I'll get coffee."

"I'm fine, Molly. I just had a huge lunch with my father." Holding Molly's portfolio up, she said, "This is fantastic! I love the pieces you selected, and I'm fine with the prices. I can't wait to get started. How soon can we get delivery?"

"The two Brittany chests and the walnut display case are at Max's shop in the City, so anytime this week is good. The fireplace surround is out in Carmel Valley, and the refectory table is in Santa Barbara. I think by the end of next week we'll have our set pieces ready to place."

"Fantastic. We can work around the painters you suggested. I'll let them know they need to get started right away with the colors you chose. Write me up a bill, and I'll give you a check. By the way, my father loves the renderings you did. He wants me to take you to one of the caves, too."

Molly almost fell off the sofa. "Caves? Uh, what caves?"

Carla laughed. "The wine caves. We have two huge caverns where we age wine. I can see I'm going to have to give you a lesson in winemaking. But don't worry, he only wants you to see some old pottery his mother bought years ago in Italy. We might be able to use it for display."

Molly's hands began to sweat. Quick with the mouth, fearless when accosted, a she-cat if threatened, she nonetheless had a deadly fear of bridges, tall buildings, and anything underground. She would walk a mile out of her way, and often did, to avoid parking garages that plumbed the depths. "I'm flattered, and I'd love to meet your father, but maybe we could work with pictures? I'm…well, I got locked in a basement when I was a kid," Molly said. "It's never left me. I'm not crazy about tunnels either. Caves would qualify, too."

Carla paused for a moment, then looked away. "It's small boats with me. My brother was drowned trying to save someone. We were on my uncle's fishing boat." Rising quickly, she said, "Look, I've got to go. But my father still wants to meet you. Why don't you and Emma come out to the ranch for dinner tomorrow night? It's not far from the winery."

"We'd love it. I'll close early. Is seven too late?"

Carla hugged Molly. "Seven is perfect. And Molly? I'm so glad we'll be working together. Daria was right. I like you a lot."

"Same here," Molly said. "And don't forget—any time you need me, okay? I've been there and I know what it's like."

"Your number is in my cell's memory. And thank you. Now, let me get out of your hair so you can sell some merch." Carla laughed again. "I love that word!"

Molly took the portfolio to her desk after Carla left and let out a big sigh. If she managed to take the two display cabinets in tomorrow's auction, three might be a problem. But then, she thought, the tasting room was huge. She'd make it work, one way or the other. On her way back to the garage, Molly couldn't wait to see the look on Emma's face when she told her they had the job. "Hey, slave!" she joked. "Mrs. Jessop just left. You've got your raise. We're doing Bello Lago!"

On the floor, with boxes and bubble wrap surrounding her, Emma looked up and punched her fist in the air. "Way to go! So now I'm at twenty bucks a week?"

Molly sometimes wondered what life without Emma would be like. The daily joy of having her around was more than she'd expected. And she was close to being her right hand in the shop. "Well, I was thinking about maybe twenty-five? But some has to go into savings, okay?"

"You're a hard one to bargain with, but I'll take it."

"How are you coming along?"

"I've got all the smalls tagged, but I think you'd better do the provenance stuff on the furniture. I'm not sure about some of the chairs, and Max's descriptions seem a little iffy." Emma got to her feet. "I'm going to take a break and run over to Bruno's. We're out of Café Français and cat food. Do you want anything?"

Molly pretended to think. "Well, maybe a few brownies?"

Emma laughed. "We could use a few."

While Molly handed Emma money for the grocery store, a man walked in. Molly smiled. "Hello. Welcome to Treasures. If I can be of help, just let me know."

Very tall, lean, and dressed in golf clothes, the man appeared to be in his early sixties. There was an affluent air about him: the sauna-and-manicure type of an upper-echelon executive. His voice was deep but not aggressive. "That's a refreshing welcome. I hate it when shopkeepers rush up and then hover."

Molly smiled again. "I hate it, too. That's why I leave people alone."

When Emma left, Molly sat at her desk and pulled out the Blue Moon auction catalog. She'd already decided to ease out of the pub-style bar. It was ungainly and far too expensive. The two display cabinets wouldn't be a problem after all, and she knew exactly where she would place them now. That was, if they were lucky and managed to snare them. The fax from Blue Moon had finally arrived, and she'd been able to get on the telephone bidding list just under the wire. The lots she'd listed would be coming up between eight and nine o'clock Eastern time. That meant she had to be up and lucid and by the phone by at least four-thirty. Molly pulled out her drawings of the tasting room and began to mentally place the auction additions just in case.

She'd paid little attention to the man wandering in the shop, and for some reason, didn't consider him a serious customer. When he approached her desk with a large silverplate water pitcher and asked about it, she said, "You must not be a hotel-silver collector." Taking the pitcher, she turned it around and pointed out the engraving. "The engraving is faint, but this came from the old Hotel Del Monte in Monterey."

"Is that so? I had no idea. It just caught my fancy. Isn't that the hotel Charles Crocker built?" Taking it back, he examined it again. "It's in remarkable condition considering its age. That hotel burned down before the turn of the century, didn't it?" He smiled then. "You seem surprised I know that. I try to learn all I can about places I visit."

"I am surprised. Most visitors tend to ask about where they

might spot Clint Eastwood. If I remember correctly, the hotel was rebuilt and then partly burned down again some years later. The Navy bought it during World War Two and it's been the Naval Postgraduate School ever since."

"Well, being an old Navy man, I guess I should buy this." He handed Molly the pitcher, then pulled out his wallet and set three one-hundred-dollar bills on her desk. "I hope you're not adverse to cash. I don't use credit cards."

Considering his bearing and appearance, Molly wasn't surprised he didn't try to haggle. Men of his age and demeanor seemed to think it beneath them. It was as if bargaining diminished their aura. Molly smiled. "Cash is always good." She wrote up the sales slip, handed him his change, then wrapped the pitcher in tissue and placed it in one of the new bags Max had sent down. A soft gray with deep blue lettering, it was as handsome as much of the merch it carried out of the shop.

Taking the bag, he nodded his thanks and headed towards the door. He stopped, then turned back. "I like that ship model you have on the desk by the fireplace. I'll have to think about it. Do you arrange transport?"

"It's not an antique. But it was built by a high-quality craftsman, at mid-century. Shipping wouldn't be a problem. Where are you from?"

He paused, then said, "Vancouver."

"I've never been there, but I understand it's a lovely city. Are you here for the golf?"

"Personal business." He reached for the door, then stopped again. "I just noticed the bookends in the window. Plato and Socrates?"

"You have an excellent eye."

"I try to stay on top of things." He opened the door, then grinned. "Keeps one young. Your daughter, in fact, reminded me of Harry Potter. That short, dark hair and those glasses caught my eye when I saw her leave."

"Emma is my niece. How astute of you to notice. Harry is one of her favorites."

He touched his forehead with his finger in a small salute. "Well, she's certainly chosen a fine hero. I'll think about the ship."

Molly watched him leave and wondered if he'd really be back for the ship. Somehow he didn't seem a mariner type. But then, what *was* a mariner type? She'd sold ship models to women and fancy dinner services to men. Collectors came in all shapes and sizes. Molly had learned a long time ago that trying to figure out what a person's particular obsession might be was a wasted use of brain power.

The remainder of the day was slow: three walk-ins who seemed bored, and two women who'd admitted they only wanted to poke around. Molly itched for the moment she could put the CLOSED sign in the front window. She made arrangements for Carla's pieces to be shipped, wrote up the invoice for her, then kept busy updating the shop's website with new photos of merch, had a coffee and brownie with Emma in the storage room, and sent an e-mail to Cleo Jones, her close friend who worked at Sotheby's in London.

After a quick dinner with Emma of waffles, their favorite Sunday menu, they watched *Sixty Minutes*, then Molly said, "I'm off to bed. I've set the alarm for four. I'll try not to wake you."

"That early?"

"The auction house is in Maine, remember? And this one starts at eight. The lots Mr. Jessop wants are in the first hour, so I've got to be up and filled with caffeine. Telephone bidding is a nerve-wracking adventure, and I'll need all my wits about me. Offers fly fast and furious, and not just from the floor or other telephone bidders. We've got on-line bidding to contend with as well."

"Can I get up with you? I've never watched you telephone bid."

"Not this time. You've got two tests tomorrow. You need to be bright-eyed. By the time you're ready to leave for school, it will be all over except for the shouting."

Emma laughed. "Think you'll be shouting?"

Molly shook her head. "I doubt it."

# Chapter 5

THE NEXT MORNING, a bleary-eyed Molly threw on her sweats. She set a jumbo mug of half regular coffee and half instant espresso on the desk downstairs, then picked up the phone and called Blue Moon. She counted ten rings before her call was answered. She was positive it was a message from on high when she was told her bidding request had been cancelled. Todd Jessop had not forwarded payment information and they could not allow her to bid without the guarantee. She'd barely had a chance to speak when she was put on hold for a moment.

"Molly Doyle? As in Elizabeth Porter? That you?"

Molly's voice was hesitant. There were few people who could connect Elizabeth Porter to Molly Doyle. After fleeing from New York and the notoriety of her husband's antiques fraud, she had reverted to her father's pet name of Molly, and her family name of Doyle. "Yes, that's me. Who is this?"

"Terry Jorgenson. A voice from your past." She heard a deep chuckle. "I worked with you and Cleo at Sotheby's on that deaccessioned art from the Met some years ago. Hey, I read all about you in the *Times*. Even saw you on CNN last year. Way to go, gal!"

Molly sucked in her breath. Every time someone mentioned her homicide involvements, she felt an ache in her chest. She quickly put an upbeat lilt in her voice. "Terry! Of course! How are you?"

"Hey, I'm good. Been with Blue Moon a couple of years now. I was handed a note about your problem and when I saw your name on it, I just had to say hello. So what's up with your client? He forget, or something?"

"He's out of town and was supposed to fax you his information."

"Look, I can get you back in the queue, but I've got to have some proof of accountability. I'm not supposed to do this normally, but since it's you, I can take your credit card info and work the sale that way. How's that sound?"

Molly's eye began to twitch. She didn't relish the idea of adding thousands of dollars on her American Express card. What she would relish was wringing Todd Jessop's neck. There was nothing more gauche than a dealer backing out of a high-ticket auction. It screamed of being an incompetent, or worse, having cold feet. Playing the game was not for the faint of heart, and Molly Doyle could snap out bids and hold her own with the best. But this wasn't the first time a client had backed out, and Molly knew that discretion was the better part of valor.

"I think I'd better pass, Terry. Bidding was a last-minute decision by my client. He's out of town and scheduled with back-to-back meetings. Either he screwed up, or changed his mind."

"No problem. These things happen. But look at it this way, we had a chance to hook up again. Listen, you take care and any time you want to bid with us call me first and I'll personally set you up."

"I'll do that. And thanks for everything. I appreciate it that you're willing to accommodate me. Great talking to you."

Molly's eye was out of control. Not willing to offer her credit card was like saying her limit wasn't high enough, or she was over-extended. The twitching was so bad, she had to squeeze both eyes shut. She thanked God she'd managed to get her ego under control and bow out with a reasonable excuse. She knew she'd been only an inch away from staying in and assuming Todd had turned it over to his assistant despite her suggestion he handle it. If he had, then his assistant dropped the ball. As a witness to Jessop's quick temper, Molly suddenly felt sorry for the assistant.

Molly wiped her hands on her sweats. The gearing-up process for telephone bidding was an adrenaline rush, and, she had to admit, addicting. Akin to being in a free fall, it was insanely competitive and sometimes dangerous to one's mental health. The advantages of seeing one's opponents, or eavesdropping on conversations, or simply getting a feel for the crowd were absent. It was like bidding against a ghost. Your telephone stand-in couldn't help but feel the competition that fueled the air. In spite of training to be calm and not transmit his or her own anxiety, it often came through and that's when it became a test of self-control. Coming down from the high was another problem. Win or lose, it often left Molly feeling as limp as a wet dishrag.

Molly jumped when the phone rang. It had to be Jessop. No one else would call her this early. She checked her watch. There was no way they could get back in now. The auction would be underway any minute. She wiped her hands again, picked up the phone, and in a calm voice, said, "You're too late. It's already started."

"I'm not too late. Your watch must be fast."

"Randall? Why are you awake this early?"

"I wanted to wish you luck. What do you mean, it's too late?"

"It's a long story."

"Yeah? I can't wait to hear it. Unlock the door. I've got dough-nuts."

Molly turned and saw him leaning against the door. She shook her head and laughed. "Got any apple fritters?"

"Of course."

Molly opened the door. "What a pal."

"Yeah, that's me. Got coffee, too. Clear your command post and bring me up to date."

Molly told Randall that Jessop hadn't forwarded his financial information, and how Terry Jorgenson was willing to let her bid, but she had to give him her credit card number. "For a nanosecond I almost stayed in and gave Terry my American Express number." Tearing off a piece of the apple fritter, she sighed. "But I came to my senses in time. The thought of being stuck with merch that expensive, which would be hard to sell here, didn't give me a warm feeling."

"Smart move."

"Smart, maybe, but I was embarrassed. Any dealer doing a phone bid for a client would have had everything in place in time."

"Hey, your reason was plausible. And you told him it was a last-minute thing, so what's the problem?"

Molly pulled off another bite, and shrugged. "I guess you're right. It's just, my big ego is a tad bruised." Molly wiped the sugar from her fingers, then laughed. "I was actually looking forward to it. I haven't been in an auction for months. Guess I miss the fun."

Randall shook his head. "You dealers are like junkies waiting for your next fix."

Molly gave him a sly look. "Yeah, but I'm in control of my habit. I think my performance this morning is self-evident."

"Sometimes I wonder." He pulled the bag of doughnuts towards him. "I forgot to get a buttermilk bar. Damn. How could I have done that? It's your fault."

"My fault? How do you figure that?"

"I was worried about you and lost my head."

"Worried about *moi*? Oh, please! I'd think by now you would know I'm a sterling individual."

"Solid gold, okay? Feel better now? At least you're off the hook with Jessop. I'd hate to be in his assistant's shoes if he delegated that little assignment." After devouring two doughnuts, he rose and said, "You need any furniture moved before I leave?"

Giving Randall one of her sweetest smiles, Molly said, "There *are* a couple of chairs out in the garage you might help me with. They're kind of heavy."

Randall followed Molly into the garage and when she pointed out the set of six chairs, he laughed. "A couple?"

The set of early-eighteenth-century, Louis XIV–style, walnut, open arm chairs with padded backs and cushioned seats was in pristine condition and very pricey. Molly ran her hand over the carved arms. "I only need two on the floor. I've got to photograph them for a new client. I promised to e-mail her today."

Randall picked one up and winced. "Must be a big house. These babies will fill up a room by themselves. Okay, out of my way."

Molly went ahead of Randall, then pointed out where she wanted them. "You're a champ to do this for me. By the way, they're not going into a house. It's for her business."

"Fancy boardroom stuff? Well, they'll make an impression for sure."

Molly bit her lip and tried not to laugh. She wondered if she should tell Randall what the chairs were really for. Best not to, she decided. Her client ran a prosperous lap dancing enterprise in the City. Molly wasn't sure if lap dancing was legal and didn't want to get Del Tinsley in trouble. Besides, she sure as hell wasn't going to blow a twelve-grand sale. Del wanted only the best, and she was willing to pay for it. "Oh, I'm sure the chairs will make a big impression."

Molly woke Emma at six-thirty, told her about the auction screw-up, then took a shower. After seeing Emma off to school, she ran over to Tosca's for her morning treat of Bennie's apple cake. Randall's fritters hadn't ramped up her energy level enough. Coming down from auction anticipation drained her, and she needed more sugar to get ready for the day. She could also have a forbidden cigarette and not worry about Emma looking over her shoulder. She and Daria had been working hard to quit, but a morning like this just blew all her good intentions to hell.

Molly e-mailed the photos of the chairs to Del Tinsley, then set about getting the shop ready for what she hoped would be a good sales day. Monday was generally slow, and Molly often thought if she were to stop being open seven days a week, which Max had left up to her, Monday would be the day to close. Maybe, since Sunset Center, the culture-and-art venue for Carmel, was hosting a traveling art show starting today, she might be lucky. She had heard tickets for the three-day event were sold out. Most likely, she thought, from the four chartered busses arriving with tourists from the Bay Area just for the art show. If the retail gods were smiling, she might sell a few things from the overflow.

But it was not to be. Between opening on time again until noon, not one person walked into Treasures. At least Del Tinsley got back to her via e-mail and loved the chairs. She promised to give her a call in the afternoon to arrange delivery. Every time the phone rang, Molly rushed to her desk hoping it was Todd Jessop apologizing for the mix-up. Instead, she had three telemarketers, two people looking for Lladro figurines, which Molly did not carry, one from Emma's counselor setting up a progress report date, and one from Randall asking her if Jessop had called.

After a quick salad for lunch in the storage room, Molly was tempted to put the CLOSED sign in the window and take a short nap. Stifling a yawn, she decided to do just that. On her way to the front window, the phone rang. No longer interested in jogging to her desk, she sauntered over and picked it up. "Treasures. How can I help you?"

"Molly? It's me, Del. Honey, I just love the chairs! The girls are crazy about them. How about if I send a few of my boys down in a U-Haul tomorrow?"

"Aren't they gorgeous? Tomorrow is perfect. I'll be ready."

"Gorgeous? They're piss elegant. I'll be driving down tomorrow, too. We're doing a private party out in Carmel Valley next week, and I want to meet the guy who hired us. I don't know him from Adam."

Molly laughed. "Maybe I can help? I mean, I might know someone who knows him?"

"I can't tell you who it is. These things are confidential. But thanks anyway."

"Gotcha."

"Figure I'll be there around ten. Keep your eyes open for more chairs. Business is booming and I'm thinking of expanding."

"Consider it done."

When Del rang off, Molly collapsed in her chair and laughed. If only her former New York clients could see her now! Purveyor to lap dancers. She couldn't wait to tell Daria. At least she'd find it humorous. Randall might not. But then, he didn't have to know.

Molly looked around the shop, hoping to find something to keep her busy. Everything was pristine. Not a speck of dust, not one cushion off-center, all the silver was shining, the French copper molds glowed, crystal sparkled, even the working fireplace was ash-free and burning gently. She placed the CLOSED sign in the window. She stretched out in her favorite tatty wing chair in the storage room and set the small alarm clock to wake her in an hour.

Molly had no sooner closed her eyes when the phone rang again.

She eyed the monster next to her on the table and considered ignoring it. With a deep sigh, she picked it up and before she could speak, Carla Jessop said, "Hi, change in plan for dinner tonight. We're still on, but instead of the ranch, we'll be at the tasting room. My father wants to see what we're doing and his cook will fix us up there."

Molly hesitated. She'd forgotten about the invitation and really wasn't in the mood to break bread with Jessop after this morning's fiasco. But she couldn't bow out now. Sooner or later, she'd have to face the jerk. Maybe he would still be out of town. "Works for me. Is seven still okay?"

"Seven it is. Oh, by the way, I'll pick up Emma when I get Michelle, okay?"

"Thanks. I'll call Charles and let him know."

Molly dialed Bitsy Morgan's number and spoke to Josie. Charles and Josie were the married couple who took care of Bitsy's gigantic house in Pebble Beach. When the decision to send Emma to Santa Catalina in Monterey was made, Bitsy had insisted that Charles would drive Emma to and from school. Monterey and Carmel were relatively crime-free, but Bitsy was adamant that Emma have safe transportation. One just never knew these days, she'd insisted. And one just never argued with Bitsy Morgan.

"Hi, Josie. Carla Jessop will be picking Emma up today with Michelle, so Charles won't have to go."

"Good thing you called. He was going to leave early to do some errands. Oh, Bitsy called today. She's coming home early."

"Bored already?"

"Are you kidding? Bitsy bored? No. She said shopping in Palm Springs wasn't much fun anymore unless you were a wanna-be tramp, and she was too old for that look."

Molly laughed. "Somehow I can't see her in navel-baring hip-huggers and four-inch heels."

Molly hung up and shut her eyes again. If the damn phone rang once more, she'd just let the machine pick up the call. When it did ring later, Molly jumped with a start. As she reached for the phone, she saw the clock and almost fainted. The alarm hadn't gone off and it was just past four. How could she have slept so long?

Randall's voice was blaring in her ear. "Hey, what's wrong? Why is the 'closed' sign in the window? You okay? Emma okay? What?"

"I fell asleep."

There was a pause, then a laugh. "Are you kidding me? Molly Doyle asleep in her shop? Impossible."

"Yes, isn't it. It's been a slow day, and well, I just thought I'd shut my eyes for a little while and the damn alarm didn't go off."

"Hey, don't bellyache to me. You're the one who said you'd bid for that jerk."

"Aw, come on. A girl's gotta do what she's gotta do."

"He call you?"

Molly paused. The last thing she needed was Randall to give her grief. "No, and I hope I won't see him tonight at dinner."

"Better count on it. I just passed him on Junipero when I was heading into the station's parking lot."

"Great. I wish I didn't have to go, but Carla invited Emma and me. We're going to the tasting room and her father will be there to see what we've planned."

"Good luck."

"You're such a comfort."

"If Jessop shows up, just don't knock him off, okay? Carmel Valley is in the county and out of my jurisdiction. Wait until he's back in Carmel. I'll be able to get you off then."

"I'm going to hang up if you keep this going."

"Okay. Give me a call when you get home."

Molly blew out her breath. "Why?"

"So you can tell me I was wrong about the guy. How's that?"

"Swell. I'll do just that." Molly hung up, and then jumped from the chair. Irritated no end, she wasn't sure if it was with Randall for thinking she'd been jerked around by Jessop, or with herself for losing most of the afternoon snoozing. And getting caught. By Randall, naturally.

# Chapter 6

MOLLY LOVED driving through Carmel Valley. Once a vast area of small horse ranches and farms, it was still countrified enough to be able to ignore the hundreds of homes and golf courses that seemed to alter only a small portion of the miles of rolling hills. New McMansions and private vineyards dotted much of the steep slopes just past the area known as Mid-Valley, and rather than disfigure the region, they achieved the creation of a California version of Tuscany. As Molly turned onto the long driveway toward Bello Lago's Tasting Room and Gift Shop, she was struck by the beauty of how the nighttime setting would be. The gravel drive was bordered by dozens of oak trees strung with what seemed like thousands of tiny lights. The imposing two-story building, faced with Carmel stone, reminded Molly of European monasteries hidden atop towering cliffs. The roof line and the tall, arched stained-glass window, depicting clusters of purple grapes with twining dark green leaves, was lit from below with a soft blue light. Molly parked in the visitor's zone, and as she approached the massive carved double doors, she stopped to admire the pair of monumental patinated-bronze reindeer perched on rockwork bases standing sentry at the entrance.

When Molly pushed open one of the doors, she was engulfed in mouthwatering aromas of garlic and basil. Daria had told her that Dando Osa, Mr. Mattucci's private cook, frequently had offers from local restaurateurs after they'd attended Bello Lago's annual dinners for the trade. Apparently, besides his extraordinary self-taught culinary skills, Osa seemed to be an interesting character. It was rumored he was a Spanish Basque and related to a big Nevada sheep-ranching family. And then others swore up and down he was a Portuguese from Macao who'd come into the country illegally. Osa, naturally, never said. In fact, Osa rarely spoke. More interesting, Daria had added, it was rumored that while some just thought he'd probably never mastered the English language, others said a small part of his tongue had been cut out when he'd been jailed in Spain as a youngster. Because rarely had anyone ever heard him say more than a few garbled words, the rumors had quickly become fact in everyone's mind.

Molly was surprised to see so many people gathering around the large refectory table in the center of the tasting room just off the foyer. At one end, a double-tiered wrought-iron stand held large white platters filled with a staggering array of appetizers. Bottles of Bello Lago wines were prominently displayed. Carla apparently had a different view of a family dinner than Molly did. It took her a moment to scan the faces. When she finally spotted Emma with Michelle, she smiled her way past a group of men clustered around the small bar, towards the two young girls. Carla arrived just as Molly reached them.

Molly leaned down and kissed Emma on the forehead, then smiled at Michelle. "Did you two get all your homework done?"

Emma rolled her eyes. "No problemo. Michelle and I did it first thing at her house before we came over here."

"I'm so glad you made it," Carla said.

Scanning the room again, Molly said, "I had no idea you were having so many guests. I would have changed before leaving."

Carla smiled. "These aren't guests, they're family. Well, employees really. But as close as family. My dad decided to throw one of his monthly dinners a little early." Carla gestured to two men standing nearby and waved them over. "I'd like you to meet a couple of them."

Dino Horne was the first to offer Molly his hand. Short, stocky, and bald, he had dark chocolate eyes. His pale blue button-down shirt sported a designer logo, and his khaki slacks looked like they'd just been pressed. "Nice to meet you, Molly. My wife loves your shop. I try to keep her out of there, but it doesn't work."

"Oh, Polly Horne! Of course. Don't worry about her. She's got a great eye and knows how to bargain."

Horne grinned. "That's encouraging news."

"Dino is our master winemaker," Carla said. "Without this man, there wouldn't be a Bello Lago."

"Don't listen to her, Molly," the taller man next to Horne said. "I'm Reggie Sullivan, and I'm the best marketing director in the wine business. I'm the guy that keeps Bello Lago in awards, not this old guy with a worn-out nose and palate."

Molly took Reggie Sullivan's hand. "How about if I believe you both?"

Sullivan, dressed in jeans and a silk aloha shirt, nodded to Carla. "Hey, with such diplomatic talent, I might just hire this gal."

"No thanks." Molly smiled. "I know zilch about wine. Besides, there are those who might argue with you about my sense of diplomacy."

Emma giggled, then covered her mouth. Both men laughed.

Sullivan turned to Carla. "Speaking of diplomacy, where's Todd?"

Molly saw Carla's eyelids flutter just slightly. "He's going to be late. We'll start dinner without him." Turning to Molly, she said, "I want you to meet my father."

Domenico Mattucci must have been an incredibly handsome man in his day, Molly thought as she shook his hand. As he was confined to a wheelchair, his height was difficult to guess, but his thick white hair and pale blue eyes still commanded attention. Molly remembered Carla saying he was in his early eighties. Had she not known this, she'd swear the man wasn't a day over seventy. "It's a pleasure to meet you, Mr. Mattucci. And thank you for inviting me to dinner."

Domenico Mattucci's voice was soft and slightly raspy. "It's my pleasure, Ms. Doyle. I saw your drawings for this room. The look you envision is perfect. You must have some Italian blood in you."

"Alas, no. Irish through and through. But I'm a great admirer of your heritage. No country has produced more brilliant artists or musical geniuses than Italy."

Mattucci's eyes sparkled. He nodded to his daughter. "This is your show, but I like this woman. Keep her around, *capisce?*" He turned away for a moment, then added, "Is your husband joining us tonight?" He looked at his watch. "Dinner is ready. I don't like to keep Dando waiting."

"He'll be late," Carla said. "Don't wait for him."

Mattucci wheeled his chair around. "I didn't plan to. Get everyone seated for me, will you? I'll be in the kitchen for a minute."

The other end of the refectory table had been cleared and was set for dinner. Molly noted the place cards and found she'd been seated between Dino and Reggie. Todd Jessop's place was across from her with Emma and Michelle on each side. Molly wondered if the placement of the young girls had been to keep Jessop in check. It was unlikely he would start anything with them. But she wasn't at all pleased to be opposite him.

The table had a true Mediterranean feel, with oversized simple white dishes, flatware with horn handles, and inexpensive wineglasses that could be found at Target. Apparently the Mattucci family didn't feel it necessary to serve their wine in thin crystal to appreciate its bouquet. The old-country attitude seemed more appropriate to Molly, and she immediately felt at home. Even the two arrangements of carnations and ferns were simple, but lovely. Dinner was served family style. Reminiscent of the back-room dinners at Daria's, huge platters arrived with antipasti, and oval tubs of butter and mini-decanters of olive oil for the sourdough bread. As the patron of the family, Mattucci sat at the head of the table, and Carla sat next to him.

As the platters were passed around, Molly suggested to Dino and Reggie that they might like to sit next to each other. They'd been discussing company business across Molly. "Look, why don't I trade places with one of you? It might make it easier for you to talk."

Reggie waved her off. "Not a problem. We yack like this all the time."

Molly pushed her chair back. "Really, I don't mind."

Dino rose. "Hey, thanks, Molly. Reggie and I were supposed to meet for lunch today to discuss a few things, but we both got busy."

"If you don't mind my hearing company secrets, be my guest."

Dino's face turned serious. "We're an open book around here. Hell, the whole Valley, Carmel and Salinas, knows what's been going on." He jerked his head towards Todd Jessop's empty chair. "You were at the shindig last week, right?"

When Molly nodded, he said, "Then you heard Prince Charming shoot off his mouth. Reggie and I are spending more time doing damage control over that than doing our jobs."

Molly traded chairs, then said, "I was in the middle of it."

"Yeah, that's right," Sullivan broke in, "you were with Carmel's chief of police. The big guy, Randall."

"Hey, was he really a big honcho with LAPD's Internal Affairs?" Dino asked.

Molly smiled. "You might say the biggest. And yes, I imagine he towered over everyone else as well."

"Nice friend to have," Sullivan said.

"He does come in handy sometimes."

Sullivan slapped his forehead. "That's right! You two have—"

"Been busy," Molly said as she sipped her wine.

When Domenico Mattucci tapped his glass for silence, all heads turned in his direction. He held up a bottle of wine. "You will be drinking a gift from my cousins in Italy this evening. It's a wonderful Barbera. The perfect accompaniment to pasta with a tomato-base sauce." Nodding to Molly, he said, "In case you're not a wine buff, the region of Piedmont is where the Barbera comes from. If you wonder why I say it is the best wine for pasta with a sauce such as we're now being served, it's because of the acidity in the tomatoes. Most red wines taste clumsy and too sweet. Barbera has what we call a bright acidity." He winked at Molly. "Ah, you find *that* wine, and you're in heaven."

Mattucci handed the bottle to the young server. He watched the pour, took the obligatory first sip, then nodded his approval. He kissed two fingers, then laughed. "*Magnifico*. The first glass is for our lovely new guest. May she join us often."

Everyone waited until all the glasses were filled. As if on cue, they raised their glasses towards Molly. She blushed. "Thank you all for your warm welcome. I'm very flattered, and honored to be here."

"Drink up," Carla said. "This is only the beginning. Dinners with my father are like the old bacchanals. The wine never stops flowing."

As each new platter of food arrived after the pasta, Molly soon felt the need to loosen her belt. Roasted Big Sur wild boar; all manner of roasted root vegetables; blue, white, and yellow potatoes; steamed asparagus and broccoli, and carrots with brown sugar filled every inch of the large table. Between sampling everything offered, Molly and Carla talked about schedules, and vendors to approach for the gift shop. The few times Carla left the table, Molly couldn't help but hear the conversation between Dino and Reggie. Their anger with Todd over his continuous interference in the business grew stronger with each new glass of wine. It was only Dando Osa's brief appearance that put a halt to their discussion. He was too far away from Molly to get a good look, but she could see that Osa was a surprisingly small man dressed in chef's whites. The tall, round, pleated white toque on his head was tilted at a rakish angle. When Domenico Mattucci raised his glass and complimented Osa's dinner, the mysterious cook merely smiled and waved, then quickly disappeared.

"That's a first," Reggie said. "We hardly ever see the guy."

Dino laughed. "Hey, maybe he was curious about Molly here."

By the time coffee and dessert arrived—which was, thankfully, a simple offering of biscotti—Molly wondered if Todd was going to show up. She checked her watch and was surprised to see it was after nine. Molly caught Emma's attention, and said, "We can't stay much later, Em. School, remember?"

"I know," Emma said. "Uh, Michelle was wondering if I could stay over?"

Molly shook her head. "Not this time. You don't have any of your things. How about if Michelle stays with us this weekend?"

"Good idea," Todd Jessop said as he came up behind Michelle and ruffled her hair. "Maybe you can put her to work doing something useful for once."

Molly saw Michelle stiffen and brush her stepfather's hand away.

Carla was returning to the table and saw her daughter's gesture. She shot her husband a warning look. "That would be great, Molly."

Michelle smiled at Molly. "I'd love to. Thank you."

Taking the empty seat opposite Molly, Jessop said, "Sorry I missed dinner. My appointments up north ran longer than I'd thought."

Jessop took out a large envelope and tossed it to Reggie. "I brought you some samples of labels I want you to look over. You'll love them."

Reggie rose, pushed back his chair, and threw down his napkin in disgust. He ignored the envelope. "How many times do I have to tell you we are not changing our label? Damn it, Jessop, give it a rest."

"Don't get your balls in a twist, Sullivan. It won't hurt to take a look. Time to get into the new century. Today's buyer wants to relate to *his* world, not to the distant past. Get with the times, or fall behind."

"I don't care if other vintners are changing to abstract art, funky pictures of animals, or dead pop stars," Sullivan said. "We don't sell wine to drugged-out hippies having dreams of Marilyn Monroe, or Baby Boomers who still read the comics. We sell quality, not shit." Sullivan glanced around the table. His eyes rested on Domenico. "My apologies, boss."

Mattucci's eyes were hooded. He waved at Sullivan. "Not accepted. You said nothing wrong. Sit down, enjoy your coffee."

Molly was surprised when Jessop looked at her and smiled. "And how was your day, Ms. Doyle? Exciting, I hope."

Her tone was cautious. "It was interesting. A glitch or two, but that's life."

"Well, you seem to be a big enough girl to handle a setback or two."

Molly knew Jessop was baiting her. When conversations stopped, and all eyes turned to them, it was apparent they knew it, too. "Big enough," Molly said, "to handle people who like to jerk me around."

Jessop's laugh was short, but nasty. "Ohhh, I sure wouldn't want to tangle with you."

Molly had had just enough wine to feel more than relaxed. She knew if she drained her still half-full glass, she might not pass a so-briety test. But then, there were pots full of coffee on the table and enough biscotti to sop up any damage. Molly emptied her glass, then leaned into the table. "Wise decision. A bit late however. Too bad you didn't think of that earlier."

"Excuse me?" Jessop said.

The last of the wine zipped through Molly like lightning. "No, I don't think I will. You almost made an ass out of me this morning with Blue Moon Auctions. Lucky for you, I know the auction man-ager. I was able to get out of bidding for you."

"I have no idea what you're talking about."

Molly leaned back in her chair and folded her arms. "You're a bad liar. You set me up. When I found out you hadn't arranged financials, did you think I was dumb enough to go on with the bid-ding and then pay for it myself thinking you'd reimburse me? Oh, you need to work on your payback skills. You're not as good as you think."

"What's going on, Molly?" Carla asked. "What the hell is this all about?"

Molly nodded at Jessop. "Go on, tell Carla."

Jessop looked at his wife then waved Molly off. "I told you not to trust her. She's off her skull. Too much wine, maybe?"

Molly stared at Jessop. "Really? Well, why don't you tell her how you called me Saturday night and asked me to bid on the English pub bar and the two French display cabinets Blue Moon auctions had up this morning. The apology gift you wanted to offer Carla for…for…" Molly saw the look in Carla's eyes and stopped there. Tearing into Jessop was one thing, but she wouldn't shame Carla in front of everyone.

Jessop looked at his wife, then shrugged. "This is a pure fabrica-tion. I never called you. You're nuts, or drunk. Or maybe this is just a scam? Is that it? You dreamed this up just to get back at me for calling you a lightweight." Todd rose and stared at Molly. "Well, you are. And you're a loser, too." He laughed then. "That's probably why they kicked you out of New York when you got arrested for sell-ing fake antiques. And your husband took off with another woman."

Every jaw around the table had dropped. Even the servers were frozen in place.

Like a jack-in-the-box, Molly was on her feet. She held onto the table, and leaned in, only inches from his face. "I wasn't involved in the fakes, and you damn well know it! If there's a loser here, it's you!"

Jessop's hand came up as if to strike Molly. He caught himself, then shouted, "You mangy bitch!"

Molly had no idea her reflexes were so swift. In less than a blink of an eye, she grabbed Dino Horne's full glass of wine and threw it in Jessop's face. It was a terrible waste of excellent wine, but the sacrifice was worth it.

The room was so silent, you could hear the pine trees whispering outside.

Carla gasped, Domenico Mattucci grinned, and Dino and Reggie were dumbstruck.

Molly, however, was in shock. She stared at the empty wineglass, then looked at Carla. "I…I'm so sorry."

"I am, too," Carla said. "I wish I'd done it."

# Chapter 7

HALFWAY DOWN Carmel Valley Road towards Carmel, Molly pulled onto the shoulder and hit the brakes. "Did I apologize to everyone?"

"Yes," Emma said.

"Are you sure? I…I'm still in a fog."

Emma sighed. "I think you did it twice. If it makes you feel any better, Mr. Mattucci gave you a hug and Michelle said he doesn't do that very often. Guess that says something."

Molly's free hand searched for her tote. "Find my cigarettes, would you? No lectures, okay? I think I'm entitled."

Emma found the pack and pulled a cigarette out for Molly. "Here, be entitled."

"Emma, please."

"I'm kidding. I know you're upset." She held up Molly's Zippo. "I'll flick the torch."

Molly took an unusually deep drag. It was as if the nicotine could purge her actions. She couldn't remember losing it like that in public. Not that she hadn't a worthy occasion or two. Her only saving grace was that she hadn't been the only one there who'd wanted to do the same thing. The looks of satisfaction on Reggie Sullivan's and Dino Horne's faces were almost comical. Nevertheless, what she'd done was, for her, beyond the pale. She'd have to say a dozen Hail Marys tonight. As Molly pulled into the alley behind the shop, she amended that thought. Two dozen might be better. By the time she and Emma were ready for bed, she amended her thoughts again. Screw it, she murmured as she climbed into bed.

$\sim$

On the phone the next morning with Bitsy, Molly pulled the phone from her ear. Bitsy Morgan could go on for hours about her shopping trips. It only took a few well-placed responses to not insult her, but at the moment, Molly was more concerned with how she was going to face Todd Jessop next time she saw him. Moving the phone a few more inches away, she thought about Carla's earlier call. She said that Todd had slammed out of the house this morning on a rampage. She suggested Molly keep an eye out. Not that she thought he'd come storming into the shop, but one never knew with him.

"I'm still mortified," Molly had told Carla. "I'm so sorry. I don't think I can face your family again."

"He asked for it. Look, Molly, I know all about New York, and I know the truth. After you left, Todd started in again and my father told him off. I made sure everyone there knew the real story. In fact, my father thought you were terrific. So, no more regrets. I'll deal with my husband when the time is right." Carla laughed then. "Dino and Reggie thought you were awesome."

Molly hadn't called Randall last night. She hadn't been in a mood to talk to anyone. She didn't need Randall going off half-cocked.

She moved the phone back to her ear as Bitsy continued to give her a shop-by-shop description of the tacky clothes with Rodeo-Drive prices. "Yes, Bitsy, I can just imagine. But, that's the look today. Not for us, naturally. Hmm? Yes, I'll be here today. Where the hell else would I be?" Molly laughed. "I'm kidding."

"Do you want me to come in tomorrow?" Bitsy asked. "I've tons to do, but I can squeeze a few hours in."

"No, I'm fine. I've got all the merch Max sent down to place. But if you could handle next Saturday, I'd love you forever. Emma's been itching to hit the garage sales, and she wants to take Michelle Giordano with us."

"I'll be there," Bitsy said. "Oh, Lord! How self-centered I've been! Did you get the job with Carla Jessop? How did it go with her husband?"

Oh, if you only knew, Molly thought. "Piece of cake," Molly replied. "She loved all the pieces I picked out."

"Oh, darling! I'm just thrilled for you. Well, listen, I'd love to chat more, but I've got to run. I'm on my way to the salon. My hair is a shambles. Call you later."

Molly had to laugh. Bitsy Morgan's snow-white chignon was never a shambles. She was always beautifully dressed, always *au courant*, and always a gorgeous seventy-plus dynamo. No one knew what the plus figure was, but it didn't matter. Bitsy had enough energy for two people. She claimed her secret was clean living and good bourbon.

When the bell over the door rang, Molly looked up and saw Daria coming in with a bemused look on her face. "Okay, spill. It's all over town, but I want your version."

Molly sank into her chair. "Shit."

"That ain't the half of it. Randall's coming down the block like he's chasing a face on a wanted poster."

Daria pulled one of the lap dancer's chairs to Molly's desk. "Hmmm. This is comfy. I could use these at the restaurant. I see 'sold' tags. Who's buying them?"

"Oh, great. That's all I need now. I didn't want him to know."

"Too late, my dear. You keep forgetting this is a small village. So, who bought the chairs? Got any more?"

Molly sighed. "Four more, but all sold, and you wouldn't believe me if I told you."

"Try me," Daria grinned. "No, don't. That *lady* from the City, right? The, uh, the one with the dancers?"

Molly's first real smile of the day felt good. "Now you're a mind reader? She's become a good customer, so no smart cracks."

Daria's shrug was good-natured. "I don't question my customers either. For all I know, I've fed embezzlers, polygamists, and maybe a few card sharks. Not to mention one or two Tony Soprano lookalikes."

Randall stood in the open door. He scanned the shop for customers, then said, "Okay, what the hell happened last night? Didn't I warn you about that prick?"

"Grab a chair and simmer down," Daria said to Randall.

Molly felt as though she were on the witness stand. The urge to disappear was overwhelming. Randall took hold of the other chair that matched Daria's. "Well? You were supposed to call me."

Molly filled them in. "I don't want to hear any more 'I told you so's. It was the *mangy* part that got to me. I guess that's when I lost it."

Daria was laughing so hard, she was holding her sides. Randall's face was impassive.

"That's it. All of it. End of story. *Fini.*"

"You call me if he shows up, understand?" Randall said.

"He won't show his face here, don't worry. I'm not on his hit parade," Molly said.

"Poor choice of words," Randall shot back.

"Come on! Let's not blow this up. He's—"

"He's rude, arrogant, and an all-around piece of shit. But I'm stuck with him for the present," Carla Jessop said as she walked in and headed for Molly's desk. She was waving an envelope in her hand like an electric fan run amok. She handed it to Molly. "For your bill. I hope this check is the right amount. I pulled the figures from memory and added an apology bonus." Nodding a hello to Daria and Randall, she said, "So, how are two of my favorite people? Here to interrogate Molly, Chief? Guess you heard about last night. I guess everyone has. I was at the post office before I came here, and two of our wine clients asked me if Molly Doyle really threw a punch at Todd. Can you imagine what people are going to have Molly do next? Throw him off the Bixby Bridge, I guess."

Molly shook her head. "No, not there. I'll never go over that bridge again."

Randall and Daria laughed. Carla asked, "Something I should know?"

"Some other time," Molly said. "Over a few Jack Daniel's maybe."

"Well, get in line, Molly. There're a few people ahead of you who'd like to kill Todd. By the way, that little to-do was the highlight of the evening. Even my father thought so. And that is saying a whole lot. In fact, he said to be sure to invite you to his birthday party on Sunday. It's at my house in the Highlands. No fancy dress. It's a barbeque." Patting Randall on the shoulder, she added, "He especially would love to have you come, too. Daria already has her invite, so I'll expect you all."

"I won't be able to make it, Carla," Daria said. "I've got to go up to the City to interview chefs. Julio is returning to Florence in a few weeks. Give your dad a kiss for me."

"We'll miss you. But business comes before pleasure, right?" Turning to leave, she said, "It goes without saying, no gifts. The man has everything he wants." She paused, then added, "Except a son-in-law he likes." She gave them a wave. *"Ciao!"*

"How the hell does she manage?" Molly asked.

Randall snorted, "Just don't say, *'Men,'* okay? Like we're all bastards."

Daria leaned over and pinched his cheek. "Oh, not you! You're just a sweetheart."

Molly laughed. "Yeah, right." When she saw Randall squint, she said, "I mean it, okay? You're a prince. I tell everyone I know that."

Randall rose. "Sure you do." He winked at Daria. "She lies well, doesn't she? But hey, it comes with the job. Antiques dealers are all—"

"Don't say it," Molly said.

Randall hitched up his slacks, turned to scan the shop, then said, "Okay. I won't say it. Shop looks good." He meandered down the main aisle, and then stopped in front of a ship model. "Nice work." He glanced at the tag, and then nodded. "Good price. I'll think about it. You sure it's *The America*, the racing yacht?"

"I double-checked. There's a picture of it in *Miller's*," Molly said. "If you really want it, better grab it now. A man was in the other day and he was interested."

Randall winked at Daria. "There she goes. Right into her dealer spiel. I hate hard sells, don't you?"

"It's the truth! But go away, Randall. Please?" Molly said. "Go catch a bad guy, or something."

Randall was facing her now. "That's why I'm here." He walked to the door, then turned. "Watch your back, Molly. Jessop isn't going to take what you did to him lying down. His type can't handle public humiliation You still got me on your speed dial?"

Molly's jaw dropped. "You're serious?"

When Randall just looked at her, she said, "Uh, yes. You're there."

"Good. Keep your cell with you."

After Randall left, Daria said, "He's right, Molly. Be careful."

"I can't believe Todd Jessop would do anything stupid." Then she remembered Carla's bruised face the other night. "But I'll be careful."

"We still on for dinner tonight?" Daria asked. "Roast duck, risotto and mushrooms?"

Molly smiled. "I'm never going to learn how to cook if I keep taking advantage of your hospitality."

"Just find me more silver. You can always learn later." Picking up her bag, she said, "Got to go. Got a new waiter to check out. Seven, okay?"

"We'll be there. Oh, Bitsy is coming in on Saturday, so Emma and I will hit the garage sales. Silver will be my top priority."

At quarter to seven that night Emma was still on the computer. "Hey, we've got to go," Molly said.

They raced down the stairs and headed into the alley where Molly's El Camino was parked. Molly did a double-take when she reached the door. The entire side of the pickup looked as if someone had run a key across it. And not just once, but several times. Emma saw her face, and said, "Wait until you see this side. The new paint job is history."

Molly went around to where Emma stood. "I don't believe it. This is Carmel. These things don't happen here."

"Time to call the gendarmes?" Emma asked.

Molly hadn't told Emma about Randall's warnings. After Randall and Daria left earlier, she started thinking about what Randall had said. She thought he was just being a cop and overreacting. But now, she wondered if he was right. "No. Just get in. We'll tell Randall when we see him at Daria's." On the way to the restaurant, Molly decided to tell Emma about Randall's warning.

"Maybe we ought to listen to him? Michelle said Mr. Jessop has a really bad temper. He even kicked her cat once when it got in his way. She hates him and wishes her mother would get rid of him."

"I don't think Mr. Jessop did this. Kids do this kind of stuff. But, we'll be careful just the same. Alarm on at night from now on, okay?"

"I'll remind you." Emma laughed.

"What would I do without you?"

"Oh, *puleeese!* You say that all the time."

Inside Daria's private back room, Molly found Randall already there and reading. She'd discovered that he and Loomis were dyed-in-the-wool mystery fans. Last Christmas, she and Daria and Emma had found two Sherlock Holmes–type hats and long-stemmed pipes and put them under the huge tree at Bitsy's. It was, Loomis had said, the best gift he had ever received. Randall, however, wondered if he might trade it for a train conductor's hat. They all knew he was an astute collector of trains. Emma agreed it was the best Christmas she had ever had, too.

"What are you reading now?" Molly asked.

Emma gently poked her in the ribs. "Tell him!"

Randall set down the book. "Tell me what?"

"Uh, well, I seem to have a problem with the El Camino."

"Okay."

"Well, what I mean is—"

"Some jerk keyed it pretty bad," Emma blurted.

"Let's take a look," Randall said.

Molly shook her head and sat down. "Don't bother. I'll get it fixed. I just thought you should know."

Randall's eyes flicked to Emma. "Or Emma did. You have a habit of forgetting to tell me things."

Molly's face flushed. She knew Randall was referring to major elements she'd held back a bit longer than necessary in the last two cases she'd helped him solve. "That's a low blow."

Randall ignored that. "Did you call it in? Report it, like good citizens do?"

Molly could tell Randall was gearing up for one of his lectures, and she wasn't in the mood. "No. I didn't think Forensics would be interested," Molly said.

"That's not funny."

"I don't think much is funny today, okay?"

"While you two kids kibbitz, I'll tell Manuel we're ready to eat. Come on, Emma, keep me company," Daria said.

Randall waited until they left, then said, "Look, Molly, I'm not trying to be a hard-ass, but trust me, huh? Todd Jessop is a control freak. When things don't go the way people like that want, they act out. Maybe he didn't key your pickup, but if he did, what's next?"

"I set the alarm before we left," Molly said with a touch of pride.

"Good. Just keep doing it, and keep your eyes open. Listen, about that invite to her father's birthday party. I don't care much about going, but because she's now a client, I guess you're stuck. I'll accept, but only to keep an eye on you."

Molly smiled. "That's very gallant. I'm touched."

"Hell, can't I do something nice without you giving me heat?"

"I'm serious! I really am."

Daria and Emma were in the open doorway and saw Molly reach over and kiss Randall on the cheek. Emma nudged Daria, and whispered, "Isn't that cute?"

Daria leaned down and whispered back, "For God's sakes, don't let them hear that!"

# Chapter 8

RANDALL INSISTED on walking Molly and Emma to the pickup after dinner. Molly protested. After all, she said, they were parked only a few doors down from the restaurant. Randall ignored her.

The strong odor hit them the minute they stepped outside. Dolores Street was virtually empty. It was past serving time for many of the restaurants, and few cars remained. Molly's eyes widened, Emma pulled the collar of her T-shirt up over her nose, and Randall said, "What the hell? Do you smell what I think I smell?"

Molly and Emma wrinkled their noses. "Smells like skunk," Molly said.

Emma shrugged. "Is that what a skunk smells like?"

"It's a damn skunk, all right." Randall moved a few steps, then the grin on his face turned sour. "Stay here." He approached Molly's pickup, then stepped back. "Did you lock this thing?"

Molly had a feeling she was about to get another lecture. "Probably not. Don't tell me—"

"You got it. It's coming from the El Camino, and I can see the perpetrator from here." He drew closer, then said, "Don't move. You've also got four flat tires." He pulled his cell out and called the station. "Get a towing service and Animal Control over to Daria's. We've got a vandalized vehicle with a live skunk in it. Stop laughing and just send a damn patrol over to write this up. I'll be waiting."

"Don't chew your nails, Aunt Molly," Emma said.

"It's better than screaming," Molly said.

Emma asked Randall, "How come you didn't say 'perp'?"

"They only say that in mysteries. Real cops speak the King's English. Especially here in Carmel."

Emma laughed. "Baloney. You're just trying to make jokes so Aunt Molly won't pound her fists or throw things."

"We're outside," Molly said. "There's nothing to throw." She leaned back against a storefront window and closed her eyes. She thought about last week when life was calm and good. When all she had to worry about was selling merch, making sure Emma did her homework, providing the cats with food, water, and a clean litter box, and hoping Carla Jessop liked her proposal. Did it all go to hell last Sunday? Yes, it was Sunday. And it started with Todd Jessop. Molly moved away from the shop and stood by Randall. She kept her voice low so Emma couldn't hear. "What do you make of this?"

"If I were a dumb cop, I'd say it was kids pulling a prank. The M.O. is classic. And I'd say your pickup was a random choice."

"But, since all and sundry know you're not a dumb cop, what say you?"

"You want the truth, or the real truth?"

"Either one will do. Do you think it was Jessop?"

"The truth is yes and no. Yes, I think Jessop was behind it. No, he didn't physically do it. He's too smart for that, and he's a city boy. He has no clue how to trap a skunk. The real truth is, it could be just vandalism."

Carmel proper is a small village of three-thousand-plus inhabitants. The downtown area of approximately ten square city blocks is even smaller. It only took five minutes for a patrol unit to arrive. When the officer got out of his car, his head jerked back. "Whoa! What is that? Smells like a skunk. So, this is why you wanted Animal Control?"

"Excellent deduction, Wilkins," Randall said. "I didn't think you wanted to net the little critter."

Officer Wilkins nodded to Molly. "Sorry about your pickup. Did you see who did this?"

"No," Molly said. "But if I had, you'd be calling the M.E. now. The bastard would be dead meat."

"Don't put that in the report, okay?" Randall said.

Wilkins grinned. "If you say so." He opened his notebook, took out a pen and made a tour of the pickup. "Pretty thorough key job, too. Someone's got a bone to pick with you, huh? Sell him a phony antique, or something?"

That was all Molly needed. "That's not funny, Wilkins. You need to work on your humor."

"Stay here until the tow truck comes. I'm taking the ladies home," Randall said.

"Where do you want it towed?"

"To the station. I want it dusted," Randall replied.

"Huh?"

Randall turned so fast, the young officer had to step back. "Are you deaf?"

Molly was surprised to hear the harshness in Randall's voice. She put her hand out to calm him, but he turned his back on her. She hoped her terse remark to Wilkins hadn't set the stage for Randall's anger. Molly felt bad for Wilkins. He was a nice young man and didn't deserve this treatment. But she knew the best thing was to remain silent. She reached into her tote for her keys and handed them to the officer. "I think you might want these," she said. She reached for Emma's hand, then turned to Randall. "Should I go over to the station and fill something out?"

"No, didn't you hear me tell Wilkins I was walking you home? You deaf, too?"

"Don't snap at me! I heard you fine."

"Good. Glad to know that. You can fill out a report later. If whoever did this is hanging around, I want him to see me walk you two home. I also want him to see me go in with you, okay? You're gonna turn all the lights on and leave them on for an hour or so. I'll leave by the back stairs and wait in the alley for a few minutes. Got all that?"

Molly was tempted to give Randall a salute and then snap out a "Ten-four," but noting that his eyes were in slit-mode, she decided just to nod. She was furious with herself for bringing this on. There was no sense in taking it out on Randall. She had no doubt Todd Jessop was behind the paint damage and the flat tires. She knew she could have played the scene last night at the dinner differently. She

knew what he'd been up to and should have ignored him. She could
have turned away and talked to someone else or left the table for a
moment. She could have called him in the morning and discussed
it then. *Would have, could have, should have:* the perpetual Monday-
morning-quarterbacking trinity. But no, she let her temper and ego
get the best of her and now she was paying the price. Carla was
right. She wasn't watching her back. Well, she would from now on,
and woe to anyone who crept up on her.

"What the hell are you mumbling about?" Randall asked as they
crossed over to Ocean Avenue.

"I'm not mumbling," Molly said.

"Your lips are moving," Emma said.

Molly ignored them. They were two shops away from Treasures
now and she counted the minutes till Randall would leave. When
they reached the outside stairs to the apartment, Randall swore,
"Dammit, Molly! Your light over the stairs is out again."

Molly's shoulders drooped and she sighed. "I forgot to replace it
again. It keeps burning out. Max is having someone check it for
me."

"Is the alarm on?"

"Uh, no."

Randall shook his head. "You said it was earlier. I gotta watch
you every minute. Gimme your keys. Stay down here until I call
you."

"You're ready to rip, aren't you," Emma whispered as Randall
went up the stairs. "I'd wait until he leaves. He's just worried about
us, that's all."

"I know, but he could be a little less gruff. Poor Officer Wilkins.
He didn't have to tear into him like that."

"Okay, it's clear. Come on up," Randall called.

"You go first," Molly said to Emma. "He likes you better than
me."

Emma laughed. "Sometimes you're a little dense, you know?"

"It's a bad family gene. I'm just glad you didn't inherit it."

Molly set her tote down in the living room, then headed for the
small kitchen. "Would you like a coffee, Chief Randall? It's the least

I can do to thank you for your diligence." She knew she was being snarky, but it was too late to take her words back.

Randall was standing by the French doors to the balcony. He pulled both handles to make sure Molly had locked up before she'd left. "Got any more of those lemon cookies?"

"It just so happens I do. Does that mean we're friends again?"

Randall smiled at Emma, and then tapped the side of his head with his finger. "She's nuts, you do know that, don't you?"

Emma laughed. She moved closer and hugged Randall. "Thanks for playing hero. It's really cool when you get into your cop mode."

Molly came back from the kitchen with a box of cookies and three mugs on an old wood tray. "Coffee and cocoa will be ready in a minute."

Randall smiled. "I'm sorry I was testy, okay? Those cookies still fresh?"

"Probably not," Molly said as she set the tray on the cut-down dining table that served as an oversized coffee table. "But when did that ever stop you?"

"Very funny," Randall said. "Stop beating yourself up over last night, will you? It's over. Spilt milk and all that."

Molly sank into the down cushions of the sofa and sighed. "I know, but it shouldn't have happened. I don't know what came over me. Well, that's a lie. I do know, but it's too late now. I can't rewind the film."

"Will Max be mad when you tell him about the El Camino?" Emma asked.

"No, the insurance will cover it. And Max wouldn't be mad anyway," Molly said. "But it looks like we might not be able to hit the garage sales on Saturday. I don't know how long it will take for the repairs."

"Don't worry about wheels," Randall said. "You can use my car. Hell, last thing I want is to see you two moping around because you missed a sale."

"Oh, I just love you to pieces," Emma said. "Now, I won't have to tell Michelle we can't go."

"That's very nice of you," Molly said. "Thanks."

# Chapter 9

MOLLY WAS ON the phone with Max first thing the next morning. "Oh, Max," she said, "I'm just sick about this. After all it cost you to repair and paint the pickup after that Bixby Bridge incident, and now—"

"Molly, my love, please don't get worked up. The insurance will pay for it. Maybe it's time to retire the old dear. It's over thirty years old. How about one of those snazzy SUV things?"

"I wouldn't dream of having you spend that kind of money for a shop car."

"But they are practical. And at least you could protect merch better. It's a sight better for the image as well. How about it? You pick something out and I'll take it from there. Really, it's only money. And at my age, what the hell else can I spend it on?"

Molly laughed. "More merch for your shop?"

"Oh, please. I can hardly move in the shop as it is. Just get something with side airbags. And be sure it has one of those GPS thingies so next time you get into trouble Randall will be able to find you."

"Very funny," Molly said. "I'm already in trouble again. Well, not like before, but this Todd Jessop is really one for the books. I still can't believe I threw that glass of wine in his face."

"Ohhh, I wish I could have seen that! You can be such a sassy thing when you get riled up. Are you still planning on going to the big birthday bash for King Mattucci?"

"Is that what people call him? How do you know so much?"

"Darling, I made it my biz to know who all the money people were down there when I inherited the shop and the complex. Domenico Mattucci has been a big player for eons. His grandfather started out as an immigrant sheep rancher. The family bought up land in the Valley like it was going out of style. We're talking about millions and millions of dollars. This Jessop is flirting with ending up on the street."

"But I thought he was loaded," Molly said.

"Hmmm. Not like his father-in-law. I know a few dot-com players who told me that Jessop has been bragging that when 'the old man' is gone, he's going to clean house and put Bello Lago on the map."

"I don't think that's going to happen," Molly said. "I had a front-row seat the other night when he tried to push some new labels on the marketing director. He was told in no uncertain terms to mind his own business."

"Well, that's what I'm talking about. Cleaning house."

"Max? Do you think I should go to the birthday party? I mean, after what I did?"

"You have to, love. If you don't, it will look like he's won."

Molly sat up in the chair and nodded. "Right! You're absolutely right. I wouldn't give the bastard that satisfaction."

Max laughed. "I knew you'd see it that way."

Molly was in a better mood after talking to Max. She set about adding the new merch into the inventory on the computer. She'd been at it for an hour when the bell over the door rang. Molly put on a smile and was about to get up, when the man who'd bought the silver water pitcher last week entered, and asked, "Is that ship model still available?"

"Hello. Yes, it is."

"Don't get up," he said, "I'll just give it another look if you don't mind."

Molly swiveled around in her chair, about to return to the computer when she saw Bitsy Morgan coming in. She braced herself. That quick stride of Bitsy's could only mean one thing: She was upset about something. Molly was glad it wasn't her for once. Not that they argued, but Bitsy had set ways about life. And they were all *her* ways. She frequently rearranged merch in the shop after Molly had set it out, moved furniture, and had even been known to take apart flower arrangements because she didn't like a certain color.

Molly sat back in the chair and folded her arms. "Okay, what's bugging you? I can see you've got something on your mind. But it's good to have you back home."

Bitsy stood in front of Molly's desk and shook her head. "I cannot believe what I just heard! Everyone's talking about you and how you poured a bottle of very expensive wine all over Todd Jessop's head and when you went after him, you had to be pulled away. And what's this about a live skunk in your pickup in front of Daria's? I heard the same story at the post office just a few minutes ago."

Molly's mouth fell open. "What? That's crazy!" Then she remembered the man at the back of the shop. "Shh. There's a customer here in the shop."

Bitsy's head did a complete swivel. "Oh, Lord. Where?"

"He's in the back, so keep it to a low roar, okay?"

"I see him now. He can't hear us. Well, young lady?"

"It's not so," Molly said.

Bitsy pretended to hold onto the desk to stop herself from fainting. "Ohhh, thank God for that!" Then she gave Molly a look. "How did this get started? You must have done something. These things don't just fall from the sky."

Motioning Bitsy to sit at the chair next to the desk, Molly put her finger to her lips. "That man is looking at the ship model. Fourteen hundred bucks, okay?"

Bitsy sat in the chair, crossed her legs, and tapped one foot. "I'm waiting."

Molly grinned. "You're making me feel like a little kid getting scolded. Stop it, okay? The real story is…well, it's a long one, but the short version is that Todd Jessop called me a mangy bitch and I lost my head and threw a glass of wine at him. But I did not go after him. And yes, the El Camino was trashed, skunked, keyed, and the tires flattened."

Bitsy patted her chignon, shrugged ever so elegantly, then looked up at the ceiling. "Dear Lord, help me save this woman, would you please? She knows not what she does. Please tell me it's not too late."

"You'd have done the same thing, so don't get dramatic."

"Not with a client, I wouldn't," Bitsy said.

"He's not the client, his wife and her father are. And evidently her father likes me. So there. As for the truck, I think it was kids."

"We don't have kids like that in Carmel," Bitsy said.

"Then last night was a first."

"At least the job was saved. That's all that really matters, isn't it?"

Molly laughed. "You're incorrigible."

Bitsy's eyes twinkled. "Yes, I've been told that." She turned away from Molly and looked toward the back of the shop. "What the hell is he doing? Counting the planks on that old ship? Maybe I should meander down his way and—"

"He's been in before. He doesn't like hovering."

Bitsy rose. "I don't hover, darling. You should know that by now. I saunter. And I sell. Just watch me."

Molly knew Bitsy was right. She had never seen an antiques dealer close sales like she did. The woman simply oozed charm. Max said that she could turn the Bush family into Democrats.

Molly also knew it was useless to try to stop Bitsy once she'd zeroed in on a potential sale. She watched her slowly move towards the back of the shop, stopping now and then to reposition a vase to her liking, check a lampshade for dust, and rearrange a stack of old leather books. Molly decided to go back to the inventory. She hadn't the heart to watch. No sooner had she turned away when a woman close to Bitsy's age entered.

"I'll bet you're Molly Doyle," she said. With short, spiky red hair and barely five feet tall, the woman wore a gorgeous mocha wool suit that Molly figured cost as much as a first-class cruise to Mexico. If it wasn't a Chanel, it was a damn good imitation. Her outstretched hand sported an emerald ring that had to be at least four carats. "My card," she said as she handed Molly an oversized beige vellum card. In bold black letters, it read: L.A.P.D. The fine print underneath brought a big smile to Molly's face. "Del Tinsley? Is it really you?"

"In living color."

Molly laughed. "I love the card! A friend of mine would get a kick out of this. He, uh, used to work for the LAPD."

"Most of my clients would rather not have their wives find a card that read 'Lap Dancer' in their pocket." Stepping back, Del eyed the pair of chairs Molly had set near the display window. "Oh, these are mine, right? I still can't believe you managed to find six of them. So classy. Just perfect."

Returning to Molly's desk, she pulled out a check. "The boys with the truck will get here around four. I won't be able to stay. I met my client and I decided not to do his party."

Molly took the check. "Have a seat while I get your bill. Why are you passing on the party?"

"I always ask to see the guest list. I have to be sure my girls will be treated right. Most of my business comes from referrals, so a lot of the guests show up at more than one appearance. There are a few men I'd rather not have my girls entertain. Let's just say they don't follow the rules. Anyway, one of those guys is on the guest list here. When I asked that he not be invited, I was told that wasn't possible. So, I turned the evening down."

Molly handed Del her bill. "Well, in that case, I don't blame you. I, uh, imagine things can get a bit—"

"Yes. They do. But I have strict rules as well." Del checked her watch, then turned in her chair and scanned the shop. "I should have come in earlier so I could browse." Her hand flew to her mouth and she let out a laugh. "Oh, my God! Is that Bitsy Morgan?"

Molly's head jerked between Del and Bitsy. "You know Bitsy?"

Del roared. "Know her? Honey, I used to work for her!"

For the second time that morning, Molly's jaw dropped. She knew Bitsy, who had been a childhood friend of her mother, had lived in Reno some years ago, but that was when she'd been married. She watched nervously as Del headed down the main aisle.

"Bitsy Morgan! You little scamp! What the hell are you doing in Carmel?"

Molly's eyes were riveted on Bitsy. She wasn't sure what to expect. She saw Bitsy turn away from the customer. She was relieved to see the smile on her face as Del grew nearer. But her mind raced as she wondered about the connection.

"Del? Is that you? Oh, my Lord!" Bitsy threw out her arms. Both women embraced. The man interested in the ship stepped back and smiled. After a moment, he moved around the two women as they chatted and approached Molly. "It's nice to see old friends run into each other. Thank you for letting me browse. I'll think about the ship when I get home. It's large, and I'll have to find room. If you'll give me one of your cards, I'll get back to you."

Molly was about to hand him a card, when he picked up Del's off the desk. "Oh, I can take this one."

Molly wasn't quick enough to stop him. She blurted, "No. I mean, that's not mine."

Molly saw his lips tighten as he read the fine print under L.A.P.D. "I should certainly hope not." He set the card back on the desk and gave Molly a long look. "What interesting friends you have."

Before Molly could explain, he turned and left the shop. She sat back in the chair and blew out a breath. "Great!" she mumbled, "just what I needed to round out the day. I can only imagine what that man must be thinking." When Molly saw Bitsy and Del seated on two chairs by the fireplace chatting away like well-heeled grand-mothers bragging about the latest addition to their families, she couldn't help but laugh. Life, it seemed, was not meant to be dull for her. She picked up the phone and called Randall.

He answered by saying, "Don't bother me. I'm busy. I've got a town to watch."

"Where is my pickup, and when can I have it back?" she asked.

"If you're smart, which I know you're not, you won't want it back. It should be junked. That skunk smell will never leave it."

"Max more or less said the same thing. He's buying me new wheels. But I have to do something with it, don't I? I mean, send it somewhere to be junked? Oh, were you able to find any prints, or whatever you do?"

"I changed my mind about dusting it. No point in it. If it were kids, they wouldn't be on file anyway. What's he gonna get you?"

"I haven't a clue. He wants side airbags and a GPS system."

"A GPS?" Randall laughed. "Afraid you'll get lost in Carmel?"

"No, smart ass, he said it would be easier for you to find me next time I get in trouble."

"There ain't gonna be a next time. I'll call him. You should have a Chevy Tahoe. You can haul all that stuff you buy for pennies from unsuspecting people."

"I could hang up on you, you know."

"Go ahead, but first let me tell you there are some crazy rumors running around town about you and Todd Jessop."

"Thanks, but I've heard them. Bitsy filled me in."

"Then you know about the one where you threatened to kill him?"

"Oh, my God! Where did you hear that?"

"I was having coffee this morning at the Village Corner. One of our local mystery writers who hangs out there told me. She thought it was a hoot and said she ought to do a book about you."

"Swell. Like I need more press? How am I going to face people now?"

"With a smile," Randall said.

"Can you meet me at Tosca's in a few minutes? Bitsy is here. I'll ask her to watch the shop for me. You've got to help me sort this out."

"I'm on my way."

Bitsy and Del were still gabbing a mile a minute when Molly approached them. Bitsy was delighted to take over for Molly. "We're having such a grand reunion that Del has decided to stay over. You go right ahead. Take your time."

*Grand reunion?* Molly almost winced. If she didn't have her own reputation to worry about at the moment, she'd be hard-pressed not to sit in on the gab fest. It blew her mind to think of Bitsy Morgan as a bordello madam. How else, she wondered, could Del Tinsley have worked for her? Somehow she doubted it was selling antiques.

# Chapter 10

MOLLY RUSHED to the storage room and ran a brush through her hair. She found an empty small café table next to the three-tiered fountain in the center of the courtyard. She figured the sound of splashing water would make it hard for the nearby table to hear her conversation with Randall. Tosca's was a self-serve operation, but its owner, Bennie Infama, was always on the move clearing tables and chatting with the regulars. Bennie spotted Molly right away. "Hey, gorgeous, you taking a break? What can I get you?"

Molly fiddled with the Zippo. "I'm waiting for Randall. Maybe just coffee? Mind if I smoke? The tables next to me are empty."

Bennie smiled. "Sure, go ahead. I can relate. It ain't a good day for you, huh?"

Randall arrived just then, and said, "It ain't a good day for either of us."

Bennie Infama, short, wiry, and never without his Giants baseball cap, just shy of thirty and the proud owner of Tosca's, took a step back. As well as he'd come to know Randall, he was still intimidated by his presence. His smile was weak when he said, "Uh, yeah, I've heard the rumors. Take a seat, Chief. Double espresso on your mind, maybe?"

Randall pulled out a chair across from Molly. "Maybe a full pot might work."

Molly's shoulders slumped. "Now what?"

"A lesson in village dynamics. The rumor mill is on fire, and I think you'd better call Carla Jessop and clear the air because I'm not going to put up with this shit."

"Look, I appreciate your concern. I'll call Carla, but I'm just going to ignore—"

"It's not just you now. I got a call from the mayor before I left. I'm on the hot seat now for telling Todd Jessop he might not see daylight. Which is being interpreted that I'm gunning for him."

Molly's hands flew to her mouth. "Omigod. I remember. Last Saturday night in the shop when those two women walked in on us. But that's just a figure of speech."

Randall's laugh wasn't very merry. "So is 'my fellow Americans.' When did you ever believe a politician felt like he was one of us?"

"But still? I mean, how can anyone take these rumors seriously?"

Before Randall could answer, Bennie arrived with a tray. "Two double espressos and apricot tarts. I figured you'd need some sugar since this looks like a meeting of the minds."

"Sit down, Bennie," Randall said. "What else is being said?"

Bennie shook his head as he set out the cups. "About what?"

Randall just looked at him.

Bennie pulled out a chair and flopped down. "Okay, probably what you've already heard. You and Molly want a piece of a guy named Tim Jester."

Molly couldn't help laugh. "You'd think they could get the name straight!"

"Naturally," Bennie added, "I said it was baloney. I mean, hell, Randall, you're the chief of police, for crying out loud! And Molly sells antiques. Besides, who the hell is Tim Jester? He's not local. I'd know him."

Randall sipped his espresso, then grinned at Molly. "Maybe we'll beat this rap."

"This is insane, damn it!" Molly said. "I can't go to that party for Carla's father now. And neither can you."

"What party?" Bennie asked.

"Domenico Mattucci's birthday party this Sunday."

Bennie almost fell out of his chair. "Whoa! Mattucci? You know him?"

"Slightly," Molly said. "I know his daughter, Carla. I'm helping her redecorate the tasting room at Bello Lago."

"Whew," Bennie said.

Molly threw up her hands. "Please don't give me a running history of the family, okay?" She shot a look at Randall. "I've heard it all. I know they're big wheels, I know I came close to losing the job and I'm sick to death about what I did!" She tapped her neck. "And I'm up to here in advice, so spare me."

Bennie said, "Then you know about—"

"Bennie!"

"What, Bennie?" Randall probed. "I'm all ears. It's gossip day in Carmel-by-the-Sea anyway." He picked up his cup, then halted. "Unless you were going to tell me that Mattucci's father was connected. I already know about that."

Molly almost choked on her pastry. "Connected? As in...in—"

"Yeah," Randall said.

"But only slightly," Bennie said.

"There ain't no slightly, Bennie. Not with that crowd."

"I'm going back to the shop," Molly said. "I'm going to scoot Bitsy and...and her friend out, put up the 'closed' sign, and then go take a nap."

"It's kind of early for a nap," Bennie said.

"Time waits for no migraine," Molly said. She rose, reached for her tote, then remembered she hadn't brought it. "I seem to be without funds." She looked at Randall. "Your treat."

Molly's head was pounding when she returned to the shop. Bitsy and Del were still by the fireplace, only now two more women had pulled up chairs to join them. Molly headed their way. When the new arrivals turned in her direction, Molly was stunned by their beauty. Del rose. "You're just in time to meet my associates before they head back to the City."

The first one to offer her hand was a tiny brunette with flowing hair down her back. She was dressed in a luscious ivory silk pantsuit. The to-die-for yellow jade earrings she wore made Molly want to lick her lips. "I'm P.J. Coldren," she said. "Del has told us so much about you. It's so great that we had a chance to meet the woman who is finding us such perfect chairs."

Molly smiled and shook her hand. "I'm, uh, thrilled you like them."

The second woman, another stunner, was taller than Molly. Her wavy, thick auburn hair hung down past her waist. Molly wondered if long hair was a prerequisite for the job. Lavender was obviously her color and she was dressed in a silk pantsuit as well. Molly noted the expensive cut and wondered just how lucrative being an *associate* was. "Good to meet you, Molly. I'm Alma Faye. Keep finding us chairs, huh? A little cushier would be great, too." She laughed. "On the arms, I mean."

"I'll do my best," Molly said as she took a few steps back. "Great meeting all of you, but I, ah, well, I'm closing early, so if…"

Bitsy rose, shook out the wrinkles in her skirt, then gave Molly a wink. "Good idea, you look tired. The ladies and I are going over to the Pine Inn for drinks. Del and I have years to catch up on."

As the women moved past her, Molly said, "I'll put a note for your movers on the door, Del. I'll be able to hear them from the storage room when they knock."

Bitsy said, "They've been and gone. Oh, I sold two lamps while you were out. The tags are on the desk." Bitsy winked at Alma. "This lovely lady helped make the sale. The man was so taken with her, I damned near had to push him out the door."

Molly's smile was weak. "Oh, great. Thanks."

"It was fun. The customer said he was with IBM and if I ever decided on a career change I should look him up." Alma's eyes took in the shop. "Nice place, Molly. I might even think about an antiques shop."

Molly wanted to say, Great, just stay out of Carmel, but said, "I'm sure you'd do fine in any sales profession. You, uh, didn't give him your card, did you?"

"Of course I did," Alma said.

Molly was ready to explode. It was a good thing Bitsy saw the look in Molly's eye. She quickly hustled everyone out. "We've really got to run, Molly. I'll call you later, okay?"

The minute they left, Molly locked the door and put out the

CLOSED sign. She stormed into the storage room, kicked off her shoes, and lit a cigarette. "If this shit keeps up, I'll never be able to quit," she shouted. She moved Tiger off the armchair and sank onto the tattered upholstery. A stiff drink would be perfect, but after the apricot tart, she didn't need more sugar. She was already battling ten extra pounds. Just looking at Del's *associates* was enough to make her realize how much she'd let herself get out of shape. All her plans to resume the beach walks were already distant memories. Those women had to be size three and spend all day at the gym. She knew damn well their profession wasn't very energetic. What really bugged her was, they didn't look or act like, well, exotic dancers. They were absolutely gorgeous! It wasn't fair.

Molly stubbed out her cigarette and fanned the air. She was out of the spray she used to hide the smell of smoke. Emma would smell it and be on her case the minute she got home from school. Molly sank deeper into the chair and held her head in her hands. She had no one but herself to blame for this mess, but she had to do something about these insane rumors. It was even more crazy now that Randall was involved. Well, she thought, at least they had the name wrong, but she'd better call Carla Jessop and warn her. Molly picked up the storage room phone and hit the speed dial.

Carla picked up on the first ring. "Yes, Molly," she said. "I've heard all about it. It's hysterical! I can't believe how out of hand this is!"

"I'm glad you think it's funny. I sure as hell don't. I'm twice mortified now. At least they have the name wrong."

"Poor Randall." Carla laughed. "He must be having a fit. Now listen, before you tell me you're not coming on Sunday, forget it. The worst thing you could do is not show up. Besides, my father said he hasn't had this much fun in years. He really liked you. And he has a lot of respect for Randall."

Molly sighed. "Okay, under those conditions we'll be there."

"By the way, I'm sorry about your pickup. We've got plenty of cars around here if you need a loaner." Carla laughed again. "I'll bet that skunk smell kept some of those blue-nosed Carmelites up all night."

"It sure as hell kept me awake. Thanks for the offer of a car. Max thinks it's time to get a new one, so I'll be fine."

"Before I forget, Molly, can Michelle take a rain check on staying over Friday night? My son is coming in from Davis on Friday and we'd like to have a family thing."

"No problem, we'll have her over another time."

Molly was relieved that Michelle wouldn't be staying over. She had forgotten all about it and hadn't picked up a futon for Emma's room. She was dying for another cigarette but knew Emma would be home very soon. Molly eased out of the chair and surveyed the storage room. She needed to replace the two lamps Bitsy had sold. She could use some distraction right now, and filling two holes in the shop could work.

She stared at the three six-foot shelves that lined one wall of the narrow room. They were filled with merchandise ready to roll. She looked over the lamps on the top shelf that she had made from interesting vases and large statues, then pulled one off the shelf and set it on the floor. She thought about filling the other empty space with a statue. Her eyes roamed the shelves filled with silver trays, coffee sets, and odds and ends of flatware. She passed over the smaller statues and figurines, then paused at a group of odd sets of china, crystal, leather books, decorative desk accessories. She needed something different, something dramatic.

And then she remembered the boxes of Orientalia Max had sent. Going out to the garage, she looked over the mix of Chinese and Japanese bowls and chargers Emma had tagged and placed on the folding tables. The three different figures of Guanyin, the Chinese goddess of mercy, would make an interesting display. She thought about grouping them with potted orchids when her eyes locked on a lovely pair of Foo Dogs.

"Eureka!" she shouted. At least a foot tall, they were glazed a beautiful green and blue. They were heavier than she'd expected. It took some effort to carry one under each arm into the shop. Molly carefully set them in front of the display window. Within a few moments, she was able to position one statue at each corner of the window. That ought to do it, she thought. Skeptics laughed at Feng

Shui, but not Molly Doyle. She knew the ancient legends surrounding these figures of half dog and half lion. They were the sacred guardians of Buddhist temples and could be found all over Asia guarding homes, businesses, and temple gates from evil spirits, and that was good enough for her. From now on, she thought, if anyone wants to mess with me, they'll have to get past these babies.

# Chapter 11

BY MIDAFTERNOON on Friday, Molly had all the new merch from Max on the floor and she was ready to scream. Treasures looked like a gypsy caravan had unloaded all its worldly possessions with no thought to form, color, or era. She couldn't believe she'd made such a mess. A natural when it came to layering, composition, and style, Molly suddenly seemed to be lost in a dark tunnel. She'd placed a late nineteenth-century multi-veined black-and-white marble-topped center table with a gesso base next to a dark oak coffer, then settled an oversized and much too busy-looking Chinese *famille verte* bowl on top. It looked horrible. The coffer had to go: it was too informal and plain. Once she pulled the coffer out of the way, the Chinese bowl looked fine. To the average eye, the combination wouldn't have seemed out of place, but Molly didn't create displays for "average." Much as women didn't dress for men, but for other women, antiques dealers—the genuine articles—set out their shops with a competitive eye geared for the *cognoscenti*, and naturally, to invoke envy from their competitors.

Molly stood in the center of the floor and folded her arms. What had happened to her sense of proportion? Her eye for color? Her talent for mixing periods and layering? Her gaze rested on a pair of Staffordshire figures of shepherds she'd positioned next to a Davenport potpourri vase and a Victorian Minton Parian model of *Una and the Lion*. She rubbed her tired eyes and shook her head. Layering had to have form and aesthetic appeal. This tableau was ridiculous. The colors were off and the size of the items didn't complement one another. She picked up the Parian piece and carried it back to her desk. Setting it down carefully, she sat in her chair and stared at the fifteen-hundred-dollar statue. Molly began to wonder if she was losing her touch. Most likely, she thought, she'd been in too much of a hurry to get everything on the floor. She ran her hand over the smooth surface of the statue. Her fingers gently followed the curve of the lion's mane while she finally admitted to herself that the reason for her manic schedule was that she was spooked.

The vandalism to the pickup had unnerved her. Between Carla's and Randall's warnings, she felt wary every time the bell over the door rang, even though her brief moments of logic told her that Todd Jessop would be crazy to do anything in public. And yesterday's arrival of the new Chevy Uplander Max had delivered did little to cheer her. In fact, she already hated the new van and missed the old El Camino. It took her over an hour to read the manual, and she still didn't understand how the GPS system worked. The El Camino had been so easy: Put in the key, hit the gas, and off you went.

Molly thought of calling off dinner at Daria's tonight. Tuesday and Friday were, as Daria proclaimed, family night in her back room. She had to get this hodgepodge in the shop rearranged before tomorrow. The weekends were her biggest sales days, and she'd be damned if she'd let a customer or Bitsy see this mess. She scanned the room and still couldn't believe some of the combinations she'd created. What had she been thinking when she'd placed those two Windsor-style chairs on either side of the early-nineteenth-century Scandinavian walnut commode? And then set the rare Paillard gramophone next to a mother-of-pearl-inlaid papier-mâché stationery box? She *wasn't* thinking, and that was the problem. She knew she was allowing the rumors about her threatening Jessop to rattle her. That realization set her blood racing. Her anger jolted her upright. "Screw Todd Jessop," she said aloud.

When Emma got home from school, Molly said, "Roll up your sleeves, Number One, we've got two hours to get this place in shape. We need to do some rearranging. A bonus will be forthcoming as well."

Emma surveyed the shop. She walked over to the marble center table. "Who went nuts?"

Molly's grin was playfully tight. "A bonus can be rescinded real easy." She steered her away from the table and moved her to the back of the floor. "Let's see what kind of an eye you've developed. I'll take the front and meet you in the middle." Molly checked her watch. "We have to be at Daria's for dinner in exactly one and a half hours."

Emma raised her arm. "Ready, get set, and go!"

Daria's call caught Molly just as she and Emma were about to leave. "I've got two kitchen helpers off sick and I've got to fill in. Rain check for tomorrow, okay?"

"Of course. Can I help out? I can wash dishes, or something," Molly said.

"No, we're okay, but thanks. Oh, Randall had to opt out, too. He said he was on his way to the City."

"Well, call me if you need an extra hand, okay? Maybe an early night is a good idea. Emma and I are hitting the sales tomorrow and there's a six A.M. sale with silver listed."

"Six? Egad. You're a glutton for punishment."

"It's the biz, kiddo," Molly laughed.

The early sale the next morning was a co-op block sale. Molly bought every piece of decent silver she could find. By the time she and Emma loaded the van with trays, coffeepots, sugar-and-creamers, salt-and-pepper shakers, and three water pitchers, they'd run out of empty boxes.

Heading to the next sale on Molly's list, Emma said, "I can't believe people don't want to keep silver anymore. Some of those trays are just beautiful."

"Uh, hang on a minute," Molly said while she readjusted her seat. "I'm still trying to get the feel of this van.... I think people don't want to bother with cleaning them. Here on the coast, silver and copper tarnish fast."

"You've changed that seat and the rearview mirror three times since we got in this morning," Emma said. "Why are you so nervous?"

"I'm not nervous. I just need to get everything set, that's all."

"Is it about the party tomorrow at the Jessops'? And those crazy rumors?"

Molly laughed. "Don't be goofy. I'm fine."

They'd sped through four more sales in the next hour, when finally they found one that caught their interest. Emma made a beeline for a set of crammed bookshelves, while Molly headed for a long table filled with smalls. But she hardly glanced at the offerings. Emma was right. She was antsy about the party, and she was sorry Emma had noticed. If for no other reason, she would go to show her that facing her accusers was the right thing to do. She knew she would be the object of stares and sidelong glances, and she'd had enough of that the past two years.

Molly spotted Emma waiting for her at the van. Her arms were loaded with books. Molly opened the door for her. "Quite a haul there."

"Most of them are children's books. Fairy tales. And only fifty cents each. I'm going to give them to the library for their book sale. I bought a couple of books for you, too. I thought that maybe if you read a little before you went to sleep, it might relax you."

Molly climbed in and was about to adjust the rearview mirror but caught herself again. "Well, thank you. I haven't read much lately. I'll give it a try. What did you get?"

"Mysteries. Reading in bed is soothing, so I thought you might like them."

Molly laughed. "Oh great! Just what I need to scare me more. Mysteries!"

Bitsy stood in the doorway between the storage room and the garage watching Molly and Emma unload the van. "How much silver can Daria use? Good Lord! The woman has enough to supply two restaurants."

"I don't know, but she wants all I can find," Molly replied.

"How much did all this set you back?"

Molly set down the last of the trays. "Eighty-five bucks. Can you believe it? Two of them are marked Tiffany and Company."

"Maybe you should keep those for the shop," Bitsy laughed.

Molly gave Bitsy a look. "That woman feeds Emma and me like royalty twice a week."

Bitsy waved her hands. "Oh, darling, I know that. Just kidding. Anyway, all set for the big party tomorrow?"

Molly forced a smile. The last person she wanted to know that she wasn't thrilled about going was Bitsy. "Sure am. And thanks for filling in for me again. By the way, I'm dying to know how you and Del Tinsley know each other."

Before Bitsy could reply, the bell over the door rang. Bitsy patted her hair. "Oh, I love that sound! Del? We'll talk later. And wait until you find out why she cancelled the engagement out in the Valley."

Leave it to Bitsy, Molly thought. How she managed to know everything that went on was mindboggling. While Emma took the children's books to the library, Molly began the messy job of cleaning the silver for Daria. After an hour, she realized Bitsy hadn't popped her head in. She washed her hands and went into the shop.

"Am I glad to see you! It's been a zoo. Six good sales. Oh, that man who was in the other day when Del was here? He stopped back. He bought the ship and took it with him. I offered to send it, but he insisted. What a nosy old coot. He kept mentioning Emma and how much she reminded him of someone he knew. And then he asked about you, and why she was living here and not with her mother. I was frankly getting a little nervous."

"What did you tell him?"

"As little as possible. I just said Emma's mother was overseas with a new job and would be back this summer. I told him she was a delightful child and we all adored her. And then he wanted to know who I meant by *we*. So I said, our close friends, the chief of police and our district attorney. I figured those were good names to drop in case he was one of those perverts."

"Good thinking. I'll keep a lookout for him."

When Molly returned to the garage, Emma was folding bubble wrap. "I picked up the mail, too. It's on the table by the Chinese bowls. There's a pretty postcard from Rome. But there's no message. Guess it's from a friend of yours and they forgot to write."

Molly picked up the postcard. Her name and address were on

the same kind of printed label as the first postcard. She shook her head. "I have no idea who sent this. I got one last week from London."

Emma giggled. "Maybe it's a secret lover and he's teasing you."

Molly rolled her eyes. "Yeah, right. That's all I need now. Another mystery."

# Chapter 12

THE CARMEL HIGHLANDS, just south of Carmel and on the northern edge of the Big Sur coastline, is a small community with homes hugging spectacular cliffs on both sides of Highway One. The brochures from nearby five-star hotels proclaimed the Highlands as a front-row seat to nature for whale and sea otter watching. Once populated by a small group of metaphysical-type residents, it soon became home to a wealthier contingent, and now residential prices vied with Pebble Beach's. The oceanside homes were the most adventurous and intriguing. The architecture ran the gamut from Spanish Colonial to stark modern boxes on gigantic stilts, perched precariously on the edge of massive cliffs. The roar of crashing waves was often thunderous.

It was early afternoon on Sunday when Molly slowed the van as she approached the Jessop home. A long line of cars idled as each guest waited for a parking valet. From what she could see as she inched down the sloping drive, the home was a dramatic fusion of contemporary and Japanese architecture. The wood's weathered gray stain blended perfectly with the bark of the towering pines and the many gnarled cypress trees surrounding the structure. Windowless from the street, wide and low-slung, with its sweeping vistas of the ocean already visible from the drive, the house seemed to be clinging to the very edge of the world. Molly had a hard time visualizing Carla living there. She seemed too vibrant, too full of life to live in this almost monastic-looking house. Molly shivered and pulled the sweater wrapped around her shoulders tighter.

"When is Randall coming?" Emma asked as they crossed a small wooden bridge to the entry. Molly rang the bell, and shrugged.

"Dunno. He said he'd be a little late." She checked her watch. "I hope he gets here pretty soon, though. We really don't know anyone here."

"Hell, you know me!" a voice behind her said. Molly turned and smiled. "Dan! You walk like a cat. I didn't hear you coming."

Dan Lucero, Monterey County's district attorney, gave Molly a hug, then leaned down and pecked Emma on the cheek. "I'm taking lessons from Randall. He keeps telling me to walk softly and carry a big stick."

"Yeah? Well, you still don't have it right," Randall said as he stood in the open door.

Lucero grinned. "I'm working on it, okay?"

"Typical politician double-speak. Always working on things that never get done."

"I thought you were coming later," Emma said.

"Change in plan." Waving them in, Randall said, "Carla told me to be on the lookout for you, so I've been hanging around the front door. The party is outside on the terrace. We've got to go downstairs to get there."

Molly had no idea so many people had been invited. The guests were shoulder-to-shoulder on the large wrap-around stone terrace. It would have taken a linebacker to get through to the bar and buffet tables. Randall and Lucero were stopped several times by acquaintances as they attempted to find an empty table. Michelle appeared and pulled on Molly's hand. "My mother saved a table for all of you. Follow me."

Finally seated near the edge of the terrace, they had a magnificent view of the ocean. When Emma asked permission to run off with Michelle, Molly said, "Don't go down near the rocks, okay? And check in with me every now and then."

When a waiter approached to take their orders, Molly pulled her sweater closer against the breeze coming off the water. "I think I'll just have coffee," Molly said. Randall grinned, ordered a drink, and winked at Lucero, who had already managed to grab a glass of wine from a nearby server. "Good idea, Ms. Molly. The road is twisty enough when you're sober."

Dan Lucero set his glass down. "Is there a hidden message here I'm missing?"

"What? You mean you haven't heard?" Molly said. "Hell, I figured an indictment was already on your desk by now. I mean, aren't death threats illegal?"

Dan looked at Randall. "What the hell is she talking about?"

By the time Randall finished telling him of Molly's misadventure with Todd Jessop and the rumors in town that had quickly included him as well, Dan was on his second glass of wine. "I leave town for a few days and everything comes apart. Is that what you're telling me? Can't you two stay out of trouble?"

Randall laughed. "It seems to follow our Molly here like a magnet."

"You're on the bubble, too, you know," Molly said.

Randall waved her off. "That's baloney. What I said to Jessop was just a figure of speech. I didn't throw wine in the guy's face, you did."

Lucero played with his glass. "A figure of speech, as you well know, can be damning these days."

"Aw, come on, Dan! This whole thing is out of hand. I'm a cop. I could have been talking about putting him in jail. Same thing. In fact, I should have nailed the bastard then. Only Carla wouldn't co-operate."

"Be quiet," Molly said. "Here she comes."

"Hey, the gang's all here!" Carla said. "Thanks for coming. Dad saw you all arrive together and was so happy you were able to make it. He'll be over soon. Dando has outdone himself today. Wait until you see the buffet. He's had the catering crew working day and night."

"Is he gonna show up for once?" Dan asked. He looked at Randall and Molly. "I've been to three parties that man cooked for, and I still haven't met him."

Carla shook her head. "You know Dando. Don't count on it. He's already gone back to the ranch. Anyway, I wanted to come over before the music starts. You won't be able to hear yourself think once that gets underway."

After Carla left, Dan said, "I'll bet every wine grower, boutique vintner, and rancher in Monterey County is here." His eyes roamed the vast terrace. "Reminds me of the parties the old-timers used to give. Tons of food, enough wine to stock three stores, and music. Speaking of which, here come the accordion players. Too bad my folks are still up at Tahoe. Dad would have loved this."

"I didn't know your father knew ranchers. I thought he stuck with his fishing gang," Randall said.

"Big family history, Carla's and mine. Goes back to World War Two," Dan replied. "Italian fishermen on the coast had to be relocated inland. Carla's grandfather took my dad's family in. They stayed there throughout the war."

Molly was stunned. "I had no idea. I always thought only the Japanese were uprooted."

"Most people don't know it," Randall said. "My mother's family in the City were restaurant people, so they got a pass. But they were still watched."

Before Molly could comment, the three accordion players were only a few tables away and further conversation was impossible. She saw Randall's lips move and leaned into the table. "What did you say?"

"Not for pristine ears. Todd Jessop is coming this way."

"Let's hope somebody stops him to talk," Molly nearly shouted.

Lucero leaned in, too. He jerked his head toward Jessop. "God loves us. Someone has. The coast is clear. Just make sure your glass is empty, Molly."

Molly laughed. "I'm drinking coffee, smart ass." Molly rose. "In fact, I think I'll mingle. Anyone else care to offer Mr. Mattucci best wishes? He's over by the wall."

Randall and Lucero followed Molly to a low stone wall at the edge of the terrace where Domenico Mattucci was talking with a group of men. "Happy birthday, Mr. Mattucci," Molly offered.

Taking her hand in his, he said, "Thank you for coming, Molly. We've got another feast today. Better than the other night, if you can believe that. Stick by me, and I'll fill you with more of my private stock."

Molly laughed, "I think I'll be staying with coffee from now on."

Domenico roared. Turning to the men with him, he said, "Maybe that's a good idea! That was such a waste the other night. But I have more Barbera. We'll have another bottle later." Turning to Randall and Lucero, he said, "I'm glad to see Molly in such good company. You boys take good care of her, *capisce?*"

Randall shook Mattucci's hand. "She's a handful, but I'll make sure she stays out of trouble. Happy birthday, and many more."

Lucero edged Randall away. "Hey, don't pay any attention to him, Dom! Molly can handle herself. From what I've heard, I think you got a taste of that already. Happy birthday, you old coot."

If Molly thought being surrounded by friendly faces would keep Todd Jessop away, she was wrong. She saw a small group nearby shift as Jessop moved towards her. Standing against the wall with the ocean behind her, Molly had no clear way to avoid him. Hemmed in as she was, her only option was to get between Randall and Domenico, but Jessop was already in front of her. When Molly saw his arms stretched toward her, she threw up hers to ward him off and managed to squeeze aside, leaving her place at the wall the only spot for Jessop to end up. She felt Randall holding her back, when Jessop turned to face her. His lips parted as if he were about to speak, but only a sharp intake of his breath could be heard. He seemed to falter, then threw out a hand to take hold of the wall. His eyes were bulging in shock as he looked down and saw blood spreading across his shirt.

Randall caught Jessop as he slowly collapsed. Lucero pulled her away, and then moved Domenico close to Molly further down the wall. "Stay put."

Molly couldn't move. She watched Jessop unwind and felt sick. Her throat felt seeping acid. She clung to the wall. Once Lucero cleared the crowd back, she saw Jessop's body on the stone pavers. Her heart was hammering and her hands began to shake. She felt for the small crucifix beneath her sweater and closed her eyes. After a moment, she remembered Mr. Mattucci was only inches away. She touched him on the shoulder and leaned down. "Are you okay? Can I do anything for you?"

He reached for her hand. "I'm okay. It's Carla I'm worried about. Can you see her?"

Molly's eyes scanned the crowd, which had retreated several feet. "No. I can't make her out. There's so many people."

"Someone will find her. Watch for her, please."

Lucero was still moving people out of the way. He had to raise his voice over their noise. "We've got an accident here, move back, please. We need room." He joined Randall as he knelt by Jessop's body. Randall had his cell out and was talking to the dispatcher at the sheriff's office. "No rush on the ambulance. He's dead. Right, I'll secure the scene until your team gets here."

Randall said to Lucero, "We need a six-foot perimeter."

"Done," Lucero said.

To the crowd standing by in shock, Randall said, "Everyone please stay where you are. We've got a situation here. The sheriff's department will be handling this, and they're on the way. You're all on a guest list, so I'll caution you not to leave. Unless you're a physician and on call, I'm going to ask you all to turn off your cell phones."

Randall saw Reggie Sullivan a few feet away. "Reggie! Take care of the catering crew for me. Get a head count and make sure everyone stays put. Same with the waiters and valets. Same rules about cell phones." He was about to commandeer Dino Horne to help, when he saw Carla Jessop making her way through the crowd. "Stay back, Carla. Don't come any closer. Please."

Carla ignored Randall and pushed Dino's arm away. She stood a few feet from the body of her husband. Her face was still. It was difficult to see her breathe as she stared at Todd. "What happened?"

Randall wasn't surprised by her calm voice. People react in strange ways when confronted by a dead body, spouse or not. He'd seen rage, hysteria, and ice-cold control. He knew Carla was a strong woman and could take the truth. "He was shot."

Carla's eyes met Randall's. "Is he—?"

Randall nodded.

Carla lifted her chin, then took a deep breath. "Cover him up."

"I can't touch him, Carla. The crime scene people would have my head."

Carla turned away. She moved to her father. "Are you okay?"

Mattucci nodded. "Listen to Randall. Come over here, out of the way." He caught Molly looking at him and winked.

Molly was shocked. She wondered if anyone had seen him do that. She found a chair and nearly fell into it. Her next thought was of Emma. She had an idea the two girls were watching movies in the den. She knew she should check on them, but she was too numb to move, and Randall had said not to leave. All sorts of horrors filled her mind. What if the killer was still here? What if he was hiding in the house and felt cornered? What if he found Emma and Michelle and decided to use them as hostages? She had to know they were safe. It was worth Randall's wrath. Molly looked around to see if there was a way to sneak away without being seen. Pushing through the crowd of guests now herded to the other end of the terrace, Molly signaled Lucero. When he reached her, she said, "I have to find Emma and Michelle. I'll make sure they stay in the house."

Over the wails of the sirens from the sheriff's units pulling into the drive, Lucero said, "Jesus, Molly! You can't! Didn't you hear what Randall said? This is a crime scene now, and you were right there."

"I have to find them! I don't dare let them walk out here and see...the body. Besides, Michelle might worry about her mother." Molly began to turn away when two sheriff's deputies stormed in. Lucero mumbled, "Oh, shit. Not Reynolds? Randall is gonna love this."

"Is this the guy that gave him such a bad time last year when—"

"Yeah. The very same. Better figure he's going to want to talk to you."

"Me? Why?"

Lucero looked at Molly. "Come on, Molly. You were right there. Everyone saw it."

"But so were other people! You were there, and so was Randall." She held out her hands. "Want to check me for powder? Hidden pockets where I stashed my gun?"

"Calm down. He'll eventually hear about the rumors, so don't lose your cool. The guy's a prick. Don't antagonize him."

Molly turned away. "Well, then keep him busy while I'm gone. I'll sneak back in."

She found Emma and Michelle in the den. Michelle hit the remote to freeze the film. "Is it time for the buffet?" she asked. "The movie is almost over, can we..." She saw the serious look on Molly's face. "Oh, oh. What's wrong now? Did old Todd shoot off his mouth again?"

Molly winced when Michelle said "shoot." "Uh, no. But there's been an accident. What I mean, is...well, Todd has been shot." Both girls sat upright on the sofa, their eyes widening.

Emma grabbed Michelle's hand, and said, "Oh, no! Oh, this is awful."

"I want both of you to stay here until I come and get you. Lock this door. Don't let anyone in here. The sheriff's people have just arrived and...well, just stay put. Your mother is fine, Michelle, so don't worry about her."

"We'll stay here," Emma said. "Is he...I mean, did he die?"

"Yes," Molly said. "Almost immediately."

Michelle's eyelids flickered, and her voice was shaking. "Who did it?"

Molly shook her head. "I've no idea. It happened so quick, I'm not sure about anything." Just that I'm in the thick of things again, she thought.

# Chapter 13

"I'LL TAKE OVER NOW, Mr. Randall," Lieutenant Reynolds said. He jerked his head dismissively. "You and Lucero join the crowd. I'll get to you both later." To the large throng of guests, he announced, "No chit-chat, people. Understood? I won't keep you longer than necessary, but I have to insist on your cooperation. I can't have a low roar going on while my people are doing their job."

Randall didn't move. "I issued a closed cell phone order, and—"

"I said, I'd take over now." Reynolds said.

Randall shoved his hands in his pockets and smiled. "Am I supposed to salute you now, too?" He winked at Lucero and said, "Come on, I'll buy you a beer."

Lucero was grinding his teeth. It was a bad habit he had when he wanted to punch someone out. He'd developed it as a young man growing up on Cannery Row. You had to be tough to work the fishing boats, and tempers were often short after eighteen hours without sleep. Only his dreams of pitching for the San Francisco Giants and caring for his hands kept him out of most brawls. Randall, on the other hand, had played football and was happy to brawl. His parting shot to Reynolds seemed to offer an invitation. Lucero knew the bad blood between the two men wasn't going to spill out here. Randall would save it for later. Reynolds's curt dismissal hadn't been lost on the guests or on Domenico Mattucci. A pin, as is said, could have been heard dropping. The blatant lack of professional courtesy was also obviously noted by two other guests, both reporters from the local newspapers. Lucero could only imagine what they planned to do with that bit of news.

Lucero moved closer to Randall. His voice was low. "Screw him. So, what's your take on this?"

Randall looked up beyond the roof to the towering pine trees on both sides of the house. "An unusually gifted marksman who knows how to climb a tree. And cautious enough to use a silencer."

Lucero followed Randall's gaze. "You're kidding me. Not on the roof?"

"I'd bet on the trees. When they do the triangulation, they're going to be all over those Monterey pines for trace evidence."

"That's one hell of a shooter. Pro? Can't be a local hunter. No one around here is that good, and I know a lot of them."

"Then Reynolds has his hands full." Randall looked at Lucero, then grinned. "Couldn't happen to a nicer guy."

They joined the nervous guests corralled at the far end of the terrace. Randall said to Lucero in a low voice, "These people are going to start getting antsy and pulling rank pretty soon if Reynolds decides to drag this out."

Nodding to some of the guests he knew, Lucero whispered back, "Yeah? Who they gonna call? I'm about as high rank as they can find, and I'm sitting here with you like some bum off the street."

"Maybe you should do some quiet schmoozing and remind everyone to be patient until after the crime scene techs and the M.E. are gone. I'd do it, but I don't want Reynolds to think I'm butting in. I don't need grief with that prick."

Lucero laughed. "What is this? The indomitable Randall backing off?"

"I choose my battlegrounds, pal. And I've got a feeling I'll be needing one soon enough, but this ain't it."

Lucero saw Molly heading their way. "Better set one up for Molly, too. We know he's going to zero in on her."

When Molly joined them at a table they had managed to commandeer, Lucero left to make his rounds. "Where the hell have you been?" Randall said. "Didn't I tell you to stay put?"

"I had to find Emma and Michelle and tell them to stay in the den."

"Damn, but you've got a hard head."

"Don't start. I'm already a wreck. What's going on now?"

Randall put his finger to his lips. "Reynolds has decreed there be no loud talking, so keep your voice down and be ready for the third degree from him."

"No talking? He can't tell us not to talk, for God's sake!"

"Molly, please, okay? Just humor him. He's an ass. We all know that. But this is his show so don't color outside the lines." He reached for the sweater she had tied around her shoulders and pulled it around her. "You're shivering. You okay?"

"No, I'm not. If I…if I hadn't moved away—" Her breath caught. "Could that bullet have been meant for me?"

"That's crazy. Who the hell would want to kill you?"

"What about my pickup? The postcards?"

"What postcards? What the hell is going on now? You back to keeping things from me? I thought we worked that out."

Molly clutched the ends of her sweater sleeves, rolling the cuffs between her fingers, searching for some tiny bit of comfort. "I've been getting some strange postcards. Addressed to me, but no message, no signature, nothing. One from London, and one from Rome."

"When did this start?"

"A week ago. But at first I thought it might be a client, maybe in a hurry. When the second one arrived, it made me leery. And then I wondered if maybe they're from my sister Carrie telling me she's okay."

"Or maybe your errant hubby taunting you? Hell, I'll bet he saw your face plastered all over CNN last year."

Molly began to tremble as the body of Todd Jessop was wheeled past her. Her eyes fixed on the black body bag. When it was gone, she stared at the crime-scene area taped off with small pylons and markers. The chalked outline of Todd Jessop's body brought on another shudder. "Molly, look at me, not that stuff," Randall said gently. "The techs and M.E. are leaving. So, do you think the cards came from Porter?"

"It's not Derek. The last thing he'd do is give me a clue where he is. He knows I'd be on the phone with the New York police."

Randall was about to reply when Reynolds arrived at their table. "I thought I'd ordered no chit-chat. Button it up here."

Randall rose. He said nothing, but the look in his eyes said volumes.

Reynolds stepped back. He hooked his thumbs into his belt and said, "I expect you, of all people, to cooperate."

Randall smiled then. "I don't know what handbook you're working from, but you're out of line asking for complete silence. So, do me a favor. Buzz off and get your people working on statements. You have no right to keep these people longer than necessary."

Reynolds nodded to the two officers coming his way. "I'll be with the victim's family. Leave the D.A., and the chief and his girlfriend for me." To Molly and Randall, he said, "Stay put. I don't want to have to go looking for either of you."

Randall returned to his chair, but his eyes remained on Reynolds. He wasn't about to give him the satisfaction of correcting his relationship with Molly. He knew it was a barb designed to rattle Molly.

When Lucero rejoined them, Randall said, "Let the games begin. Reynolds is going to keep us waiting until every single statement has been taken." He looked at his watch. "I figure that will be a good two hours. Maybe you should pull rank so you can give yours and hit the road."

Lucero laughed. "What? And miss all the fun when he digs into you and Molly? No way. I'm here for my friends and for the record."

While they waited, Domenico Mattucci wheeled himself to their table. "This is a sad day, my friends, but there's no reason why you can't enjoy the buffet while you wait for that jackass to finish strutting around. So, please, help yourselves. Dando has outdone himself today. I'd hate to see all his work go to waste. I've told the other guests to do the same once they're through with the cops. It's not disrespectful, and we won't be following Jessop to hell for filling our stomachs." To Molly, he said, "Emma and Michelle are fine. Don't worry about them. Dando has taken them back to the ranch. I hope that was okay. I'd like to ask that you let Emma stay with Michelle for a day or two. We'll take good care of them. Carla will be, well, busy and knowing Emma is with Michelle will be a relief to her."

Molly didn't know what to make of Domenico Mattucci. Either he was a genuine pragmatist, or he knew he hadn't long to live and no longer cared what people thought of him.

But she sensed he was innately kind and that he loved his family. "Of course," Molly said. "If I can help in any way, please let me know."

After a few more minutes, when guests began to trickle towards the buffet, Lucero found an empty drinks tray and filled it with three plates of food with wineglasses wedged between. "Domenico is right. No sense in letting all this food go to waste," he said as he set the tray on the table. "Come on, *mangia*."

Randall pointed his fork at a fat sausage on Molly's dish. "Try that sausage. You'll never find this at the market. Well, maybe one or two down in Gonzales or Greenfield, but not at a big-box."

Molly's appetite was less than zero. "A sausage is a sausage."

"Randall's right," Lucero said. "These are something else."

"How can you get excited over a sausage? Sometimes I wonder about you two. A man was shot and killed in front of us, and you act as if you're at a picnic."

"Occupational hazard," Randall said. "Give us a break, okay? We're trying to get you to calm down. Trivia is a big help."

"Sorry," Molly said. "Okay, tell me all about this special wiener."

"You're impossible," Lucero said. "I don't know why we put up with you sometimes. These babies are made only by Swiss-Italians in the Salinas Valley. Secret recipes handed down from the old country." He took a big bite, chewed it slowly, and then beamed. "There's only a few guys left that make these anymore. They're so paranoid, they cover the windows while they put the stuff together. Dando's one of them, even though he's not Italian."

"Maybe he knocked an old-timer off for the recipe," Randall said, and laughed. "I hear he's some character."

Lucero grinned. "Don't say that too loud around here. Men shake in their boots when his name is mentioned."

"Come on!" Molly said. "Daria told me he's shy and can't speak. Something wrong with his tongue. If Mr. Mattucci trusts him, so do I."

"Yeah?" Lucero said. "Story is, he got some of it cut off in prison in Spain when he was a kid. His father and big brother were ETA suspects, and they threw the whole family in jail."

Molly took a bite. Her eyes widened in surprise. "Oh, this is good. What's ETA?"

"Basque separatists," Randall said. "In some camps they're called terrorists, and in others, patriots."

"If you lose, you're a terrorist. If you win, you're elevated to a patriot. Same old story throughout history," Lucero said.

"I thought we were going to lighten up," Molly said as she cut into another sausage.

Randall checked his watch again. "I'd venture to say we've got another hour and a half before Sherlock shows up. Grab another bottle of wine, Lucero."

"I can't. I'm the D.A. I'm a big shot. I can't be seen waiting on you." He rose and headed for the banquet table, but before he could return, he was stopped by three angry guests. Molly and Randall watched hands slicing the air, chins jutting out, and flicking wrists as watches were examined. Reggie and Dino joined the exchange for a moment, then headed for Randall.

"What kind of bullshit is this?" Reggie asked. "Who the hell gave that nutcase a badge?"

"Pull up a chair and calm down," Randall said.

Horne saw the empty wine bottle on the table. "Wait for me. I'll get us another bottle." He winked at Molly. "Maybe two."

Reggie sat down with a thud. "I can't believe this crap. We've been shoved into a corner, our wives are pissed off, and everybody is either thirsty or starving. Those jerks were told to get more than a brief statement. They were told to get full interviews. Hell, guests that were at the other end of the terrace who didn't even see what happened were treated like suspects."

Dino set two bottles on the table. "You have to do something about this, Randall."

Randall said, "It's not my call. This is Monterey County jurisdiction. I haven't got a leg to stand on here. Reynolds is running the show. Besides, we're not buddies, know what I mean?"

"Yeah? Well, his boss, the sheriff, is going to get an earful about these high-handed attitudes. If the sheriff wants to get elected again, he'd better think about making some personnel changes."

Reggie's hand was shaking slightly as he filled everyone's glass. "I'm not going to be a hypocrite and say what a tragedy this is, and I've got to tell you, watching that bastard fall didn't faze me at all." He looked at his hands, and laughed nervously. "On the other hand, it's the first time I've been around someone who was murdered."

No one spoke. It was as if the word "murdered" was a foul sound. It was obvious that Jessop hadn't keeled over from a heart attack, but still, no one had uttered the word until now.

"Could have been an accident," Dino said. "You know, some kid fooling around with his father's gun."

Reggie snorted. "Where was he then, goofing off on Jessop's roof shooting at sea otters?"

"Damn, I don't know. I just never considered it wasn't an accident," Horne replied. He looked at Randall and Lucero. "You guys are the pros here. What's your take on this?"

Lucero said, "We can't talk about it even if we wanted to."

"But we're all friends here," Reggie said.

"This is a homicide investigation. Friendship takes a back seat. End of story," Randall said.

"Okay, how about you, Molly?" Reggie pressed. "What do you think?"

Molly sipped her wine, then paused. "I think I want to go home. That's what I think."

"Duck out the back way," Sullivan said. "The front of the house is blocked by media vans and satellite trucks." He looked at Horne. "This isn't the kind of advertising we want, but hell, Jessop got his wish. He wanted to be big-time. Now, he'll be front-page news for a few days."

Molly looked at Randall. "I don't think I can handle this again."

Randall shrugged. "Put your sweater over your head when you leave. Not much else you can do."

"I'm always good for a photo op. I'll draw them away," Lucero said.

"How am I going to get my van? The valet kids parked it."

Lucero reached in his pocket and took out his keys. He tossed them to Molly. "Take my car. It's just outside the iron gates. I told them to park it there in case I had to leave."

When Sheriff's Deputy Lieutenant Reynolds finally arrived at their table, he jerked his head to Sullivan and Horne. "Time to find another spot, gentlemen. I've got some statements to take here." He waited until they left, then pulled out a small notebook and said to Molly, "Let's start with you."

After establishing her identity for the record, Reynolds said, "I understand you and the deceased were involved in a dispute. I'd like you to tell me what prompted him to seek you out today."

"I have no idea," Molly said. "And I don't know that he was seeking me out specifically. His father-in-law was next to me. Maybe that's who he'd intended to talk to."

Reynolds looked at her. "That's not what I was told by several witnesses. Jessop, they all concurred, was going to you. Why were you here if there was tension between you and the deceased?"

"Because I was invited?"

"Don't get smart-ass with me."

"I wouldn't think of it. I'm not in the habit of crashing private parties. I was invited by Carla Jessop and her father. But, excuse me, I thought you were taking a witness statement. This is beginning to sound like an interrogation."

"It's not important what you think. I can ask any questions I see fit."

"Okay, then take this down. I was invited to the party, I was standing at the wall with Chief Randall and District Attorney Lucero when I saw Mr. Jessop approach me with his arm raised and poised in a manner I considered aggressive. I moved away. He made it to the wall, and after he turned to face me, he clutched his chest and fell. I have nothing more to add."

Molly ignored her shaking knees, rose, and pulled her sweater closer. "You have my statement. I'd be happy to sign it if that's required. In any case, I'm leaving."

Reynolds looked up from his notes. "You're not leaving. I'm not through with you."

Molly looked down into his face. "Oh yes, you are. I happen to know my rights. If you have further questions, then I'll want my lawyer present." Molly nodded to Randall. "I'll have coffee on if you and Dan want to stop by."

Reynolds leaned back in his chair and laughed. "I guess that was a hint to remind me you have high-ranking friends."

Molly gave him a withering look. "I'll pretend you're not harassing me, okay? And please don't bother to remind me not to leave town. I know the drill. But if you need to speak to me again, you'd better have a good reason. And I'll have my attorney with me."

# Chapter 14

BY THE TIME Molly got home, she was glad it was just past closing time for Treasures. The last thing she needed was a cross-examination from Bitsy. Molly had no doubt that the news of Todd Jessop's demise had already run its course through Carmel. Pulling into the back alley, she locked Lucero's car, then hesitated. She hadn't noticed if the CLOSED sign was in the front window when she drove past the shop. She wouldn't put it past Bitsy to wait for her return. She loved her dearly, but oh, the woman could talk the legs off a centipede. Molly decided to go up the back stairs from the court-yard to the apartment just in case. She could always open the door from upstairs to the shop and peek down to see if Bitsy had waited for her.

Molly took off her heels and tiptoed into the small kitchen. Making as little noise as possible, she pulled a mug from a cabinet, and then plugged in the teakettle. She stared at the cat clock on the wall and remembered Emma said it took forty wags of the cat's tail for the wispy tendrils of steam to emerge. Forty-two, and the teakettle screamed like a banshee. Molly wasn't taking any chances of mis-counting and pulled the water cap off at thirty-nine. Quickly making her coffee, she took two sips, then inched her way to the door leading to the shop. The minute she opened the door, she could see that the night light at the foot of the stairs was at its night-time wattage.

Relieved, she made her way down and headed to her desk. A sheet of wrapping paper was on her desk with a note in large block letters from Bitsy wanting to know why Molly's cell phone was off and telling her to call immediately. There was little doubt Bitsy had heard the news. Molly crumpled up the note and threw it in the wastebasket. She figured Bitsy would have gone over to the La Playa Hotel after closing. It was a weekend ritual she loved, and one of her major sources for local gossip. Bitsy and many of the art and antiques dealers in the village met regularly as clockwork to drink, share the latest news, boast about new acquisitions, and lie about how great business was. Molly rarely joined them. Branded with the stigma of previously being a high-end dealer in New York, which most of them aspired to be, she was politely tolerated because of Bitsy, rather then welcomed. Her past three homicide involvements with all the publicity did little to endear her to them as well. The dealers in town were quick to attribute the success of Treasures to Molly's notoriety, rather than her fine eye for top-notch merch.

Molly's first call was to Josie to let Charles know that Emma wouldn't be going to school with him for a few days. Josie had said the shooting was all over the news and warned her that Bitsy had been trying to reach her for hours. Molly told Josie her cell had been off and she would call her later. The next call was to Emma's school counselor. Molly left a brief message on her voice mail explaining that Emma would be absent and she would call tomorrow to explain. With those two calls out of the way, Molly checked her watch, wondering how long it would be before Randall and Lucero arrived. Her knees were still shaky, and small shivers continued to run through her.

In spite of the events of the day, Molly checked the day's sales tags, more for a diversion than real interest. She couldn't help but be impressed with the total of Bitsy's sales slips. *Seven thousand bucks?* She quickly scanned the floor and noticed the gaps. Two small chests, a lovely inlaid side table, and a set of French side chairs were gone. Out from behind her desk, she walked down the center aisle and saw that two needlepoint pillows had been sold, and the two lamps she'd had made from the large reproduction Sèvres vases she'd found at a house sale.

Well, she thought as she climbed the stairs, at least Bitsy had a good day.

Molly already had the coffee table set with cups and a plate of cookies when Randall called to say he and Lucero were pulling into the alley behind the shop. She made a quick dash to the bathroom to look in the mirror and see if her face was as green as it felt. Besides being a nervous wreck, Molly had an upset stomach from the wine and food she should have ignored. The dash from the Jessop house while Lucero spoke to the media and the winding two-lane road from Carmel Highlands in Lucero's car—with a stick shift she'd forgotten how to use—hadn't helped either. The image of Todd Jessop clutching his chest wouldn't leave her mind. She almost missed turning onto Ocean Avenue from Highway One on her way home. Being harassed by Reynolds was the last straw.

She was glad Randall and Lucero were here now. With Emma staying at Michelle's, she had only Tiger and the kittens to hear her venting. She had thought about calling Daria on her cell but hadn't wanted to ruin her trip to the City. Daria would hear all about it soon enough. Molly picked Tiger up off the sofa. She was stroking her back when she heard the knock on the French doors.

Molly's anxiety grew when she saw the strained looks on Randall and Lucero's face as they entered. "What now?"

"Problems as usual," Randall said.

Lucero threw his sport coat on a chair, moved to the coffee table, and helped himself to coffee. "No lemon cookies?"

"I'm out," Molly said. "They're Pecan Sandies." She looked at Randall, who had moved to the sofa. "What problems? Besides the obvious, I mean."

"There were two freelance reporters at the party. One contributes on and off to the *Monterey Herald*, and the other one to wine magazines. They're both friends of Reggie Sullivan, and apparently they've done some nice pieces on Bello Lago."

Molly sat opposite Randall and handed him a cup of coffee. "And?"

Lucero snorted. "Damn reporters. They were on the terrace when Jessop took the hit, so they were part of the outside group that got herded back. They obviously made good use of the wait by cozying up to some of the guys who were at the vintner's banquet when Randall got into Jessop's face. And either Reggie or Dino told them about your little episode. They both hit on me and Randall when we were leaving and asked for confirmation."

Molly slumped in the chair and blew out her breath. "Oh, great. That's just peachy. But why the big surprise? I mean, the village is already talking. Where have they been? In a cave?"

Lucero laughed. "What happens in Carmel rarely gets to Monterey, kiddo. You should know that by now."

"So what, pray tell, did you two say to them?"

"Come on, Molly," Randall said. "You know us better than that."

"Doesn't matter, anyway," Lucero added. "They'll use what they heard, and there's not a damn thing that can be done about it."

"Got any Jack Daniel's to put in this coffee?" Randall asked Molly.

Molly rose. "I take it there's more to tell me?"

"Yeah, you could say that."

Molly returned and set the bottle on the table. "Will I need much? I've already got a stomach ache." She gave Lucero a look. "You should have stopped me after the first sausage."

He leaned closer to the coffee table and poured whiskey into all three cups, then added fresh coffee. "It's not every day your over-whelmingly elected district attorney plays waiter. This is twice now. I only do this for special people."

Molly took a hearty sip of her coffee, and then tightened her eyes as it went down. "I'm ready."

"One of the reporters asked Randall what he thought the odds were that you two would be considered 'persons of interest,'" Lucero said.

Molly's gaze shot to Randall. She set her cup on the table with a thud. "Besides the fact that you and I were standing right there and I don't recall either one of us holding a smoking gun! Why would that even come up?"

Randall pulled out a cigar from his case. He took his time indulging in the aficionado routine, clipped off the end, then lit it with a match from Molly's antique match striker. Molly's gaze bounced between the two men. "Randall!" she finally blurted.

Randall blew out a stream of smoke, tapped his cigar in the ashtray, then gave Molly a grim smile. "Why? Because those reporters want a story. They will mention an undisclosed source close to the investigation. They will manufacture a phony leak that will be pure bullshit and impossible to verify. And then, Reynolds will have to go along with it and haul both of us back in for questioning. If he doesn't, he'll have egg on his face. That's why."

"Molly," Lucero began, "this is the way a lot of reporters get space, okay? I'm not saying they're all like this, but if they can add some spice to a story, they'll do it. It's called insurance for a follow-up. Next thing you know, there will be another leak from the sheriff's office when Reynolds calls you two in, and the photographers and TV news media will be there to cover it. Careers will be enhanced, the networks and cable news will call their local stringers, and then—depending on how long the investigation takes and if it gets juicy enough—it could be 'New York, here I come' for someone."

"Providing, of course, the local stringer doesn't flub his lines or get too carried away with false tips or innuendos, in which case we might have grounds to sue the twerp," Randall said.

"I'm not going through that again," Molly said. "I'll leave here if I have to." She looked at both of them. "I mean that."

"Calm down. Besides, if you do become part of the investigation, and I think Reynolds will make sure you do, you can't leave without permission," Randall said.

"I won't let it get that far," Lucero said. "You seem to forget that jackass has to come to me with some of this. He can't make demands on either of you over gossip or a minor altercation." He looked at Randall. "You know that, so why the hell are you scaring Molly?"

"I just want her to be prepared, that's all," Randall replied.

"Gee, thanks," Molly said. "But what are we going to do if—"

Randall waved her off. "There's no *if* about it. We answer his questions. End of story."

Lucero added, "Reynolds will have plenty of people to question before long. Hell, Jessop got into a lot of faces besides your two. Sullivan and Horne should jump the queue. I hear they both had shouting matches with Jessop for months over Bello Lago. And then there's Carla. The spouse is always high on the list. And let's not forget her father. Everyone in the wine biz knows Mattucci couldn't stand the sight of Jessop."

Molly looked at Randall. "I'm worried about Carla. Others must have seen that welt on the cheek he gave her the night she came in to go over the portfolio."

"What welt?" Lucero said.

Molly told Lucero what had happened. "I don't know why she put up with him after that. And she said it wasn't the first time either."

"Why the hell didn't you cuff him?" Lucero asked Randall.

"Carla wouldn't cop to it. She insisted she'd run into a door."

Lucero thought that over. "She'd look good as a prime suspect then. Wives have had husbands killed for less. And she's got the dough for a top-notch hire."

Molly gasped. "That's crazy! Carla couldn't—"

"Hold up," Randall said. "Don't be going there, okay? Forget that you like her. Killers come in all shapes and sizes. Take your pick. If it were my case, I'd be looking at her pretty damn hard."

Lucero reached for two cookies, bit into one, and said, "Well, whoever the shooter is, he's damn good. If you're still thinking about trees, the closest one had to be at least five hundred yards away." He finished the first cookie, then added, "Come to think of it, that's nothing for some hunters."

"A tree?" Molly asked. "Those pine trees are ten stories high. Why not the roof?"

Randall laughed. "They're not that tall. The roof is out. Too much time to get off and he could be seen. The shooter needed a quick getaway or a blind where he could wait and then leave without being seen. I'm guessing he was up there before the party even started. He waited for Jessop to get into position so the bullet would end up in the ocean."

"And when he approaches Molly at the wall, Molly moves away, Jessop turns to face her, and bang!" Lucero said cocking his finger like a gun.

"The bullet is lost, and they'll never find the shell casing. He would have painted it so when it hit the ground he'd spot it right away," Randall added. "The only thing they'll find is his spike marks in the tree."

"What about…uh, what do they call it, forensics? Won't they find fibers or stuff like that?" Molly asked.

Randall shrugged. "Maybe, maybe not. He probably wore camo gear so he'd blend in. Hell, they sell that stuff all over now. It would take weeks to make a match. The shooter would have paid cash anyway. No paper trail to follow."

Lucero stared at the second cookie in his hand. "So you think this was a pro, then? No jealous lover pining after Carla, no guy with a grudge against Jessop?"

Randall set his cigar in the ashtray, and filled his cup with more coffee. "With the way people are glued to all those damn 'CSI' shows, who the hell knows? You can get a how-to-kill-and-get-away-with-it primer off the Net with just a click of your mouse."

"I don't like it when you're not butting in," Lucero said. "You've got that look on your face. What's filtering through that brain of yours?"

"I was just thinking about what Michelle told Emma about her grandfather. Not Mr. Mattucci, her other one. Something about not seeing him very often because of some bad blood after her father died."

"Testino Giordano? That's ancient history," Lucero said. "Giordano and Mattucci have been at each other's throats for years. It goes back a couple of generations to the old country. Something about a sale of land, I think. Hell, they grew up hating each other. The only time those two families had any peace was when Carla and Tony took off to Reno and got married. After that, they had little choice but to bury the hatchet. But when Tony died in a chopper crash on a hunting trip, Giordano claimed Mattucci was behind the crash. Nah, forget about all that. Giordano is close to eighty-five. What's the point now?"

"Settle an old score before he bites the dust?" Randall said. "If anyone should understand the *vendetta* mentality, we should, huh? Family honor means everything."

Lucero shook his head. "Why now? And why Jessop?"

"Why anything?" Randall said. He got up from the sofa, picked up his cigar, and looked at Molly. "You look done in." He nodded to Lucero. "What say we hit the road."

Lucero rose, took a last sip of his coffee, then moved to Molly and kissed her on the forehead. "Lock up tight, huh?"

Molly smiled. "That's usually Randall's line. But I will, and thank you two for coming by. I feel a little better now. More or less."

Molly followed them to the French doors. She almost fainted when Randall followed Lucero's gesture and kissed her on the cheek. "If Reynolds shows up, call me. I'll be right over."

"If he calls you in," Lucero said, "call me right away. I'll get you an attorney if you really want one."

"Will I need one? I mean, really need one?"

"Only if Reynolds decides to show off," Randall said.

Molly looked at Lucero. "Make sure she's a ball-breaker then."

# Chapter 15

MOLLY NESTLED Tiger and the kittens next to her on the bed. She felt a need for company and hoped their soft purring might help her fall asleep. She hadn't left the lamp beside her bed on for months, but tonight was one of those nights. Snuggled deep under the blankets she said her prayers and decided it was time to talk to the Big Guy.

*It's been awhile since I've had to talk things over with you. I mean, you've always got your hands full, and we're supposed to handle our problems on our own, but if you don't mind my saying so, I'm a little pissed right now and scared as hell. I should be praying for Todd Jessop's soul and begging your indulgence for his sins, but to be honest, he's your problem. Here's the thing—I don't need to be a "person of interest." And I'd like your intervention if you have a moment. I know I suffer from a quick mouth and can't handle too much wine, but this is getting serious. It might have been better if you'd let me pass out instead of throwing that wine in Jessop's face. Is my being there today payback for putting those Foo Dogs in the front window? You know you're the top guy. But a little Feng Shui when you're busy shouldn't be a problem, right? Look, I just don't want to get involved in another murder investigation, that's all. I'm sleeping well these days, and I'd like to have that continue. Give me a slow month in the shop for penance, and I promise I'll be good. Honest.*

But sleep was not in Molly's immediate future. The harder she tried, the more frustrated she became. Tiger and her brood had decided the crook of her knees was better than the second pillow on her bed. Worrying about disturbing them wasn't helping either. She tried to burrow under the comforter, but that only made her too warm. Flinging it on and off aggravated her even more.

When the old hook latch on the window facing Ocean Avenue

snapped and her window flew open at a quarter past six, Molly finally gave up. Her head ached, her eyes were gritty. She suddenly felt
hungry as she headed for the shower. She was downstairs and at
Tosca's by seven for a stop-worrying-about-the-diet breakfast of
croissants and her personal concoction of espresso with lemon and
cream. She knew Bennie would have heard about Jessop's murder,
and she was ready. Bennie, she could handle. Bitsy was the problem.
She'd want to know every detail, every nuance, every blink of an
eye. For that marathon, she needed at least two espressos. Daria was
probably sleeping in after her trip from the City. She'd call her later.
By then she would have her routine down pat.

The early morning fog made sitting inside Tosca's an easy decision. Molly waved at Bennie as she entered. "Yes, I was there. No, I
don't want to talk about it until I've devoured at least two croissants."

Bennie came from behind the counter with a tray. "Okay, I won't
give you the third degree for at least five minutes, or let you see the
newspaper." He set out the croissants and espresso, then sat down,
grabbed a magazine a customer had left yesterday, and pretended to
read. After a moment, he looked around the small café, and said,
"Go ahead and smoke. The early regulars won't be in for another
half hour."

"I'm stuffing my mouth at the moment, but thanks for the offer."

"Randall called. He's on his way. Guess you two really got a front
row seat, huh?"

Molly gave Bennie a look. "My five minutes aren't up yet. So why
did he call?"

"He calls every morning around this time so I'll have his sweet
rolls warm and ready. I thought you knew that."

Molly squeezed lemon into her espresso, then topped it with
cream. "I don't know his every routine. I was just curious. I mean,
what? He can't wait for you to warm them when he gets here?"
Molly pulled out a pack of cigarettes, lit one, and then exhaled.

Bennie laughed. "Hey, he's the chief of police. I obey the law."

"Yeah? Then why the hell are you letting her smoke in here?"
Randall said, as he entered with a cigar between his fingers.

It was Molly's turn to laugh. "Oh, that's rich. Look who's talking!"

"It's in my hand, not in my mouth. I smoked on the way over," Randall answered.

Bennie looked at the clock on the wall above Molly's head. "Your time is up. What's the scoop about yesterday?"

Molly stubbed out her cigarette. "It was awful. We were all standing on the terrace—"

"We? Who's we?"

"Jesus!" Randall said. "You gotta know every comma? Molly's talking about me and Lucero. We were there with her and Domenico Mattucci, okay? Got all the players now lined up in your mind?"

"Aw, come on, chief! I just want to get a picture of everything." He grinned, then looked back at Molly. "Go on."

"Todd Jessop fell over when he was shot. That's all I know," Molly said. "I really don't want to talk about it."

"Aw, come on," Bennie said.

"What the hell more do you want?" Randall said. "How much blood was splattered? You've been watching too much TV. Maybe if you'd been standing where Molly was, you wouldn't be so interested."

"I was just asking. You cops see that stuff all the time. You're used to it."

Randall gave Bennie a stern look. "We never get used to it."

Bennie's face reddened. "Point taken. Sorry."

"Forget it," Randall said.

Bennie rose. "I'll get your sweet rolls and coffee."

"That was a little mean," Molly said. "Bennie's a good guy, he didn't mean to sound—"

"Yeah, I know." Randall ran his hands over his eyes. "Occupational hazard. Let's leave it at that. Did you by chance see the news on TV this morning?"

"No. I particularly avoided turning it on."

"Good thing. They caught you on tape leaving the Jessop house, running for Lucero's car. Bastards even ID'd you."

Molly cringed. "Damn!"

"Worse than that. Someone yapped to the press and told them

the three of us, you, me, and Lucero, were close to the line of fire. They also mentioned some of the gossip going around town about you and me having a beef with Jessop."

Molly nearly screeched. "Who the hell told them?"

"Keep it down, okay? I don't know, but it's out, and it could be a big problem now. We talked about it last night, remember? Well, now it's here."

"Wait a minute!" Molly's cup clattered on the saucer. "Maybe Todd Jessop wasn't the target."

"Oh? You playing detective again? Stay out of it, okay?"

Molly moved her chair closer to Randall and lowered her voice. "Hold on, hear me out. I'll buy the trashing of the pickup as vandalism. And the skunk, too. Same kids, probably. But maybe the killer was after you or Lucero, or even Mr. Mattucci? It's possible, isn't it?"

Randall thought for a moment. "Anything is possible. Lucero and I both have a laundry list of enemies, and so does Mattucci. Carla's former father-in-law, for one. But knocking off me or Lucero could take place anywhere. The shooter was after Jessop. It was a clear and clean shot. The angle was wrong for Mattucci in the wheelchair and for Lucero and me. This shooter knew who he was looking for."

Molly chewed that over. She scooted her chair back an inch or two. "Do you really think Carla might have something to do with this?"

"Like I said, if it were my case, I'd be looking hard at her. But it's not, and Carla, you, and I are likely in for a nasty ride."

"Carla, I can understand. But why would we even be considered? Just because we didn't get along with Jessop isn't grounds for murder, for God's sake."

Randall laughed. "You haven't learned a thing yet, have you? A motive for murder can damn near be anything, and every cop knows it. Even Reynolds can wrap his head around that."

"Yes, but he needs solid evidence before he can do anything, right?"

Randall didn't answer. That made Molly even more nervous. She tore into her second croissant and waited. Bennie appeared with Randall's sweet rolls, a large carafe of coffee, and a smaller one filled with espresso. He set them on the table. "Shorthanded this morning," he muttered. "I gotta run. I'll be back later."

"Sorry I jumped you, Bennie. We still pals?"

Bennie grinned. "You know we are! Later, okay?"

Molly nodded to Bennie, but her eyes were still fixed on Randall. "Well? The evidence? He's got to have something solid, doesn't he?"

"Yeah, right. Of course."

"Are you listening to me? You've got that faraway look on your face."

Randall poured his coffee and picked up one of the sweet rolls. "I'm thinking, that's all."

Molly grinned. "I can't wait. Now what?"

"I just might decide to find the killer myself."

Molly sat back and folded her arms. "Really? How, pray tell, do you plan to do that when this is out of your hands? You can't go around interviewing people, and you don't have access to all the reports."

"Suffice it to say I have other avenues available."

"But Lucero can't tell you a thing, not if Reynolds considers you a suspect."

"I'm not talking about Lucero. Besides, I wouldn't think of compromising him."

Molly's eyes lit up. "Loomis! You can have Loomis snoop around. Now that he's got his PI license he can do the legwork, right?"

Randall's smile was slow and wide. "I always said you were a smart cookie. Loomis is due back tonight. But he's not the only one I can reach out to."

"So, where do we start first?"

Randall shook his head. "Oh, no you don't. And I mean it this time."

Molly laughed. "Really? Well, just try and stop me. I can't let you be arrested for murder, you know. Who would I get to move heavy furniture? I'd have to break in a new chief of police."

～

Molly set an even loftier new record for opening the shop: She was actually ready for business two hours ahead of time. She used the opportunity to make several telephone calls. Her first priority was to call Emma at the ranch. It took a moment for her to come to the phone, and when she did, Molly said, "Everything okay with you?"

"Uh-huh, but do I have to stay very long? I know this is a terrible thing, but honest, Aunt Molly, Michelle isn't a bit upset. She's not in shock or crying her eyes out. I don't think I really need to stay. Besides, there's a lot of yelling going on between Michelle's mother and her grandfather. It's hard to pretend I don't hear them."

Emma had already told Molly that Michelle wasn't crazy about her stepfather, but she'd expected at least some sadness. It was clear, the Mattucci household was not a place of mourning, and she quickly agreed with Emma. "I'll send Charles over for you. I'll call Carla and make some sort of excuse, okay? I can't leave right now. I've got fax orders for merch from some out-of-town customers that I need to pack up for shipping. Remember that couple from Fresno? And the lady from Phoenix?"

"Oh, right! The linen press lady and the walnut pedestal desk couple. Ohhh, big sales, huh!"

"About fifty-seven-hundred big. And they want the stuff like yesterday."

"You don't have to call Michelle's mother. I already told her I thought I was coming down with the flu and I was going to call you."

Molly laughed. "You're a monster in the making, you know? Lying now, eh?"

"Please? I'll be good forever after. I promise."

"Okay, but I wish you would have talked this over with me first. I could have given some other excuse rather than have you lie."

"You keep telling me that part of growing up is learning to anticipate problems and be ready with solutions. So, I'm practicing."

"Point taken. But this isn't quite what I'd meant. I'll call Charles now."

Molly dialed Bitsy's number. She immediately reassured her she was fine and told her what little she knew. She asked if Charles could pick up Emma. After that, it was mostly a one-sided conversation as

Bitsy filled her in on the latest gossip, which was a rehash of the earlier misinformation. She next called Daria, whom she'd awakened, and told her much the same. As it turned out, Lucero had beat her to it last night and had reassured Daria that Molly was fine. Molly then called Emma's counselor and asked if Charles might pick up Emma's assignments for the next two days. Molly decided to wait for a few hours before calling Carla.

The flurry of phone calls had at least given her some respite from thinking about her conversation with Randall. But now, with a good hour before any customers might drop in, she knew the best thing she could do was to pay attention to business, to get those shipments arranged and to forget about wondering who wanted to kill Todd Jessop. Those good plans quickly evaporated. The challenge was embedded in her mind. It was difficult to concentrate. She almost faxed the wrong invoices to her out-of-town clients.

And now, Mrs. Brooks, a first-class pain in the ass, was knocking on the door. No doubt, Molly thought, to try to convince me to let her consign her collection of costume jewelry again. This must be the third time. Would the woman never learn? It wasn't that Molly hadn't thought about adding jewelry to her inventory. Jewelry was very popular and a lucrative and easy addition to sales. But Molly hadn't found the right type of locked case to store the baubles, and until she did, it was too risky. Mrs. Brook's collection, was, unfortunately, merely cheap necklaces, earrings, and brooches from department stores and not of a quality Molly was interested in offering.

Molly forced a pleasant smile onto her face. She wondered how she was going to diplomatically reject the woman again. She braced herself as she opened the door. Before Molly could even say hello, Mrs. Brooks thrust the morning newspaper at her, and said, "Don't ever expect to see me at your shop again, young lady! You seem to have a penchant for getting mixed up in unsavory events, and I no longer wish to have my collection offered by your store."

Molly held onto the paper, then stepped back from the angry woman. She flinched when Mrs. Brooks began to shake her finger at her. "And furthermore, our village is not pleased with any of this or you."

Molly bit her tongue so hard she was afraid she might have inflicted some serious damage. She closed the door in the woman's face, and locked it. In two angry strides, she was at her desk. She unfolded the paper and stared at the front page. There she was, in all her glory, running to Lucero's car. The caption above read AGAIN, MOLLY DOYLE? WHAT IS IT ABOUT YOU?

Molly's face was crimson as she speed-dialed Randall's private number. When he picked up, she shouted, "Why didn't you tell me I was on the front page of the *Herald?*"

"I figured you'd see it sooner or later. I didn't want to be in your line of fire."

"That's not funny! How the hell am I going to show my face now? What about the shop? Who's going to come in now? People are going to think I'm a magnet for murder and not want to be around, just in case!"

"Slow down. I told you this kind of crap was going to begin. But hey, at least they put Jessop and Carla's photo on there, too."

"Really? How nice. Call me self-centered, but I didn't look past mine."

"Ease off, you'll have a stroke. Be ready for your phone to ring off the hook if it hasn't already."

"It hasn't, thank God. But I can't unplug it. I do have a business to run, you know."

"It will. Trust me. Just leave the recorder on and screen your calls."

Molly sighed. "I know you're right, but this is just too damn much." She told him about Mrs. Brooks. "I wonder if people really are upset with me."

Randall laughed. "Are you kidding? You're damn near neck-and-neck with Eastwood on keeping Carmel on the map. Before you know it, they'll have bus tours driving past the shop and pointing you out. I'd say that would really boost business."

Molly plopped down on her chair and put both feet on her desk. She didn't care if anyone going by saw her. "I could hang up on you right now."

"Do that. I've got a full agenda today. I don't have time for cry-babies."

Molly finally laughed. "You're such a charmer."

"How's Emma doing out at the ranch?"

"She's coming home. She's very uncomfortable with all the yelling that's going on. Charles is going to pick her up for me."

"Yelling? I want to know about that. Meet me at Ruby's around six-thirty for Chinese. Loomis will be with me."

"Dare I leave the store? I might be accosted."

"Then call me, and I'll rescue you."

# Chapter 16

RANDALL WAS RIGHT. Just after she got off the phone with him, the calls began. By eleven A.M., Molly had seven messages from reporters wanting to set up interviews. Emma was already home and upstairs working on the homework Charles had picked up from school. Molly put the CLOSED sign in the window early and joined Emma in the kitchen. She wasn't hungry, but she knew she had to eat something or she'd order way too much later at Ruby's. Molly's weakness for Chinese food was almost as bad as her love of Italian food. She poked around in the fridge but found nothing to entice her. She'd already had her calorie quota this morning with the croissants, but her nerves were jangling, and only food or a smoke could relax her.

"I'm going back down," Molly said. "I can't find anything alluring."

"I had a huge breakfast at the ranch. Mr. Mattucci's cook, the one who doesn't speak? He fixed Michelle and me pancakes, eggs, bacon, and biscuits with country gravy. Ummm, so good."

Molly laughed. "And you're already hungry?"

Emma lathered what looked like an inch of mayonnaise on two slices of bread, then began adding sliced tomato, avocado, and lettuce. "I'm a growing girl."

"Okay, growing girl, I've got a request. Since you're already into adult wiles, would you mind telling Randall tonight what you heard at the ranch? About all the yelling? It might be important. We're meeting him and Loomis at Ruby's for dinner."

Emma sliced her sandwich, then paused. "Ruby's, huh? Is this a bribe?"

"You could call it that. Actually, no. It was Randall's idea. To meet there, I mean. And, well, to ask if you'd snitch."

"Is this because your picture was in the paper this morning? And you and Randall are on the hot seat?"

Molly leaned against the tile counter and blew out her breath. "You could say that."

"Sure. I'll tell you everything." Emma kissed Molly on the forehead. "I was going to anyway. There's something screwy about that family."

"Screwy? Like how?"

"Well, no one cried or felt bad about Mr. Jessop being dead. They just yelled about Michelle's brother arriving late to the party and that he hadn't given his grandfather a hug when he showed up. And how Nicky, that's Michelle's brother, had gone over to see his other grandfather first when he got back from Davis. A bunch of family stuff, you know? Oh, and that his grades were slipping, and if he didn't get his act together, he was going to be pulled from school and put to work in the vineyard picking grapes. Oh, and the publicity for the winery was going to be bad and could hurt sales. That kind of stuff."

Molly threw her hands up. "Not even one tear? Not from Mrs. Jessop either?"

"I didn't see one. She was more worried about the television people and the shame to her family. And what people would think."

"Randall's right. You never know about people, huh?" Molly snatched the half sandwich on Emma's plate and said, "That looks good." Taking a bite, she grinned, "You don't mind, do you? I'll eat it on the way down."

Molly unlocked the shop door, removed the sign, headed for the storage room, and lit a forbidden cigarette. She was amazed she'd only smoked two all day. Considering what was going on, that was quite an achievement. She pulled the can of air freshener off the shelf and had it handy in case a customer came in. She'd barely had a chance to take two drags when she heard the bell over the door ring. She quickly put the cigarette out and returned to the sales floor.

A woman was standing in front of her desk. She was dressed in an expensive teal wool running suit, the type Molly had only seen in Europe. Molly took a deep breath, hoping this wasn't another

angry Carmelite here to tell her to get out of Dodge City. It was
hard to tell for sure, but Molly guessed the woman to be in her early
fifties. Her light brown hair, cut just below her ears, framed a square
face with a high forehead. "Hello, welcome to Treasures," Molly
said. "Please feel free to browse." She smiled. "If I can be of help,
just let me know."

"Are you Molly Doyle?" she asked. When Molly nodded, the
woman said, "May I sit down?"

Molly moved to her desk and pulled out a chair. "Of course, are
you okay? Can I get you something? Water or coffee?"

"No...no, I'm fine. I...I just need to talk to you." The woman
waited for Molly to sit, then said, "I'm Susan Jessop, Todd's wife."

Molly's mouth fell open.

"Yes, I can see you're a bit surprised. But then, imagine how I
feel?"

Molly tried not to sputter. "Uh, well, yes...I mean his...his
death—"

"I'm not talking about that. I mean to learn he has another wife.
Well, actually, she's not legal. Only I am."

"I don't know what to say," Molly finally managed.

"There's isn't much you can say, is there? Todd evidently fooled
me and this woman who claims to be his wife. I won't pretend to be
a grieving widow because frankly, I'm not."

"But why are you here, talking to me? You should be seeing the
sheriff and telling him. And your attorney."

"I'll see them later. My first priority is you. I saw your picture in
the paper this morning, and I read about you. I want to hire you to
help me."

Molly tried not to laugh. "Hire me? I'm an antiques dealer. How
am I supposed to help you? Forgive me, but I don't sell antique
coffins."

Susan Jessop smiled. "I hadn't thought about that. But even that
would be more than he deserved. You helped solve some murder
cases here, and I need you to find Todd's killer. I'd like to congratu-
late him."

Molly couldn't have stopped her laugh even if she'd tried to.

"You've got to be joking! Those...those were...well, something I fell into. I'm not a sleuth. Really, I'm not. In fact, I'm a genuine coward, and I leave my light on at night. You need to hire a pro, but first you need to see the sheriff." Still in shock, Molly had no idea what to say but knew it was important to keep her talking. Since Randall was bent on beating Reynolds to the punch, she might be able to pick up something important.

When Susan began to rise, Molly said, "Wait! Uh, tell me more. Let me see if I can point you in the right direction. I mean, after you've talked to the sheriff. I do know a private investigator who might be able to help you. I'm...I'm really shellshocked here. I'm doing a decorating job for Carla Jessop, and well, you might say I am a bit involved."

Susan Jessop sat back and said, "I imagine you're wondering how I didn't know what was going on? Todd's absences?"

"Well, yes. That's a good place to start."

"I knew he had an apartment in Carmel but not that home in the Highlands. That was another surprise. It must have been bought with her money, not ours. I'd have known. The story he gave me was that he was setting up a consortium to purchase a winery here. He'd lost out on one in Sonoma and was bitter about that. So, his many trips here were expected."

"How long have you been married?" Molly asked.

"Five years. Todd worked for my husband and me in our software company in San Jose. He was our marketing director. When Chuck died, Todd was an enormous help, and well, it progressed from there. At his urging, I sold the company and put up the seed money for a winery."

"That's quite a change," Molly said. "I mean, going from software to wine."

"I didn't mind selling," Susan Jessop said. "Chuck and I didn't have children, so there was no reason not to sell. I was tired of working. When Todd became involved in meetings and tours to find a winery, I traveled. It wasn't long before I suspected he was playing around. I hired a private detective, and I have proof he was involved with someone. In fact, I told him weeks ago that I knew about the affair. I told him to end it, or I'd divorce him. Well, he didn't. We had a row the morning before he was killed. I was yelling and he was laughing at me. I told him I didn't appreciate being laughed at when I was paying the bills. I came down here Sunday to tell him I'd already filed divorce papers. He wasn't at the apartment. And then Sunday night, I saw the news."

Molly was itching to call Randall. She wondered how long she could keep Susan talking. "I'm confused," Molly said. "Todd has been married to Carla for three years! Weren't you suspicious about how long it's taken to find a winery to buy?"

"Suspicious? No. It takes time to find the right company. Todd was always very thorough. I just can't see though how he managed to supposedly marry this Carla woman and keep us both in the dark. And what really upsets me is, that damn private detective I hired never found it out! Unless he was holding that information back and planning to prolong his investigation so he could hit me up for more money. I'll worry about him later."

Trying on her best Barbara Walters look and sympathetic voice, Molly crossed her arms on her desk and asked, "But Susan, surely you must have suspected something. There just aren't that many wineries here in Monterey County to spend three years looking at them. Do you have any idea who might have wanted Todd dead?"

"Besides me? No, not really. I'm sure there is a long line of candidates. That's where you come in. I want to know all about this woman he's supposedly married to. You're working for her. Tell me about her."

Molly was impressed by how easily Susan Jessop had put her in a corner. She'd been up front with her information and now expected Molly to do the same. But then, Molly wondered if this woman was really who she said she was. She might even be one of those tabloid reporters, making up some crazy story to get her to reveal what she knew about Carla Jessop. "Forgive me, Susan, but do you have any proof of who you say you are?"

Susan Jessop laughed. "Oh, you are clever, aren't you?" She pulled out her wallet and handed Molly her driver's license and two credit cards. "Will that do?"

Molly looked over the DMV card, then the credit cards. "But you might be his sister, instead of a wife," she said. "Even if that were true, I can't blame you for wanting to get to the bottom of this, but so does the law, and I really think you should see them first."

Susan Jessop took back the cards, carefully placed them in her wallet, and rose. "I appreciate your caution. Tell you what. I'll see the sheriff, then I'll be back. Have that private investigator's name and number ready for me."

"I'll do that. In fact, I'm having dinner with him tonight. I'll let him know you're interested."

Susan Jessop moved to the door, then stopped. "You have a lovely shop. I like Carmel. I should have visited with Todd." She laughed then. "Wouldn't that have thrown a kink in the works? I might just buy a place here. I'm sure I'll want to redecorate."

Molly ignored the bone Susan Jessop threw, and let it fall on the desk without a reply.

The minute she was out the door, Molly called Randall. "You won't believe who just came in the shop! Todd Jessop's wife. The real one!"

When Randall didn't comment, Molly thought she'd lost the connection. "Hello? You still there?"

"Clarify that, please."

"Okay, but don't interrupt. If you do, I might forget something." She filled him in on what she hoped was every single word, down to Susan Jessop's body language and facial expressions. "I think that's about it. I'm sure she's real. Her clothes are too expensive for a reporter. And she has a driver's license and two credit cards with her name on them."

"Okay, I'll fill Loomis in. If she comes back, don't talk to her about Carla."

"I don't plan to. In fact, I think I did a good job skirting that."

"Okay, see you at Ruby's. I gotta go."

"Wait! Have you talked to Lucero today? Anything new?"

"Yeah. He gave me the name of an attorney for you."

"I didn't need to know that," Molly said.

# Chapter 17

MOLLY AND EMMA walked into Ruby's just steps behind Randall and Loomis. Randall asked for the big booth in the back. Molly could tell he wasn't in one of his better moods. She nudged Emma and whispered, "A quick hug for both of them, and that's it. I don't think Randall is very cheery right now."

"Gotcha." After a hello hug to both men, Emma scooted into the center of the large booth. She picked up a menu and pretended to read it.

"Great to have you back home, Loomis," Molly said. "Catch any fish?"

Almost as tall as Molly, but twice as round as Randall, balding with a gray fringe of curly hair crowning his ears, and a walking advertisement for Ralph Lauren, Loomis said, "Fish? Fishing expedition is more like it. I was on a case with an old fishing buddy."

"Something got lost in the translation, I guess," Randall said. "So shoot me."

Molly laughed. "Isn't he cute? Maybe after we've given Ruby our order he might be in a better mood."

"I'm in a good mood. I'm just thinking. I filled Loomis in on everything, so let's give him a chance to run it through his computer brain before we start yacking. Then Emma can tell us about what was going on at the ranch."

As usual, they ordered enough food to feed a small army and were surprised when it arrived. Everyone's laughter helped ease some of the stress continuing to build in Molly.

Randall offered Emma the plate of spring rolls. "I don't want you to think you're being a snitch, okay? We've got a situation where any bit of information can help us understand the dynamics of—"

"I know," Emma quickly said. She helped herself, then passed the spring rolls on to Loomis. "I look at my information as a contribution to the investigation, even though you're not authorized to perform one."

Randall's eyes popped open. "Excuse me? I happen to be a law enforcement officer who is obligated to extend any and all courtesies and leads to my counterparts in the criminal justice community. It is within my purview to question and elicit the cooperation of any and all persons who might be able to provide said information."

"Gulp," Emma said.

Neither Molly nor Loomis thought laughter was appropriate at the moment. The exchange was funny, but considering Randall's method of delivery, Molly wasn't sure whether he was serious or pulling Emma's leg. Emma's first comment was a bit smart-mouth, and for all they knew, Randall could be demonstrating a lesson in humility. Molly kept quiet. Emma had to learn sooner or later there were some borders one did not cross.

"Now that we've got that clear, you can just sit on what you have to say until we finish dinner," Randall said.

Emma's face was a bright shade of pink. "I'm sorry. I was just trying to sound grown up. It came out wrong, I guess."

Loomis handed Emma the teapot. "Did I ever tell you the story of—"

Randall gave Emma a smile. "Apology accepted."

"He's a stuck-up sourpuss," Emma said.

"Emma!" Molly blurted.

"Michelle's brother, Nicky. He swaggers around like he was the king, or something. And he told Michelle that their other grandfather thinks Mr. Mattucci had Mr. Jessop killed just like he had their father."

Randall looked at Molly. "You didn't tell me that."

"I didn't know," Molly said. She put down her chopsticks and stared at Emma. "Why didn't you tell me that?"

"I was kinda saving it for my ending."

"This isn't a TV mini-series, Emma. I don't want cliffhangers, okay?" Randall said.

"Nicky said that Mr. Giordano wants him to change from viticulture at Davis to animal husbandry so he can take over his big ranch when he dies. He told Nicky growing wine was for sissies, and cattle was for real men."

"Nicky said all that in front of you?" Loomis asked.

"I guess he thought I was asleep. He came into our bedroom to talk to Michelle."

Randall looked at Loomis. "Looks like you've got your work cut out for you."

"You're singing my song," Loomis said. "How long were the Jessops married?" He looked at Molly. "Not the other one. I mean Carla Jessop."

Molly paused. "Three years? I think that's what I heard."

"No," Emma said, "two years. They lived up the coast until four months ago when they moved here so Mrs. Jessop could be closer to her father."

Randall folded his napkin, and set it on the table. "Okay, Emma, spill. Might as well get it all out now."

"All of it this time, okay?" Molly said to Emma.

By the time Emma related all that she had told Molly, the table had been cleared. Molly quietly sipped her tea, wondering if it might be a good idea to ease Emma away from Michelle until tempers cooled down and the killer was caught. They would still see each other at school, but sleep-overs should be a thing of the past. She also decided that once the furniture and accoutrements for the tasting room arrived and were placed, she was out of there as well.

Until the murder was solved, she thought that a low profile was in order. She couldn't risk continued notoriety for herself or for Emma. They'd certainly had enough for one lifetime. So spooked by seeing herself in the news again, not to mention hearing the rumors that had been flying around town, she hadn't even picked up the mail at the post office for two days. Grocery marketing was most likely going to be a challenge as well. She would have to shop in Monterey for a while. With her orange El Camino pickup in trashed-car heaven, the white minivan was a sudden blessing.

"That's it? All of it? You're sure?" Randall asked Emma.

"All that I can remember. Honest."

"Okay, great job, Sherlock. You hear anything else, you let me know."

"I think," Loomis said, "we have enough to get started. I'll talk to my buddy in the sheriff's department and see what I can weasel out of him."

"You know someone there?" Molly said.

"Sergeant Farley and I are old friends. He's from Oxnard originally. I ran into him one day at Brinton's. Talk about surprise! He's been up here for a few years now. He'll be our pulse. He owes me big-time." Loomis pulled out a small notebook and made some notes. He looked at Randall for a minute, then said, "I think I'll head up to Palo Alto tomorrow and do some digging on this new wrinkle."

"Ohhh," Emma said with renewed interest, "what's that?"

Molly hadn't told Emma about her visitor. The less she knew, the better. Her passing on what she had heard at the Mattucci ranch was the end of her involvement. She didn't have to give Randall a high-sign. She knew he would handle it.

"Another case, Nancy Drew," Randall said.

"Okay, I get it. Butt out, huh?"

"Right. Stick to algebra and chemistry or whatever the heck they teach you kids these days."

"Say, Molly," Loomis said, "I meant to tell you about my pal in the sheriff's department. He collects duck decoys. You ever get a bead on any of those, let me know."

It was apparent Loomis's intent was to move the conversation away from the murder, and Molly was glad to cooperate. A few Hail Marys would be worth a small lie. "Uh, I just might have a lead for you," she quickly said. "Let me check my dealer list. I think there's one in the City who specializes in them. I'll get his name and number for you."

"Great. He's also into paperweights. I'll bring him by the shop. You still have a few of those left?"

"It just so happens I do. Come by anytime." Molly said.

Randall made a show of looking at his watch. "I'm gonna pass on dessert."

"Me, too," Molly said. "I can't keep eating like this." She smiled at a silent Emma. "We'll hit the beach tomorrow morning and get back on schedule, okay? I need to get rid of some of this blubber."

Emma stole a quick glance at Randall, then said, "Good idea. Guess that means it's early to bed then."

"Before anyone reaches for the bill," Loomis said. "It's my treat. No arguments."

"You want us to walk you two home?" Randall asked.

"No, we're fine," Molly said. "I'm not being stalked by the paparazzi yet, and we're only three blocks away. Besides, I have to stop at the post office and get my mail. I haven't been there for a couple of days, and the box is probably jammed full."

Molly quickly shoved the post card from Berlin into her tote before Emma turned away from the posters on the bulletin board in the post office. "Can you take some of these catalogs?" she asked. "I've got a load of them again."

Emma reached for them and said, "Any good ones this time? All you get are auction catalogs and women's clothes. Don't they have any for people my age?"

"Better you don't get addicted," Molly said, and laughed.

The walk home took twice as long as usual. Molly purposely took her time, stopping every now and then, pretending to check out a few of the new antiques dealers who had opened up recently. The postcards were now becoming a gnawing problem. As if she didn't have enough on her mind, she needed this as well? Three blank cards in ten days were more than a busy customer or friend in too much of a hurry would send. If the sender were a secret admirer, she was worried instead of being curious or impressed. Molly stared into one of the art galleries and realized she hadn't turned this latest card over. Maybe this time there was a message. She decided she would examine it when they got home and Emma was in bed.

As they neared Ocean Avenue, Emma said, "I'm not impressed with that new shop, Hall's, are you? Those old pharmacist's jars they had in the window were in bad shape. Did you notice the gilding was gone? And the gilt scroll banner was all scratched up?"

Emma paused and touched Molly's arm. "Aunt Molly? Hello?"

"Sorry," Molly said. "I was, uh, thinking the same thing. You're right, not very good quality."

"You looked a million miles away. I wasn't sure if you'd heard me. You're not mad at me, are you?"

Molly stopped at the corner. "Why would I be mad at you?"

Emma linked her arm in Molly's as they crossed the street. "Because I was smart-mouthed with Randall? I was. I know it."

Hugging her close, Molly smiled. "Yes, you were. I think maybe this was a good lesson for you, huh? And maybe for all of us. We forget sometimes that you're—"

"Still a kid. I know."

"Well, yes, but even though we sometimes forget your age, there are some conversations you shouldn't join. And good manners you should remember."

"I can't help it if I have an inquiring mind."

Molly laughed. "No, you can't. Thank God that you do. But just keep it focused on your studies and not this terrible tragedy. We're not involved, and we're going to keep it that way."

They were about to climb the outside stairs to the apartment when Emma said, "Shoot. You forgot to change the lightbulb again. Good thing Randall and Loomis didn't walk us home."

Molly sighed. "Amen to that."

When they entered the shop, Molly saw the red light on her recorder blinking. "I've got some messages. You go on up. I won't be long." Molly settled her tote on the floor and saw that there were three messages. She found a notepad, grabbed a pen, and then hit the play button. The first call was from Bitsy. "Molly! Call me the minute you get home. I have some breaking news you just have to tell Randall about." Molly paused before she pressed the play button again. She was torn between calling Bitsy right away and retrieving the rest of the messages. She knew Bitsy had a flair for the dramatic, but one never knew.

Well, it would only take a moment to find out who else called.

The second call was a man's voice. He didn't leave his name, only that he'd recently purchased a ship from her and would be back to see her tomorrow. Molly immediately remembered him. He was the older man who had also bought the silver pitcher from the Del Monte Hotel and who had asked Bitsy so many questions about her and Emma. What could he possibly want now? The third call was from Susan Jessop. She left a number and asked Molly to call her as soon as she got in.

Damn! Molly thought. I don't need this. I'm not calling her back. And I am not going to get involved, and that's final!

She punched in Bitsy's number and waited for her to answer.

"I was about ready to come looking for you!" Bitsy told Molly. "I think you should consider a trip out of town until all this blows over. Todd Jessop's murder hit the inside of the *San Francisco Chronicle,* and you and Randall were mentioned as being interviewed by the fuzz. Max and I have been on the phone, and this is what we've decided. You and Emma are going up to his condo in Sonoma, and I'll take care of the shop, and then—"

"Whoa!" Molly said. "I am not leaving town, and that's final. It isn't necessary. I've done nothing wrong, and neither has Randall. Besides, I was already told by Detective Reynolds not to leave. We've both given our statements, and that should be the end of it."

"This doesn't look good for the shop, Molly."

That did it. Not only was Molly furious to know Bitsy and Max were back running her life, they hadn't had the courtesy to consult with her first. "The shop will survive this. In fact, its reputation has been enhanced by my, uh, previous involvements."

"What about Emma?" Bitsy threw in.

"What about her?"

"Well, I was thinking it might be best if she didn't spend too much time with Carla's daughter for a while. You know, in case, well, in case Carla is involved."

Molly's voice was a bit colder than she'd planned. "I've already taken care of that. Emma understands."

"You're angry with us, aren't you?"

Molly sighed. "No, not angry. Just maybe annoyed that you and

Max are making assumptions and plans without talking it over with me."

"Point taken, darling. Don't mention this to Max. I'll call him and say that I'd thought it over and that maybe we were overreacting. How's that sound?" Bitsy said.

Molly immediately realized that all of this was Bitsy's idea, and that she didn't want Max to know she'd been meddling again. "Great. I'll leave it up to you. I appreciate both your concerns, and I know they're from love. Oh, by the way, uh...I'm dying to know how you knew Del Tinsley? I don't recall you ever mentioning her. She said she used to work for you."

The long pause from Bitsy's end spoke volumes to Molly. She didn't let her off the hook, and waited her out. Finally, Bitsy said, "Oh, honey, Del and I go back centuries. I knew her in Reno. She worked at one of the casinos I frequented. I forget which one now."

"Really? What did she do?" Molly asked.

"Do? Lord, I can't remember. I think she was a hostess, or something. Look, sweetie, I've got to run. I'm having a late dinner with some of the girls. We'll talk tomorrow, okay? Give Emma a kiss for me when you tuck her in."

Molly was laughing when she hung up. It wasn't often that one found Bitsy Morgan in a rush to get off the phone. Molly listened again to the message from the man who'd bought the ship, and the one from Susan Jessop. She looked at her notepad and stared at Susan's number. She decided not to give her Loomis's name and number. Loomis would have his hands full with Randall's needs. She threw the note in the wastebasket and turned off the desk lamp.

As far as she was concerned, that lady was on her own.

# Chapter 18

AT SIX A.M. SHARP, Molly threw off the duvet, turned off her alarm clock, and headed for Emma's room. It was time to get back to the beach and try to knock some pounds off. She also hoped she might shake off her lingering doubts about not becoming a part of Jessop's murder investigation. She tapped on Emma's door. "It's Tuesday morning, it's glorious outside, and we're off to the beach. Last one ready to go is a lazybones."

Molly scooted into the kitchen, plugged in the electric teakettle, and then ran to her room to throw on her sweats. She slipped into her sneakers and raced back to the kitchen to find Emma there filling two mugs with hot water for Molly's Café Français and her instant cocoa.

"Ha! You're the lazybones this time!" Emma laughed.

"You cheater! You were ready when I called you!"

"Yep, back to anticipating."

Molly threw her arm around Emma's shoulder. "What would I do without you?"

"You say that all the time, but I love it." She hugged Molly back. "Ditto."

They sat on the bottom of the back stairs just off Tosca's courtyard and drained their mugs. Molly stretched her arms and took in a deep breath. "Smell those pines? Oh, wow! What a wonderful way to start the day. Come on, brat. Let's roll."

By the time they reached Carmel Beach, only five blocks away and all downhill, Molly was out of breath. When they reached the walking path above the beach, she waved Emma on. "I'll come down in a few minutes and catch up with you. Don't get close to the surf, okay? Remember what Randall told us."

"Right. Don't turn your back to the sea, or it'll get ya'."

Molly was still short of breath and nodded. She realized it was a mistake to start out with a brisk walk. If she hadn't wanted to show Emma she could keep up with her, she'd be down on the sparkling white sands with her right now. Vanity, she thought. And too much good food. At least she had been able to curtail her smoking enough not to place all the blame there. But then she realized that was just an excuse. She was going to be forty in three months, and a pack-a-day habit for too many years to admit to was rearing its ugly head. She had resented Emma's teasing about her smoking at first, but now she was glad Emma had. Not that she was completely free of the habit, but knowing that little imp was looking over her shoulder, she had managed to drastically curb the need. Even Daria had cut back. The thought of Daria reminded her of the silver she'd found for her. Molly made a mental note to call her. Tomorrow was going to be dinner night instead of tonight, and she would drop all the pieces off then.

At the staircase down to the beach, Molly stopped to take in the awesome view. The Carmel Bay was preening today. Azure sky met a deeper blue ocean. The small whitecaps farther out were shimmering. The sand sparkled in the early morning light and at least a dozen morning strollers, many with their dogs on leashes, made a postcard-ready photo. It was a scene that never changed, yet always seemed different somehow. Molly often felt like stretching her arms wide then slowly drawing them in, capturing the majesty and holding it in an embrace.

Molly watched as Emma stopped to greet some of the walkers they knew. As she descended to the beach, she noticed a man sitting on newspapers he'd spread out on the sand. There was something about the way he held himself that made Molly think she'd seen him before. She was close enough to know he wasn't a regular. And his tweed sport coat, slacks, and loafers made him look as if he were ready for breakfast at the Lodge at Pebble Beach instead of sitting on the sand. Molly shaded her eyes against the sun. When he turned his head, Molly realized he was the man who had bought the water pitcher and the boat. The man who had left her a message last night. She moved back, out of his view, and watched him. Her breath caught in her throat when she saw him turn his head again to follow Emma as she continued to jog down the beach. Molly moved back up the stairs and beckoned Emma to join her. She wondered if Bitsy was right about him. Perverts, like murderers, came in all shapes and sizes. Expensive clothes, too.

Emma's face was flushed from running. "Aren't you coming down?"

Molly saw the man get up off the sand. He picked up the newspaper, turned in their direction, and watched them as he folded the paper into a neat square and tucked it under his arm. She turned away from the man. "We're heading back."

"We just got here. What's wrong?"

"Don't look around, but did you notice that man sitting on the newspaper?"

"Nope. Oh, wait—yes, I did. He was dressed kinda funny to be ocean watching."

Molly linked her arm in Emma's. "He's been in the shop twice. He bought the silver pitcher from the Del Monte Hotel, and that big ship model we had in back from Bitsy. He asked her a lot of questions about you, and he made her nervous."

Emma skidded to a halt. "Do you think he followed us? We should tell Randall right away."

Molly pulled Emma along. "Don't stop walking. He couldn't have followed us. He was already here when we arrived. But I will tell Randall, just in case. I don't want you leaving the shop or the apartment today."

Molly decided not to tell Emma that the man had called and was planning on coming into the shop today. Until she knew what he was up to, it was best to keep her in the dark. Emma had exhibited too much of a liking for mystery, and she didn't want to encourage her.

"We're still going to have croissants at Tosca's, aren't we?"

Molly made a joke of patting her hips. "Maybe we should pass on that today. We ate a ton at Ruby's last night, and we won't be getting a full walk in today."

Later that morning, Molly was about to pull the CLOSED sign from the window when she saw a sheriff's patrol car slowly driving past. She left the sign and hurried to her desk. She picked up the phone and called Randall.

"Calm down, it's not Reynolds. He's with Lucero in a meeting."

"How do you know that?"

"I know everything."

Molly laughed. "Of course. Excuse me. But, uh, what might they be discussing? He's almost past the magic hours isn't he? The solve-it-in-forty-eight or get ready to hit the street?"

"No doubt the meet is a case update."

"Susan Jessop left me a message last night. I didn't return her call, and I'm not going to. And I'm not giving her Loomis's number either."

"Keep your distance from her as best you can. If she comes in and gives you heat, call me."

Molly then told Randall about the man on the beach. "He's coming in today. I'm almost tempted not to open. Between Susan Jessop and him, I'm ready to pull the covers over my head or go read a good book."

"Okay, call me if either one shows up. I can be there in five minutes. Damn, it, Molly! I can't believe the messes you get into."

"What is it about me? My charming smile, or do I just look like I love problems?"

"I don't know, but it's not something I'd want to bottle and sell."

Molly pulled the sign from the window, squared her shoulders, and braced herself for a full day. She spent the next few minutes checking for dust, put two fresh logs on the grate in the fireplace and got a lovely fire going, rearranged a stack of leather books on a nineteenth-century, French Provincial, bowfront, kingwood commode (whose price, she decided, was light by five hundred bucks), then headed for the storage room to set up the five-disc CD player. While she made a new tag for the commode, she remembered the postcard she had shoved in her tote. She pulled it out. Almost dreading to turn it over, she counted to five, then flipped it onto the desk, hoping it would land upside down. She almost felt as if touching it further would burn her fingers. Her eyes widened in amazement. A rabbit had been drawn on the message side. What the hell? Whatever trepidation Molly may have felt, it was now quickly morphing into a red-hot anger. She had half a mind to throw the damn thing away. If this was a joke, she was not amused. She set the postcard aside and finished making the new tag for the commode.

Molly had just replaced the tag when she heard the bell over the door. When she turned to see who had come in, she had to hold onto the edge of the commode to steady herself. Lieutenant Reynolds from the sheriff's department was standing at her desk with a bland look on his face. "If you'll spare me a few minutes, Ms. Doyle, I have a few questions."

Molly took her time walking down the center aisle. Randall must have bad information, or else Reynolds's meeting with Lucero didn't last very long. She hoped he didn't notice that her hands had already begun to sweat or that her knees were beginning to stiffen. "Of course, I have all the time in the world. Have a seat." She turned to enter the storage room and said, "I'll just unplug the teakettle first. It has a habit of boiling over." Molly reached for the portable phone on the shelf and speed-dialed Randall's direct line. She prayed he was in. When he picked up on the second ring, she clattered a few cups and saucers so Reynolds couldn't hear her. "Your intel sucks. Reynolds just walked in."

Back on the floor, she moved around to her desk, sat down, and smiled. "How can I help you?" Before he could answer, she jumped back up. "I'm sorry, I should have asked if you'd like coffee? Or maybe tea?"

"Nothing for me. But you go right ahead."

"Be just a minute." Molly returned to the storage room, plopped a teabag in a mug, and took her time filling it. She dunked the teabag several times, buying precious seconds with each dip, then picked up the portable phone and punched in her second line.

When it rang, she poked her head around the door and said, "Excuse me, I'll have to take this." At her desk, the mug in one hand and the phone in the other, she said, "Treasures, good morning."

Molly kept a smile on her face as she set the mug on her desk, then engaged in a one-sided conversation. "Oh, yes, I do have a Gallé piece. No, not expensive at all, at least not for Gallé. I have a small vase. Yes, a cameo thistle, and it's in excellent condition. Hmmm? I believe it's priced at around two hundred. I'm at my desk, but I can check for you. Lalique? No, not at the moment. I had a lovely perfume bottle last month though. Oh, yes, they're gorgeous. Oh, of course, I'd be delighted to keep an eye open for you. Could you give me your name and number?" Molly gave Reynolds an apologetic smile as she reached for a notepad and pen. "Is that Hannigan with one 'n' or two? Great, got it all. So nice of you to call. Oh, no bother at all. Certainly, any time is fine. I'm open seven days a week from ten until six. Wedgwood luster? Hmm, no, I haven't run across any lately. Oh, aren't they the devil to find? Shall I put that on your want list as well?"

Molly could see Reynolds was becoming impatient. There was no sense in aggravating him more than necessary. Randall should be here any moment. She ended the call, then apologized. "I'm so sorry, but business is business, right?" When he didn't answer, she gave him a smile, "Are you sure I can't offer you anything to drink? I only have instant coffee, but it's actually very good."

Reynolds was looking at his notebook, and shook his head. "You've been here in Carmel how long now?"

So much for courtesy, Molly thought. She paused, pretending to think. "Well, let's see. A little less than three years now."

"You don't own this store, right?"

"No. I manage it for Max Roman. He owns the entire complex as well."

"If you don't own it, then why are you out going to garage sales all the time? You do a little personal business on the side?"

Molly laughed. "How do you know I go to garage sales 'all the time'?"

"It's my job to know these things."

Molly could feel that old Irish creeping up her neck. "Is it your job to delve into the private lives of ordinary citizens just for the hell of it, or do you know my comings and goings for a specific reason?"

Reynolds ignored her, checked his notes again, and gave her a hard stare. "My question is—do you do other business on the side? It's relevant to my next question."

Molly suddenly knew where this was going. She tried to look past Reynolds's shoulder to see if she could spot Randall. He should have been here by now. There was no point in stalling anymore. "Then your so-called relevant question must be how I came to be involved with the Jessops, right?"

When Reynolds didn't answer, Molly said, "Yes, I do *other* business on the side. My employer encourages me to attend sales and offer my buys here in the shop alongside his merchandise. I've also branched out into interior decoration to broaden my client base. Carla Jessop approached me because of my reputation, and asked me to assist her in redecorating the tasting room at Bello Lago."

"Oh, right. Your reputation. Things are beginning to make sense now."

"Yeah? What's that supposed to mean?" Randall said as he entered the shop.

The lieutenant's head jerked around. Molly could see the cold anger in his eyes as he stared at Randall. "You'll have to excuse us, *Chief.* This is a private interview."

Randall pulled his cigar from his mouth and grinned. "Sounds more like harassment to me."

The lieutenant rose and stared Randall down. "I'll ask you to leave just once more."

Molly rose as well. "Oh, this is an *interview*? I thought you only had a few questions."

It was apparent that Reynolds had a change of heart when he said, "Relax, this is an informal interview."

"In that case," Molly said, "there's no reason why Chief Randall can't stay, is there?"

Reynolds shrugged. "As long he doesn't interrupt."

Molly sat back down. "What else do you want to know?"

Reynolds remained standing. He flipped his notebook closed and put it in his pocket. "Well, I'm just a little concerned about your recent altercation with Todd Jessop about an auction that went south. Oh, and then that vandalism to your pickup you reported to the Carmel police last week? I hear you're claiming Jessop was behind that. See, all these incidents put you in a shadowy light, Ms. Doyle. Perfect scenario for anger, maybe thoughts of a little payback?" Reynolds let that sink in for a moment while he turned away and pretended to look the shop over.

"Anger," Molly said, "is not necessarily lethal rage. It's also just being pissed off."

Reynolds turned back, glanced at Randall, who was leaning against the open front door, then smiled. "Pissed off? I'd say the killer was that, too. See, I have to look at things like that when I'm looking for a motive. Now, you just have to go on my list. Especially when you were next to the victim when he was shot. I have to say, the setting was picture-perfect. You there, by the terrace wall, you throw your arms up in the air, you move a foot or two, the victim takes your exact location, and then bang-bang, the man is dead. If we were watching a movie, I'd say your throwing your arms up was a signal to the shooter, wouldn't you?" He laughed then. "No, no, don't answer. Anything you might say, blah, blah, blah."

Reynolds was still laughing when he tipped his hat to Molly. He turned to Randall and said, "You can stop playing bodyguard. I'm through for now. But, like our great governor, I'll be back."

Randall moved aside. "You should start watching more intelligent movies, pal. The one you just described would never make it to the big screen."

Molly held her breath. The animosity between the two men was reaching flashpoint. She was at a loss to understand why Randall continued to bait the lieutenant. She prayed Reynolds would leave it alone. She saw his body stiffen, and when he went into macho mode and shifted from one foot to the other, she was ready to hide under her desk. But miracles did sometimes happen. He said nothing and walked out. Randall locked the door, reached into the front window, and leaned the sign against one of the Foo Dogs.

"Do you have to be so damn snarky with him all the time? You're not helping my image with him, you know."

Randall laughed. "It's a cop thing. You wouldn't understand."

Molly wasn't in a laughing mood. "A man was shot in front of me on Sunday, some freak is sending me unsigned postcards, Todd's real wife is bugging me to help her, and oh yeah…some pervert is asking questions about Emma, and now you're pissing off a cop who thinks I set up a killing shot? Oh, hell, try me. Maybe I need a good laugh!"

Randall pulled up a chair and stretched out his legs. "Okay. It's like this. The more I stay on Reynolds's back, the madder he gets, right? Ergo, the harder he has to work. He's rattled already. I can smell it on him. He's damn near his forty-eight hours, and if he doesn't come up with a suspect…a real one…pretty damn soon, he's up a creek without a paddle."

Molly crossed her arms. "And isn't that where you want him? So you and Loomis can find the killer first and show him up?"

Randall's smile was slow, but Molly saw how sly it was. "Nah, I wouldn't do that."

"Baloney. It's exactly what you're doing. Just keep me out of it."

"I'm trying to do just that, Ms. Doyle. Now, tell me about this pervert, and what makes you think he is one."

Molly told him about the man's first and second visits to the shop, Bitsy's worries, his phone message, and seeing him at the beach this morning. "It's probably nothing, and I was going to mention it to you later, but Reynolds arrived, and…well, I'm telling you now."

"Not much to pin a pervert tag on the man. If he shows up today and you're still worried, call me." Randall ran a hand over his eyes. "Damn, Molly! I can't believe how much your life fills up my calendar."

Molly smiled. "Are you complaining?"

Randall gave her a slow look. "Not at all."

Molly was thankful Randall's cell phone rang. There was a chance he missed the flush on her face. She watched his eyes narrow as he listened.

"No shit," Randall said to the caller. He was silent for a good two minutes, and then said, "That's trouble. Okay, I'll take it from here."

He punched in a number before Molly could ask what was wrong. He put up his hand to hold her off from speaking. "Maili? Hey, how you doin', little mama? Good, good, listen to the doc. I don't want to have to put you under house arrest. You still feel up to doing some computer sleuthing for me? Great. I'll stop by in about an hour. Yeah, in fact, I'm with her right now. I'll tell her." Randall laughed. "Right, Molly Doyle's at it again. Sure, she's just thrilled to be on the front page again. No problem, so don't get agitated. I want you back on the job in one piece after that little sweetheart pops out, you hear?"

Molly waved. "Tell Maili hello and that I'll stop by again."

Randall passed on Molly's message. As he continued to talk with his detective, who was on maternity leave, Molly pulled out the first two postcards and placed them with the current one on her desk. She liked Maili Montgomery, and was proud of the way she'd handled the emotional aftermath last year when she'd been involved in a shooting. Maili was home now as the last month of her first pregnancy neared. Molly, Daria, and Emma often stopped by to visit, loving the excuse to play surrogate aunts-to-be.

When Randall got off the phone, he said, "That first call was from Loomis. His contact at the sheriff's department passed on some interesting news."

Molly leaned her elbows on the desk and rested her chin on her hands. "Am I going to need a drink to hear this?"

"Not yet. Maybe later. The postmortem on Jessop was completed this morning. Pretty damn fast, if I say so myself. Reynolds must be pulling out all the stops."

"He was shot! Everyone saw that. Why the need for an autopsy?"

"Come on, Molly. You know it's procedure. Anyway, it appears Mr. Jessop—" But before Randall could go on, his cell phone rang again. He answered, then mouthed, "*Lucero,*" to Molly. "Yeah, I heard. I just got off the phone with Loomis. I appreciate it. Hey, goes without saying, I heard it elsewhere. No, I'm at Molly's. Yeah, I know about that, too. We'll talk more tonight."

Randall set his cell phone on Molly's desk. "It appears Reynolds has more than his hands full. He's got two killers to look for now."

Molly's eyes widened. "Two? Uh, explain that, please?"

"The M.E. found traces of deadly nightshade in his system. You might know it as belladonna."

Molly's mouth fell open. "He was being poisoned as well? Omigod!"

"It's also known as devil's cherries and devil's herb. In fact, it has a lot of different names," Emma said.

Molly saw Emma at the foot of the stairs. "Have you been snooping, miss?" Molly immediately regretted her words when she saw the hurt look on Emma's face.

"I just came down to borrow a history book from that set you have for sale, and I heard you say belladonna."

"I'm sorry, that wasn't fair," Molly said.

"So how come you know so much about nightshade?" Randall asked.

Emma held onto the banister, still not sure if she should go further. "Dando showed us his plants one time when we were out at the ranch. He wanted to be sure we didn't fool with them. He makes a medicine for Michelle's grandfather so he can sleep at night. He said it helps with inflammation, or something. I was curious about it, so I looked it up." Emma moved to where the book she wanted rested. "Is it okay if I take this upstairs? I'll be careful. It's about Macao in the early eighteen-hundreds, and we're studying the South China Sea region now."

Molly nodded. "Of course. Take them all up if you want."

"I only need a few of them," Emma said.

Molly watched Emma gather the books in her arms and head for the stairs. "Emma. I really am sorry. That was thoughtless of me."

Emma shrugged. "It's okay. I know you don't want me to hear what's going on. I understand."

"It's not that, Emma," Randall said. "It's that you're young, and—"

"And I might slip and say something to Michelle? I wouldn't do that. I know that sheriff guy thinks Mrs. Jessop had her husband killed."

"What makes you think that?" Randall asked.

"Michelle told me that's what her grandfather said to her mother. He's sending her someplace else. I forget where, but she said she wouldn't go until he makes up with Nicky. It's a real family mess."

"When did you find all this out?" Randall asked.

"Just a little while ago. Michelle and I text a lot. I had to bring her up to date on our history test. No one has picked up her assignments from school for her." Emma looked at Molly. "If someone comes in and is interested in the books, call me and I'll bring them right back."

When Randall heard the door upstairs close, he said, "Damn, that kid knows more about what's going on than the rest of us. So, the mysterious cook is an herbalist, too, huh? What a coincidence."

"I thought you hated that word," Molly said.

"I do. Hate it like the devil."

"Okay, while you mull this new development over, what else did Loomis have to say?"

"Your picture is on Reynolds's incident board with a big red circle around it. I think it's time to call Lucero and get that attorney's name."

# Chapter 19

"REYNOLDS IS out of his mind," Molly said to Lucero over the phone. "I'm closing up today and driving to Salinas to see his boss and give him a piece of my mind." Molly pulled the phone away from her ear, then put it back, and said, "I don't care what you think! I'm not going to have that bozo come in here and accuse me of setting up Jessop's shooter!"

Randall tried to pry the phone away from Molly. When she wouldn't let it go, he moved closer and shouted, "Ignore her, Dan! She's not going anywhere. I'll tie her down first."

Molly turned her back on Randall. "Listen good, Dan Lucero! I'll stay put, but I want to discuss this with you tonight at Daria's. So you'd better be prepared to answer some questions, understand?" Molly snapped her cell shut with a flourish and stared at Randall. "And you'd best be ready, too!"

Randall sat back in the chair and smiled. "Your cheeks are red. Don't have a stroke on me, okay?"

"Ha! I wouldn't think of putting you out. But I'm serious. I'm not going to go though this crap again."

Randall rose. "It's too late. You're on his board. You're part of his game plan now. Look, we'll talk to Dan tonight. Let's see what he thinks."

Molly's sigh was almost a bellow. "Shit. I'll never touch wine again as long as I live."

Randall laughed. "Famous last words of some pretty famous people."

"I don't want to be famous. I just want to sell antiques and be left alone."

Heading for the door, Randall paused. "We'll figure something out. By the way, I haven't told Lucero about the other Mrs. Jessop. I'll take care of that."

Molly nodded. "I wonder if she's been to see Reynolds yet."

Randall opened the door. "I'll have Loomis check."

"Wait! What about the cook? What's his name...uh, Dando?"

Randall snorted. "That's imprinted on my eyelids. I'm on that, like now."

After Randall left, Molly went to the foot of the stairs and called Emma. When she appeared, Molly said, "Pack a bag. You're going to Bitsy's for a few days."

"Huh? Am I in trouble?"

Molly laughed. "Of course not! I just want you out of the way of the media. It looks like they're going to hound me again, and you need to get back to school."

Emma sighed. "Okay, I guess you're right. No sense in both of us having to hide out."

"I knew you'd see it my way. I'll call Bitsy now and have Charles pick you up."

When Bitsy quickly agreed, she also suggested that Emma stay until things settled down. "Have Charles pull into the alley and park as close to the garage door as possible," Molly said. "I'll have Emma ready to jump right in."

After Emma left, Molly seriously thought about closing for the day. She decided to lock the front door instead. She wasn't in the right frame of mind to greet customers, and the thought of having to keep a smile on all day made her face ache. She picked up the postcards she hadn't shown Randall, and threw them in the desk drawer, then went into the storage room and sank into the chair. Just thinking about her photo on Reynolds's incident board was enough to give her the shakes.

She decided to call Max and bring him up to date. When his new assistant answered and said that Max was in Mexico City, Molly breathed a sigh of relief. At least she wouldn't have to worry him further or be concerned about closing for the day. Max would understand and would most likely have suggested it anyway. But she was a bit miffed that Max hadn't told her he was leaving. No doubt Bitsy knew. They were as thick as thieves and twice as devious.

While mulling all this over, Molly thought she heard someone rapping on the front door. She decided to ignore it. When the knocking became a loud pounding, Molly blew out a sigh. Very carefully, she poked her head around the open door and peeked past a tall floor lamp hiding her from view. She could see most of the glass in the front door from there. Molly squinted, wondering why the young woman's face seemed familiar. It took a moment, and then she remembered. She was a new TV reporter for one of the local stations. Molly pulled back and returned to the storage room. She wasn't about to talk to anyone from the media. She no sooner plopped in the chair than the phone rang. Molly had a good idea who it was. She waited for the answering machine to click on and listened. Sure enough, it was the reporter. Molly picked up and said, "Don't call me again. And don't come to the shop. I have nothing to say." She hung up, and it rang again. Her hand hovered over the phone, ready to let loose. She pulled it back and decided to let it ring. There was no point in trying to warn any of them off. She knew firsthand they were like mad dogs with a bone. She listened to the caller. It was Carla Jessop.

"I don't blame you for not picking up, Molly," Carla's voice said. "I'm not answering my phone either. I just wanted to tell you how sorry I am you've become involved. I…well, I hope this won't impact our relationship or stop you from completing the redecorating. I know this may sound a bit crass, but if you could stay with the delivery schedule, I'd appreciate it. We've closed the tasting room for the present. Can you place the pieces when they arrive? Oh, one other thing—we're not having a service, so please let Daria know, too, would you? Take care, Molly…and thanks so much for everything."

Molly was about to delete the message, then changed her mind. She decided it might be a good idea to save it. She wasn't sure why, but if she'd learned one thing in life, it was cover your ass.

Molly checked her watch. She had hours to kill before leaving for Daria's. An idle day was not a part of her lifestyle, and she found herself unable to decide what to do. She didn't dare take the van and leave. Going upstairs and watching TV was out of the question. She'd only bite her nails. With a sudden jolt, she realized she was a prisoner. And that infuriated her no end. She jumped from the chair and plugged in the teakettle. With as much defiance as she could muster, she lit a cigarette and began pacing the small, narrow room. After a moment, she threw open the door to the garage and stared at the two tables of the new merch she hadn't put away. Maybe, she thought, she should just spend the day rearranging the shop. Like the old Chinese proverb—when business is slow, paint the counter. Only business wasn't slow, but that didn't mean a fresh, new look would be out of order. But there was a problem with that, too. She'd be visible from the street. And then there was all the silver she'd bought for Daria to pack up. That would take at least a half hour if she took her time. Disgusted at her cowardice, she decided the hell with it. She was going back in the shop to move merch until she got bored. If anyone else knocked on the door, she'd just ignore them.

After an hour and four trips back and forth to the garage, Molly was on a short stepladder hanging a new watercolor when loud knocking surprised her and she almost lost her balance. She climbed down and stalked to the front of the shop. It was one thing to knock politely, but the continuous banging was uncalled-for. She skidded to a stop when she saw that it was the man who had bought the water pitcher and the boat. The same man on the beach, and who Bitsy thought was a pervert. Molly had half a mind to turn away, but the stern look on his face made her falter. What in heaven's name was this all about? Molly wondered if he was going to give her hell as well. Well, she thought, he'd better not. He didn't even live here.

Days of frustration came to a head. She was ready to tear into someone, and it might as well be him. She unlocked the door, and said, "In case you didn't notice, the door was locked. I'm not open today and probably won't be tomorrow either. If you want to return something, you'll have to do it later in the week."

She was about to close the door when he said, "I think it would be wise if you let me in."

"Really? Well, I'll be the judge of that." Molly gripped the edge of the door and stared him down. "Look, Mr. Whatever-the-hell-your-name-is…get lost before I call the cops."

"My name, Ms. Doyle, is Marshall Macomber. I'm Emma's father."

# Chapter 20

MOLLY DIDN'T KNOW what a heart attack felt like, but the sudden pain in her chest could be a preview. She staggered against the door.

Marshall Macomber's hand reached out to steady her. "I'm…I'm sorry I was so rude. I guess I should have—"

Molly's hand flew to her forehead. "I'm okay…I'm okay. It's just that—" She stepped back from the open door. "I guess you'd better come in." Molly sucked in her breath and made it to her desk. She turned to see Macomber still by the door. She gestured to the chair next to her desk. "Please. I'll be fine in a moment." Her vision was blurry as she watched him sit.

"Are you sure you're okay?" Macomber asked. "I should have eased into my announcement. I hadn't planned to be so blunt."

Molly couldn't ignore his sincerity. No matter what she might be feeling, she realized how distressed he was. "I'm not really okay, but it's not your fault. It's been a nasty few days, and I'm afraid my temper got the best of me. I was rude to you first."

"One might argue your mood is justified. It's easy to realize you've most likely been targeted by the media again."

She checked herself this time. There was no point in being defensive. She knew a few things about this man who claimed to be Emma's father. She knew he was a high-powered attorney in Seattle and that her sister, Carrie, had worked for him for several years, and they'd had a long-term affair. But then, was he really who he said was? She hadn't been sure about Susan Jessop. Why should she believe him? For all she knew, he could be a reporter.

"Before we go any further, I'd like to see some identification."

When she saw his neck stiffen, she said, "Your purchases were made with cash. I have no proof of who you really are."

"Fair enough." He pulled out his wallet, opened it, and set it on the desk. "My driver's license and credit cards. Feel free to take them out and examine them." He reached into his pocket and took out a card case. "My business cards." As an afterthought, he opened his sport coat and took out a leather folder. "My passport as well."

While Molly eagle-eyed each item, he said, "I also have a private investigator's report on you. Shall I offer that as well?"

Molly stared at him. "Really. Well then, please do."

Macomber pointed to the leather folder. "It's there with my passport."

Molly willed her eye to stop twitching. Indignation had quickly overcome her shock and was threatening to explode into full-blown anger. With more control than she'd imagined possible, she read the report.

It was all there. Damn near her entire life. Two pages, single-spaced. Filled with her father's incarceration, her marriage, her husband and his girlfriend's antiques scam, her move back to San Francisco, and then to Carmel. The last paragraph detailed the murders she'd played a major role in solving. "Apparently you know a few things about me."

Macomber smiled. "Yes, Ms. Doyle, I think the report makes that quite evident."

Molly smiled back. It was vital she didn't let on how much he'd rattled her. "Well, guess what? I know a little about you as well. But I don't know for certain that you're Emma's father. You'll have to prove that to me. But first, it would nice if you'd let me know why you're even here."

"Might we go somewhere for coffee or maybe a cocktail?" he asked.

Molly shook her head. "No. I'd rather chat on my own turf if you don't mind."

Macomber laughed. "Excellent strategy, Ms. Doyle. Cleverness must be a dominant gene in your family. Your sister was—"

"Leave my sister out of this," Molly shot back. She could have kicked herself. She realized he'd just pushed a sensitive button, and she'd reacted as he planned. Score one for the other side.

"Unfortunately, Carrie plays a major role in our discussion. Do you have a guardianship agreement with Carrie for Emma's care?"

"Until you can offer me proof that you're Emma's father, that's none of your business."

"I can, and I will if that becomes an issue. But before we continue in this adversarial mode, I think I should explain why I'm here, and what I've decided to do about Emma."

That was all Molly needed to hear. All her good intentions flew out the window. "Excuse me? What *you've* decided to do about Emma?" Molly shot out of her chair. "Until you come up with your so-called proof, you have nothing to say about Emma or her future. And even then, you'd better know I'll fight you tooth-and-nail."

Marshall Macomber put his hands together and softly clapped. "Brava, Ms. Doyle. Wonderful performance. The jury would be in tears by now. Please do sit down and hear me out. You won't be unhappy with my verdict." When Molly just stared at him, he added, "Please?"

Molly hesitated. She wasn't buying his sudden but rather pompous empathy. "I'll sit, but you'd better understand I'm serious."

"I do. And I am, believe it or not, on your side."

Molly's mouth fell open. "You are?"

"May I call you Molly?"

Still surprised by this sudden turn-about, Molly could only nod.

"I came here, Molly, with every intention of taking Emma back to Vancouver with me. I've left Seattle. Too many sad memories. When I read the investigator's report, I must admit, I was very concerned. The report, as you no doubt noticed, was merely factual. The human element, your character if you will, was missing. Also missing were your simple lifestyle, your circle of friends, and your weekly religious attendance. I needed to see, firsthand, just who and what you are. Although, I must admit, I wasn't pleased to discover your association with those...well, calling them exotic dancers is being kind."

"Those are clients who buy chairs and are not friends. I doubt you were very cozy with some of the white-collar criminals your firm defended."

"Touché." He laughed. "I apologize. That was rude of me. One does not always have the opportunity to choose one's business associates."

Molly didn't buy his apology but was surprised by sudden softness in his eyes. Was this just another lawyer trick to lull her? Her hands were in her lap. From where he sat, across the desk, he couldn't see how tightly her fingers were intertwined. "Okay, now that you've met me, let's get on with your next move. I mean, I'm sure that's what this is all about, right?"

"Until yesterday's event, I'd decided Emma was in good hands. But now I'm not sure. You've become involved once again with yet another murder investigation."

"But I'm not involved!" Molly rushed to say. "I was only a guest."

"From what I've read, Molly, you were in a dispute with the victim. He was approaching you when he was shot."

"My dispute was minor. I…couldn't help where I was standing."

"Suppose Emma had been there with you? Do you see where I'm heading?"

Molly no longer cared about lawyer tricks. She slumped in the chair and turned from Macomber's intense stare. *He can't take her, please God!* "I…I'd thought about that," she finally managed. "But—"

"Yes," Macomber said gently. "But."

Molly knew he was right. She also knew that he had good cause to take legal measures for custody. If…and that was a big if…he were indeed Emma's father. "Emma will be thirteen in a few months. She's of an age where she can—"

"I'm well aware of juvenile rights, Molly. I want only the best for her, and I can offer her much more than you're able to."

"Really? Well then, where the hell have you been all these years? Your sudden concern leaves me wondering."

"I've only just discovered that I'm her father."

Molly suddenly knew who was sending the postcards. "Carrie," she said. "Carrie has been in touch with you, hasn't she!"

Macomber nodded. "Yes. I began to receive a series of blank postcards from Europe a few weeks ago. I knew it was Carrie."

Molly slammed her hands on the desk. "Damn her all to hell! She's been sending them to me, too. The latest one has a—"

"A rabbit on it?"

Molly let out a deep sigh. She could only nod.

"Carrie had a habit of doodling. Always rabbits. Two days before I arrived here, I received a letter from her. She told me about Emma and where I could find her, and that I should tell you about my postcards. A childish whim of hers, I suppose, to tease us. She also included a lab report attesting to my being Emma's father. Apparently, she'd gone to the expense of having our DNA samples examined. Carrie is, if nothing else, thorough. I suspect she'd decided a day might arrive when she needed some insurance. I had assumed Emma was the result of an affair she'd had with one of my partners. I truly had no idea I was her father."

"I find it hard to believe my sister sat on this information all these years."

Macomber shook his head. "I don't. Carrie knew I wouldn't leave my wife for her. Unfortunately, my wife found out. The end result was tragic. And then there was the mess Carrie got into."

Molly waved him off. "I don't want to hear any more about my sister or your infidelity, if you don't mind."

Molly rose and stared at Macomber. "Excuse me for a moment." She headed for the storage room, lit a cigarette, and marched back to face him. "What is it exactly that you're proposing?"

Macomber saw the determination on Molly's face. He held up a closed hand and lifted a finger as he ticked off each demand. "Visitation rights. Financial support. A say in her education." He paused, then lifted the last finger. "Taking her away now until this dilemma you find yourself in is resolved."

"If I refuse? And decide to fight you?"

Macomber smiled. "You care too much for her to refuse."

Molly avoided looking at him. She took her time stubbing out the cigarette. She knew he was right. Of course she wanted Emma to have the best of everything. And of course he would know she'd feel that way. She wished her sister were here now so she could throttle her. How like Carrie to set this in motion. How like Carrie to be so damn sneaky and manipulating. She'd stolen from their father, she'd stolen from Macomber's law firm, she stolen from Molly, and now she was ripping her heart apart once again. Molly had little doubt Macomber was telling the truth about being Emma's father. The resemblance, now that she had a chance to really look at him, was there. The chin and the eyes were so similar, a DNA report was hardly necessary.

"I've made arrangements for Emma to stay with a close friend until this mess is over. I...I didn't want her caught up in this media thing. I think they'll lose interest in me soon enough."

"I imagine she'll be wonderfully cared for by Mrs. Morgan," Macomber broke in.

When Molly's eyes widened, he quickly said, "I'm not following her, if that's what you're worried about. I expected that was where you would send her. It was the most logical assumption."

"I don't want you contacting Emma until I've thought this over." Macomber rose. "I'll honor that wish for the time being."

Molly faced him head-on. "There is no time being. Don't you dare impose a time limit on me! You may know a lot about me, but I know nothing about you and until I do, you keep your distance, mister!"

Macomber moved closer to Molly. He stood only inches from her when he said, "Fair enough. Just don't bankrupt yourself if you decide to fight me. I have no other children, Molly. I can offer Emma so much more than you'll ever be able to manage. Remember that if you want the best for her."

Molly watched Macomber's leisurely stroll to the door and wished she could wave a magic wand and make him disappear. He turned and smiled. "I've extended my reservation at the Lodge at Pebble Beach. I've decided to work on my golf. That may take several days." He tipped a nonexistent hat. "Wish me luck."

Molly said nothing. She hoped the look on her face told him what she wished for him.

# Chapter 21

MOLLY SAT IN THE storage room the rest of the afternoon thinking about her conversation with Marshall Macomber. She could almost lay out the emotions she experienced: shock, indignation, anger, and now the fear of losing Emma. She sat still for a very long time, clutching the small cross under her sweater as she wondered how she was going to solve this new problem. She smoked one cigarette after another and drank instant espressos until her throat began to burn and her stomach felt queasy. She started to call Randall at least four times, then changed her mind each time. This was her problem, not his.

She placed the CLOSED sign in the window and continued to ignore the occasional knocks on the front door. She barely listened to the five calls on the phone from reporters, three from clients wanting to see what was new, a call from Del Tinsley, and one from Bitsy asking if she had a line on more chairs for Del.

She had to leave soon for dinner at Daria's. She wasn't in the mood, but she knew her mind and heart, both feeling ready to implode, needed the comfort and wisdom of her friends. Everything Macomber had said about what he could do for Emma was true. And it was also true, Molly knew, that not to allow Emma those advantages would be selfish. If Macomber was as affluent as Molly assumed, there was no way in hell she could match the power of his wealth if he wanted a fight. As it was, Bitsy was paying for Emma's private school tuition. The best she'd been able to manage was a new computer and moving up from buying Emma's clothes at Target to Macy's.

Not that she was poverty-stricken, but every dollar she'd managed to hold onto went for merch and a rainy day. Her salary from

Max was minimal, her commission the standard ten percent, but then the apartment and utilities were free and so was the new van. The Fund, as she termed it, was at a respectable level and used carefully. There were days when Molly felt a little guilt over her self-imposed thrift, but she had to think of the future. Max was in his mid-eighties, and God forbid, he could go at any time. The Fund was her only stake for a future shop of her own. Her days of high-end merch and the glory of being a sought-after New York dealer were gone. She knew nothing else. Art and antiques had been her only life. She doubted she'd last long in any other profession. She simply had no other skills to fall back on.

Macomber might be able to give Emma the best of everything in a material sense, but what about love? Could he love Emma more than she? How much time would he spend with her? Would he sit on the floor and watch movies and eat popcorn and pizza until he was sick? Would he pretend to be all thumbs with an Xbox? Or take her to garage and estate sales and smile with bursting pride when she bested a book dealer or edged out a buyer after the same item? He sure as hell wouldn't jog on the beach with her. Would he even eat her meatloaf or macaroni and cheese?

Molly's past experiences with the media left her no illusions as to their persistence or ingenuity. She decided to sneak out the back way and to weave through the many alleys of downtown Carmel on her way to Daria's. It took her a good half hour to reach the alley behind Daria's restaurant, but the walk had given her more time to think. She was about to knock on the kitchen door when she realized she'd forgotten Daria's silver. Molly checked her watch. She still had time to go back and get the boxes. But that meant she'd have to take the van after all. She stared at the door for a full moment, then turned and marched out of the alley onto Dolores Street. Screw it, she thought. She was through hiding. If anyone was hanging around looking for her, she'd just ignore them. She was about to step onto the sidewalk when out of the corner of her eye she saw Macomber entering Daria's.

Molly flattened herself against the wall and took a deep breath. What the hell was he doing here? Of all the restaurants in town, he had to pick this one? It only took a nanosecond for Molly to realize what he was up to. He was going to ask Daria about her. She made a quick about-face and hurried to the back door and into the kitchen. Molly brushed past the prep cooks and the pastry chef and almost ran into Manuel, Daria's head busser. "Is Daria out front?" she asked.

"The boss is in her room making the ready for you and the *jefes*. You want me to call her for you, yes?"

Molly shook her head. "I'll go right in. Thanks, Manuel." Molly scooted out of the way of two waiters and rushed to Daria's private room. She threw open the door. "Before you go out front, I have to talk to you!"

Daria set down a tray, put her hands on her hips. "Now what? I can't keep up with you!" She tried a smile. "Don't tell me Reynolds is after you, and you're on the run?"

Molly sank into a chair. "That would be the least of my worries. Him, I can handle."

Daria's face turned serious. She sat opposite Molly. "I don't like the sound of that. Spill, okay?"

As Molly told Daria about her session with Macomber, she saw Daria's face run through the same gamut of emotions Molly had experienced earlier. "He's out front in the restaurant," Molly said. "I saw him come in. He'll order dinner first, and then I'll bet he'll ask you to join him."

Daria, however volatile she could be on occasion, was surprisingly calm when she said, "Screw him. I'm not available. We'll fight him with you, Molly. We won't let him take Emma from you."

"And neither will I," Randall said as he appeared inside the open door. "Why didn't you call me?" He moved to Molly. "How long have you been sitting on this?"

Molly closed her eyes and tried not to cry. Just hearing them offer their support was reassuring. She sniffed loudly, then said, "I almost called you four times this afternoon. And then I remembered you'd said how much my life problems filled your calendar."

Randall sat down next to her and laughed. "I was kidding, for chrissakes!"

"I know, but still. I just found out a few hours ago. Did you hear everything? I'm not sure if I can repeat it again. I might start to bawl."

"Yeah, I got it all." Randall looked at Daria. "When Lucero and Loomis get here, call me. I'm going out to see the gentleman."

Molly put her hand out to stop him. "Don't. He'll think I ran to you for help. It will make me look like I'm running scared. Besides, I don't think he's easily intimidated."

"Okay," Randall said. "I'll do it your way." He gave her a hug. "For now."

"I forgot to mention the postcards. He asked me if I'd been receiving blank cards from Europe." Molly paused. "I almost fell over when he asked. I told him I had. And then he asked me if the latest one had a drawing of a rabbit on it. When I said yes, he told me he'd received them, too. He said they were from Carrie."

Daria's eyes widened. "Your sister? How did he know that?"

"He said that Carrie was a doodler, and she always drew rabbits. That's how he knew they were from her. She also told him she'd sent them when she wrote to him."

"And this all means what?" Daria asked.

"It means," Randall said, "she's up to her shit-stirring-tricks. She's also taunting the both of you. Playing with your heads and letting you know she's still out there."

"And it all has to do with Emma," Molly said. "How better to torment me? Leave her with me, let me grow to love her, and then set things up to lose her."

Daria reached across the table and took hold of Molly's hand. "Does she hate you that much?"

Molly squeezed Daria's hand, then closed her eyes. "Apparently."

Manuel popped his head in the door and said, "The D.A. is at the bar, and he tells me to say he's coming soon. He is with the Mr. Looms having the cocktail."

Daria nodded, then said to Molly, "Uh, maybe Randall might like to join them? You know…and get a glimpse of this guy?" She looked quickly at Randall. "Just a glimpse, huh? No chit-chat."

"Good thinking. Always better to know what the opposition looks like." He smiled at Molly. "I promise not to get near him, okay? What does he look like?"

Molly described Marshall Macomber. "On your honor?"

Randall winked. "Sure. Whatever. Where's Emma?"

"She's going to stay with Bitsy for a few days until the media loses interest in me."

"Good. We can talk openly then. Be right back."

After Randall left, Daria said, "That was smart, sending Emma to Bitsy. I take it she's not aware of this new development?"

Molly sighed. "No, and I'm not sure how I'm going to tell her."

Daria pulled up a chair. "If you need me, you know I'm here."

Molly reached for Daria's hand, and smiled. "You're a wonderful friend, you know?"

"Likewise. Okay, let's not get soppy, or we'll both start crying. Come on, let's get dinner on the table."

"I forgot to bring you the silver again." Molly shook her head. "I'm just not thinking straight."

"First things, first. The silver is the least of our problems."

By the time Molly and Daria had set out the usual *mélange* of platters, Randall, Lucero, and Loomis arrived. Dan took off his jacket, threw it on the French day bed at the end of the room, and said to Molly, "Don't worry about Macomber. Randall just filled us in. I'll get the brief on him and if I'm not mistaken, it won't be sterling. I mean, what lawyer has clean shorts, huh? Emma has rights, and we know what her decision is going to be. But I gotta tell you, Molly, you may have a problem with the guardianship thing."

Molly's face paled. "What kind of problem?"

Lucero looked at Randall. They both knew the roadblocks that might be ahead. "You've been in the news since you moved here. You've played a major role in helping solve homicides." Lucero saw Molly's hands clenched on the table. "Look, it doesn't matter that you helped law enforcement. What does matter is that a judge might consider your involvement as being prone to…well, hell, what I mean is…you're in the middle of another one right now."

Molly's throat was too tight to speak. She reached for her water and took a sip. All she could manage was a nod. She took a deep breath, and said, "Endangering? Is that the word you're looking for? Emma might be in an endangered atmosphere?" Molly looked around the room, noting the face of each of these wonderful friends. She was deeply touched by their love and generosity, but now she saw they, too, realized that keeping Emma with her was not going to be a slam-dunk. "We used to laugh at my being a magnet for trouble. It's not funny anymore. In fact, I'll bet this is what Macomber will try to use against me."

"Hey, knock that off," Lucero said. "We're not beat yet. I'm just saying, is all."

Randall took his usual place at the table next to Molly. Loomis sat across from him, and Daria and Lucero sat at each end. "Tell Molly the good news," Loomis said.

"What could possibly be good news after this?" Molly said glumly.

"You tell her, Randall," Lucero grinned.

"No way. It's your show," Randall said.

"Stop this!" Daria yelled. "I hate these games. What?"

Lucero reached for a bottle of wine. "We need a full glass handy so you can toast me." He handed Randall the open bottle. "Come on, pass it around! And make it quick before Daria throws something at me."

When all the glasses were full, Lucero lifted his and said, "Here's to me for personally taking Molly's photo off Reynolds's incident board." He threw up his free hand and added, "Wait! There's more. Reynolds is no longer in charge of the Jessop investigation. He's, uh, on vacation as of this afternoon."

Molly felt as if she'd been holding a balloon that suddenly burst. "Omigod, Dan! That really is fantastic news! I...I don't know what to say. I really don't."

Daria was on her feet, running to the end of the table to hug Lucero. "You big lug, you finally did something grand! How the hell did you pull that off?"

Lucero grinned. "How? Hey, I'm the people's choice around here. I work for justice, right? Besides, Reynolds didn't have cause. Simple as that."

Molly looked at Randall. "Did you know about Reynolds when you came in?"

"Yeah. But it was Dan's doing, so it was his announcement, not mine."

Molly's eyes finally began shining. "Then you're off the hook, too?"

Randall shrugged. "Hell, I never was on it. Reynolds knew that. He just wanted to see if he could make me squirm."

Loomis reached for the wine. "Fat chance of that happening."

"The truth of the matter," Lucero said, "is that the sheriff knew Reynolds was off-kilter as well. Reynolds was working too hard looking for the easy way out. There is a list of suspects a mile long, and he was skimming over those prospects just to get back at Randall. Hell, any ten-year-old watching TV would know his reasoning was shaky. The new guy, Lieutenant Jack Stuart, is a recent transfer from San Jose, and one smart investigator. He's already taken over. And he'll be sharing with me on a daily basis."

Suddenly, the baked eggplant with mozzarella looked promising to Molly. She helped herself, then passed it on to Randall. "Have you told Dan and Loomis about Susan Jessop, and that Dindo grows belladonna?"

"The man's name is Dando. Yeah, Dan and Loomis are up to snuff, so is Stuart. Loomis is already checking out Susan Jessop, and Dan told Stuart about the herb garden."

Daria passed the veal *alla Milanese* to Loomis. "Can you work independently on this case?"

"Oh, didn't Dan mention that I'm working for his office now?" Loomis said.

Daria shook her head. "No. He only tells us how great he is."

Lucero laughed. "That's all anyone needs to know. It's called BSP."

"Very funny," Daria said. "I don't even want to know what that means. It sounds like a nasty disease. But I would like to know who the hell Susan Jessop is, and what's this with Dando and belladonna?" When she encountered silence, Daria knocked a fork against a glass. "Hello? I've come to think of this room as a sub-rosa command center. Don't start with the silent treatment now. Just because we're not personally involved any longer, that doesn't mean we can't contribute."

Randall asked Molly to pass the sautéed zucchini. He helped himself to a large portion, then said, "I forgot to mention, Wilkins picked up two kids last night keying a car. They had a raccoon they were about to shove in the window. Guess that leaves Jessop in the clear."

Molly said, "Well, at least that's one mystery solved. But Daria's question hasn't been answered."

"Okay, Lucero. You're on. You fill Daria in while the rest of us dig into the *grigliata di pesce.*"

"The what?" Loomis asked.

"The fish," Randall said. "Breaded sea bass baked with garlic, parsley, and lemon."

"I knew it was fish," Loomis said. "You don't have to get fancy on me. Right, Molly?"

Molly wasn't sure what Loomis had said. Her thoughts were a million miles away. She figured a nod would work. The possibility of a judge being influenced by Molly's past experiences brought on more eye-twitching. She had to get hold of her emotions. She knew everyone here would vouch for her, and they would be witnesses to Molly's love for Emma. How many people, she wondered, could lay claim to having a chief of police and a district attorney as close friends? Daria was a pillar in the business community. Bitsy was one of the Monterey Peninsula's biggest philanthropists. They had all played a big part in Emma's being accepted at Santa Catalina School. And besides, she tried to convince herself, this newest problem, Todd Jessop's murder, had nothing to do with her at all. But there was always Murphy's Law, and that damn Irish plague seemed to crop up too much in her life.

Molly caught the tail end of something Loomis was saying. She faintly recalled him talking about a greenhouse. Everyone's eyes seemed riveted to him. "I'm sorry," she said. "I guess I was drifting. Did I hear you mention a greenhouse?"

"I was talking about Susan Jessop. I'm checking her out for Dan.

I looked over her home in Portola Valley. Big place, three or four acres." He nodded towards Lucero. "I was telling Dan, there's a big greenhouse on her property. I, ah, well, I pretended to be lost and found her gardener." He gave Molly a wink. "We got to talking about plants. Told him I was thinking about adding a greenhouse to my place. He kindly gave me a tour of Mrs. Jessop's and showed me her herb and medicinal sections."

Molly turned to Randall. "She didn't look like a green-thumb person to me."

"Like killers, huh? They have to have a look?" Randall said.

"The greenhouse is for show," Loomis said. "It's for some charity garden tour she takes a part in every year."

"Don't tell me," Molly said, "she grows belladonna?"

"I don't know a pansy from a rose," Loomis said, "but the gardener pointed a few plants out when I asked. And yeah, she's got a few nice specimens of belladonna."

"Whoa," Daria said. "That can be bad stuff. My grandmother used to make tea with it to help soothe her arthritis. A lot of the old-country women grew the plant and always had it on hand. What's it got to do with Todd Jessop?"

Randall told Daria about the postmortem findings and what Emma had learned. "So this Dando character must have the same old-world recipe your grandmother had," he added.

Molly pushed her plate away. "I can't eat. My stomach is a mess. My head hurts, and I want to sleep for a few weeks."

Daria said, "Maybe you might want to close for a few days or go up to the City and visit Max."

Molly shook her head. "Max is out of town again. Not opening has some appeal, but I'll stay open. Besides, I've got to tell Emma about her father." She saw the surprised faces. "I have to. She has a right to know."

The door opened, and Manuel said to Daria, "Excuse, but out in front there is a man who wishes to speak to you. The food he is not complaining." He entered and handed Daria a business card.

Daria read it, then looked at Molly. "You were right. It's Macomber." She threw the card on the table, and said to Manuel.

"Tell the gentleman I'm with a private party and am unable to meet with him."

After Manuel left, Molly slapped her hand on the table. "Damn it! For once, I wish I'd been wrong."

Randall pushed back from the table. "Being right is a bitch sometimes."

# Chapter 22

THE THOUGHT OF going back to the empty apartment after leaving Daria's held little appeal. Instead, Molly retraced her alley route for a few blocks. She wasn't worried about running into Macomber, or the media at ten in the evening. She finally headed up to Ocean Avenue and slowly wandered past the dozens of gift shops and art galleries. It only took her a few moments to realize how many shops had changed since she first arrived. She'd been so busy, she'd hardly noticed. Now that she desperately needed to clear her mind, to wonder how to tell Emma what faced them, the changes around her finally hit her in the eye.

Her favorite Dansk store was already gone, and so was Saks Fifth Avenue, only to be replaced by a high-priced men's store. And some of the small gift shops she'd remembered were also gone, no doubt having succumbed to the shocking rents. She wondered how long many of the new merchants would last. Carmel might have a ordinance against chain operations, but rents were reaching a point where only the chains could afford to be there. But then, what exactly constituted a chain? Some of the newer shops she passed had other locations besides Carmel. And while the village was still unique and well groomed, it was beginning to feel like a giant outdoor mall.

But then, Carmel was no longer the sleepy little village catering to a cadre of drop-outs, *avant-garde* artists, and starving poets. Property values had become so outrageous that only the deep-pocket merchants and semi-chains could survive. Except for patronizing the restaurants and small bistros, most locals didn't shop in Carmel anymore. Only tourists could afford to shop here now. She was lucky with Treasures at least. Many of her customers were locals and the newly arrived groups of property-rich Central Valley farmers and Silicon Valley *nouveaux riches*.

She remembered hearing a local person tell Bennie one morning at Tosca's that all the characters were gone. Only Bill Bates, the local cartoonist, he'd said, seemed to be still hanging around. The recollection brought a small smile to Molly's aching face. She recalled being at the post office a few weeks ago when she'd encountered a huge crowd outside protesting the removal of several of Bill's framed poster-size cartoons that had hung inside the post office for twenty years. The excuse for removing them had been a new paint job. But they hadn't been put back up because of a new standardization ruling for the interior of all post offices. That hadn't sat right with over eleven hundred locals who'd signed a petition to hang them back immediately. Even the local state assembly representative had chimed in. As she crossed the meridian to the other side of Ocean Avenue and to the shop, Molly made a mental note to see if the posters were there again.

The brief smile over the village outrage soon faded as she walked under the arch and into the courtyard. She slowly headed up the back stairs to the apartment. It would be strange not to join Emma in a nightly cocoa. She shivered as she thought about life without Emma. She heard the telephone ringing as she unlocked the French door. Racing to the kitchen, she picked it up and heard Carla Jessop's voice. "Molly? Why the hell didn't you tell me about this woman who claims to be Todd's wife?"

"Wait, hold on!" Molly said. "I didn't tell you because I didn't know if she was telling me the truth."

"What difference did that make? You could have at least warned me."

Molly shrugged out of her jacket and threw her tote on the floor. "You're right. I should have called you. But I did tell her to see the sheriff's deputy. I figured he'd call you."

"That jackass never said a thing to me. Now another one has taken his place, and I was hauled in for questioning again today."

"How did you find out about her?"

"The new cop told me, and he said you knew her."

"I don't *know* her. She came into the shop and that was the first time I'd laid eyes on her. Look, Carla, I'm sorry you had to hear this now. I mean, that Todd was…well, maybe it's not true." Molly knew Loomis had been to Susan Jessop's home, but it still didn't mean she was married to Todd. She could still be a sister. Or a mistress with a fake ID.

"Oh, it's true all right. She had a marriage license to prove it. That bastard! If he wasn't already dead, I'd kill him myself."

"Carla! For God's sake! Don't say things like that."

Carla laughed. "Why not? I'm sure I'm already the prime suspect. And if you're wondering if I *did* kill Todd, the answer is no."

"It never crossed my mind," Molly said.

"I'd love to believe that, but I'll take your word for it. Anyway, we've still got lives to lead, and until the fuzz decides to throw some cuffs on me, I've got to get back to the project. The furniture you ordered has arrived. Can you make it out here this week to set things up?"

Molly hesitated. The thought of returning to the winery left her strangely uncomfortable. But still, she reasoned, it was her responsibility to complete the commission. "How's Saturday? Bitsy will be in to work here."

"Perfect. Oh, by the way, I've found that old stuff my father wants you to see. My grandmother spent two months in Italy after the war, and she brought back crates filled with dishes, urns, and all sorts of real old things she'd bought from some local families in need of cash. She got sick soon after and they were never unpacked. They're in a storage area of one of the old wine caves."

Molly's brain zeroed in on old Italian ceramics and hadn't processed "caves" until it was too late. Even so, Molly's fingers began to tingle. The thought of maybe finding prewar stuff still in crates was jump-starting her enthusiasm after a day of depression.

"I'll meet you at eight in the tasting room," Carla said. "Maybe Emma might like to come along. Michelle will be with me."

"We'll be there."

Molly plugged in the teakettle and was about to go into Emma's room to tell her the exciting news, then stopped cold. A sudden shroud of loneliness dropped over her. She rolled her shoulders as if she could fling the sensation away. She reached for a mug and wondered if this was what it would be like if Emma should leave for good. The silence in the small apartment weighed upon her.

Molly turned to the sink and leaned against the cracked tile. She rested her arms on the window sill and stared out over the rooftops of the buildings across the courtyard. How many stressful times, she wondered, since she had come to Carmel, had she done this? It was odd, she thought, how this small window seemed to be the portal to the few Zen moments she could muster. Clear moments when she managed to push away doubt and fear. Moments when her world might not feel so unsure.

The shrill whistle of the teakettle jolted her back to reality. She turned from the window and unplugged the damn thing. Without Emma, the soothing routine of a warm drink before bed had lost its appeal. Even the prospect of possibly finding new treasures seemed meaningless.

Molly turned off the lights as she moved through the apartment to her bedroom. She clicked on the lamp beside her bed and then sat for several moments with Tiger and her kittens. When she finally got ready for bed and pulled the duvet over her, she noticed the mystery books Emma had bought. She picked one up, then changed her mind and set it back on the night table. She wasn't in the mood to read about murder right now. She'd been there already.

Randall had been standing across the street from Treasures waiting for the lights in Molly's apartment to go off. It wasn't the first time he'd done this. In the past, it had been to satisfy his need to know Molly was safe and tucked in. Now it seemed a different need had propelled him, once again, to stop. Randall was a frequent night walker in this little village he had pledged to watch over. It gave him a sense of satisfaction to know all was well, that he and his small force were doing their jobs. He liked seeing the night lights on in the shops, the doorknobs that didn't give when he randomly shook them. He often stopped in the quiet of the night and took in the faint smell of the ocean and the soft scent of the hundreds of pine trees that protected this place. This home of his.

Tonight was different. And he knew, deep down, why when he'd stopped himself twice from crossing the street and ringing Molly's doorbell. He lit a cigar and watched the flame of the match inch down until it almost burned his finger. It was time to go to the City. It was time again, he realized, to see Annie. He felt no guilt accepting the comfort and favors of an old flame who knew an occasional visit was not a commitment. He liked to think he was also a man who had managed, in spite of a realistic view of the worst of life, to hold onto vestiges of honor and respect for a woman who still considered herself married. A man who accepted the dictates of a faith they both shared.

He turned away from Molly's dark windows and headed home. But he had much on his mind besides Molly Doyle. He wanted to find a killer. It didn't matter that the case wasn't his, or that working it with Loomis wasn't kosher. It was something he needed to do. It was, in fact, what he was all about. An artist needs to paint, a writer needs to write, a cop needs to solve a crime. And Randall knew he was the best one around to do just that. Of that he had no doubt.

# Chapter 23

ON FRIDAY, Molly was up with the first light. Sleep had been sporadic the past few nights, and her eyes were gritty. Nonetheless, she hopped out of bed, and after plugging in the teakettle, headed for the shower with a forced sense of enthusiasm. Life, she reminded herself, is what you make it. So, pretending all was well would hopefully carry her through the day. The end was not near. Not even close. She knew worrying about losing Emma was most likely overblown. As everyone had said, Emma had a say in the matter. She still wasn't sure how she was going to tell Emma about her father. She'd thought about all sorts of different openings to ease into the problem, then discarded each one when she realized it was best just to come out with it. Preambles were not one of Molly's talents. She had a habit of blurting things out. No point in changing now.

Yet, even though she was no longer a suspect in Todd Jessop's murder, she still had the feeling a dark cloud was hovering over her. Not one to rely heavily on precognizance, Molly nevertheless knew there were times when warnings from the senses shouldn't be ignored or dismissed as superstition. But then, she thought as she stepped into the shower, show me a Catholic who isn't superstitious.

Molly called Bitsy just after seven before heading over to Tosca's for her morning indulgence, confirming with Bitsy that she was still coming in on Saturday. She spoke briefly to Emma, and told her that it appeared the media had finally lost interest in her and it was safe to come home. Feeling that life was somewhat returning to normal, Molly scooted down the back steps and crossed the courtyard to the small indoor section of Bennie's café. She found him seated, sipping coffee and reading the morning paper. Bennie jumped up when Molly arrived. "Hey, good to see you. Where you been?"

"Hiding out," she said as she took a seat at his table. "Damn reporters were driving me nuts. Apparently they've given up on me, thank God."

Bennie handed her the paper, and said, "While I get your espresso and croissants, you might want to read this and see why."

Molly took the paper and saw Susan Jessop's photo on the front page. The article portrayed Todd Jessop as a philandering bigamist, an unsettling intruder and meddler into the business end at Bello Lago, and a habitual client of an unnamed lap dancing establishment in San Francisco, where he'd recently been banned for aggressive behavior. The report went on to recap his murder and a brief background of Carla and her family's history in Monterey County.

Molly immediately thought of Del Tinsley, and also the private party she had cancelled. Oh, if only Del had told her who the unwanted guest was, Molly might have been able to avoid going to that damn dinner. But then, she knew she probably would have gone anyway, if for no other reason than to show support for Carla. She set the paper back on the table. Poor Carla! This was all she needed now. It was bad enough to realize she wasn't legally married to Jessop, but to have it all over the newspapers and to discover he'd been banned from a lap dancing club? And for aggressive behavior? How humiliating for her. Not to mention Michelle. Girls her age were infected with cruelty toward peers as it was, and now they had new fuel. At least Michelle had Emma to help buffer what might be an unpleasant time until school was out.

Bennie arrived with a tray for Molly. "Pretty lurid, huh? Old man Mattucci must be frothing at the mouth. You know how Italians are about stuff like this. *Faccia. Che salva la faccia!* In other words, 'face.' Saving face, to be accurate. In this case, it's *perdere la faccia*— losing face. It's what we live with, even after two or three generations. Jeeze, Molly, *fare bella figura* is banged into our heads from day one."

"And that one means?"

Bennie sat down. "Literally, it means, make a good impression. What it really means is reputation. Like, oh—upstanding, dignified. You know, honorable."

"Respected," Randall said over his shoulder as he walked to the counter, checking out the fresh pastries. "Hey Bennie, you got my stuff ready, or what?"

Bennie shook his head and smiled. "Damn, Randall. You have a bad habit of creeping up on people."

"It's part of my charm, I guess."

Bennie laughed. "Yeah, right. I'll get your stuff." He looked at Molly and said, "It also means, don't do things to make people talk about you."

"Guess I need to learn some of that myself," Molly said. "Can I buy it in a bottle somewhere?" She smiled at Randall as he took the chair Bennie had just vacated. "So, have you seen the paper this morning?"

Randall nodded. "Saw it in the *Chronicle* yesterday when I was in the City."

"So that's why I haven't seen you."

Randall pretended not to hear Molly as he reached for the tray Bennie handed him. "What? No extra butter?"

"Under the napkin," Bennie said. "Hey, you mean the *Chron* beat our paper with the news?"

"Looks that way," Randall replied. "Big stink going on up there anyway with those lap dancing places. This won't help your friend, Molly."

"She's not my friend. She's a customer. I wish people would get these things straight."

Randall waited until Bennie returned to the counter, then said, "I've got the scoop on Marshall Macomber. Dan did some checking with lawyer pals, Loomis snapped a photo of him on the links at Pebble, and then we did our thing."

Molly held her breath. "Okay. Fire away."

"He's who he says he is, Molly. And from what we can tell, clean as a whistle."

"Well, to be honest, I'm not surprised. The resemblance between them is there. Emma's got his eyes, too. I doubt that DNA report he showed me is a fake. But then, I've never seen one before."

"Have you told Emma anything yet?"

"No. I was stalling until I heard from you." Molly tore into a croissant, then took her time adding a pat of butter. "I'll tell her tonight when she comes home from Bitsy's. Bitsy doesn't know yet. I didn't want her dipping her oar into this yet."

"Amen to that. Listen, can I throw a little advice your way?"

Molly had the croissant halfway to her mouth when she stopped. "All of a sudden you're asking?" She rolled her eyes. "Go ahead. I won't be able to stop you anyway."

"Cool it with Carla for a couple of weeks. Don't go out to the winery, okay?"

"Why? I'm meeting her there tomorrow. She wants me to see some old Italian stuff. If we're lucky, they could help create that old-world look she wants."

"Look, don't ask me why or how I know. You've got Emma's father on your tail, and well, just trust me, okay?"

"You and Loomis found something out, didn't you! Is it about Susan Jessop? Do you think she was poisoning Todd?"

"What I think, and what I know for sure are two different things. That story Susan told you about not knowing about Carla is bullshit. She hired a private eye last year to tail Jessop. She's known for a good year."

"No kidding! How did you find this out?"

"The PI contacted Loomis when he found out he was down here. They're old buddies."

"How did he know Loomis was here? That man seems to know everyone."

"Maybe Loomis joined a PI association or something. Never mind how he knew Loomis was here. And yeah, he's got contacts all over the damn country. Even more than me."

Molly folded her arms and stared at Randall. "You know I hate it when you do this. You give me half a story, then leave me hanging."

Randall speared a strawberry Bennie had added to his pastry

order. "That's the breaks, kiddo. You're on a need-to-know basis these days."

"Then tell me why you don't want me going out to the winery? I should think that would qualify my intel level."

Randall sighed. "Damn it, Molly. Can't you just for once take my word for things?"

When Molly didn't answer, he said, "Okay. Fine. A little bird told me that Susan Jessop is planning to go out there with a reporter she hooked up with and make some headlines. I don't want to see you thrown in the mix."

"What? Why on earth would she want to do that?"

"Because she knows that she's been added to the hit parade, and the best defense is offense. She needs to get public sympathy on her side. It's a sisterhood ploy. Commiserate with the other wronged woman and show you're not vindictive. A kind of 'sister in arms' thing. You women all love that shit. She knows it, and it'll probably work in her favor."

"*You women?* Why, you freaking misogynist!"

"Misogynist? Me? You gotta be kidding!"

Molly pushed away from the table and rose. "Kidding? Didn't you hear what you just said?"

"Aw, come on, Molly. Sit down. I apologize, okay? I'm just saying that's how it'll probably be written up." He watched the sparks in Molly's eyes cool and grinned. "You should know me better than that."

Molly sat and picked up her espresso. "Sometimes I wonder." She drained the cup, then took out her cigarettes. "Would you mind opening the glass doors so I can have a smoke?" She watched him handle the tall, multi-paned folding glass doors, then dug into her jeans pocket for her Zippo. When he sat back down, she said, "I'm still going out there tomorrow."

"Antiques-dealer fever, huh?" he said. "Okay, have it your way. Just don't call me if you run into trouble."

Molly blew out a long stream of smoke. "I wouldn't think of it."

"I'm kidding. Want me to drop by tonight? Maybe a show of support?"

"Oh, I think Emma and I will be fine. The sisterhood thing, you know?"

"Ouch. Happy now?" Randall paused. He put his hand up to stop Molly from replying. "Look, you know I care a lot about Emma. I'd just like to, well, I'd like to let her know that I'm here, too. I mean to help her any way I can."

Touched, Molly said, "I know you adore her." She looked away. She also knew what he was about to say. "And I know she needs a father figure. Genuine, or not."

Randall didn't answer right away. The smile on his face told Molly volumes. Finally, he said, "I know you'll do the right thing for her."

The day flew by for Molly. Six tour busses from Fresno, Bakersfield, and Stockton hit Carmel before nine. Her sales weren't spectacular, mostly items small enough to take back on the bus, but every sale helped. By two in the afternoon, she took a few moments for a break in the storage room. Molly took off her shoes and rubbed a sore spot. She'd dropped a marble paperweight. It had landed right on the tip of her toes, and she'd been favoring it all day.

Molly was thankful she had been busy enough not to dwell on what she was going to say to Emma, or what Randall had meant by her doing the right thing. But now she had a moment, and she knew the "right thing" was not to discourage Emma from getting to know Macomber. In a practical sense, he had much to offer her, and she had no right to stand in Emma's way of a more secure life. But from an emotional sense, and that was the kicker for Molly, she knew she was worried deep down that he might also steal Emma's heart away. Even so, she reminded herself, she had no reason to be jealous if that happened. Emma wasn't her child. She was Carrie's and Macomber's, and it would be sinful to hope Emma wouldn't like him.

Molly picked up the telephone and punched in Daria's number.

"I'm nervous," she said to Daria. "I'm going to tell Emma to-night, and I keep thinking it's best just to blurt things out, but I don't want to spook her."

"We should have gotten together last night for dinner. We could have talked about this," Daria replied.

"Oh, I know. I just thought you could use a night off. Since the guys were out of town, it seemed like a good chance for you to go home early."

"Want me to stop by later tonight? I can pinch you if you start to falter."

Molly laughed. "No, but thanks. I think it would be better if Emma heard this without a safety net. I need her to know that whatever she decides is okay with me. I don't want her to feel pressured or to feel obligated to tell us what she thinks we want to hear."

"Good point. But call me later and let me know how she took it. Considering how Randall feels about you, I'm surprised he didn't insist on being there."

"Oh, come on, Daria."

"No! It's 'Oh, come on, Molly.' For cryin' out loud, are you that blind?"

"I just heard the bell over the door. Gotta go. See you later." Molly quickly hung up the phone. Of course I'm not that blind, she thought. I just have to pretend to be. Doesn't Daria realize that or understand why? Molly eased her shoe back on and stared at the shelves filled with merch-in-waiting. She didn't want to dwell on Randall or what might or might not be. Her only thoughts were of Emma. First things, first.

When Emma got home, Molly pretended to be on the phone with a shipper arranging a pickup and delivery for a customer from Sacramento who had just left after buying a set of six Regency mahogany dining room chairs. She had actually made the arrangements moments earlier, but she needed an excuse not to make eye contact with Emma. Her anxiety had grown with each passing hour. She pretended to ask the shipper to hold for a moment. Molly waved at Emma and blew her a kiss. "How's pizza tonight? Will you call in an order?"

"Gotcha. Two small combos—one with anchovies and one without?"

Molly nodded, then got back on the phone. When she was certain Emma was out of sight or hearing, she set the phone down and folded her hands in her lap. This was crazy, she thought. She was working herself into a basket case. She should have more confidence in Emma's affection.

At a few minutes before six, Molly set the CLOSED sign in the window at the foot of one of the Foo dogs. She patted the ferocious-looking beast on the head and muttered, "Time to bite the bullet, pal. I'm not waiting until after dinner. I'm going to tell Emma right now."

Molly summoned her courage and marched for the stairs. Her grip on the wrought-iron handrail was so tight, she actually winced and stopped on the fourth stair. She straightened her shoulders, took a deep breath, then chided herself for being such a coward. She didn't realize she was mumbling when she entered the living room, until Emma, sprawled on the sofa with a school book in her lap, said, "Sorry, I missed that."

Molly paused at the open doorway to the kitchen. "Missed what?"

Emma looked up from her book. "I don't know. That's what I asked. You said something."

"Oh? I guess I was talking to myself. Uh, I'm going to have a cup of tea. Do you want one?"

"I just fixed one. The water in the teakettle should still be hot enough."

Molly could see the steam still curling out of the spout. She quickly pulled out a mug, threw in a teabag, and joined Emma. "Are you working on something urgent for Monday, or can I interrupt you?"

Emma set down the book. "I was just reading ahead." She saw the frown on Molly's face. "You look kinda serious. Is that sheriff's guy still bugging you?"

Molly cradled the hot mug in her icy hands. "No. He isn't a problem anymore. I'll tell you all about that later."

"Whew. I guess you're relieved, huh? It was kinda cool helping figure out that mess with Frances O'Brien, but I'm glad we're not involved this time."

"Amen to that. I need to talk to you about something else." Molly set the mug on the coffee table. She stared at it briefly, holding onto an instant of calm. But she knew she couldn't go backwards now. It was time. "It's about your father."

Emma's eyes narrowed in surprise. "My father is dead."

Molly shook her head. She thought for a brief moment, searching for the right words. But she already knew there was no easy way to tell her. "No, Emma. He's not dead. He's alive, but he's not who you thought he was."

Emma's face was a mix of confusion, surprise, and sudden hope. Her words tumbled out so fast Molly hardly heard each question. "He's alive? Are you sure? How do you know? Who told you? Where is he?"

Molly put her hands out. "Whoa…whoa. Slow down. I'll tell you everything. Take a breath, okay? Remember the man at the beach?"

Emma's brow furrowed. She blinked a few times. "Oh, right." Her hand flew to her mouth. *"That's him?"*

Molly nodded. "He came to see me. I didn't believe him at first. He showed me a DNA report your mother sent him."

Emma was silent for a long moment. "She's known all along then, huh? She even lied to me about my father." Emma balled her hands into fists and pounded them on her lap. "I never want to see her again!"

"Emma, please. I know this is a shock. I've been trying to think of some easy way to tell you and there just isn't one."

"Does he want to see me? Is that why he's here? He's not going to take me away from you, is he?"

Molly moved to the sofa and put her arm around Emma. "Yes, he wants to meet you. No, I don't think he can force you to leave. Lucero said there's steps we can take. Besides, you have some legal rights, too."

Emma clung to Molly. "I want to stay here with you. Don't let him take me."

"Oh, Emma! I want you to stay, too, but you need to meet him. I mean, if he's really your father, then—"

"Well, why has he waited so long to find me?"

Molly told Emma about the postcards. "I didn't show you the latest one. It had a rabbit drawn on it."

"She used to draw them all the time," Emma said.

"Well, anyway, when she sent him the one with the rabbit, she also sent him the DNA report and told him where you were."

"Why?" Emma pleaded. "Why did she do this now?"

"I don't know. I've never been able to understand Carrie. But maybe she meant well for once. Maybe she felt guilty and wanted you to know the truth."

"I recognize his name. I know she worked for him. He's mega-rich, too."

Molly let her arm slowly drop from Emma's shoulder. "Yes, he's mega-rich. And he wants to take a place in your life. He's concerned about your education, your—"

"Tough," Emma sputtered. "We're doing just fine. We don't need him."

"I want you to meet him, Emma. It's the right thing to do, okay?"

Emma looked away. "Does Randall know about him?"

"Yes. So do Daria and Dan."

Emma's voice took on an edge. "You told them first? How long have you known?"

Molly sighed. Emma had every right to be angry with her. "I've known for a few days. We all wanted to be sure he's who he claims to be. Dan, Randall, and Loomis investigated him for me. I wanted their counsel. I...I wasn't sure where we stood legally."

"What did they say?"

"Dan said I can hire an attorney and petition for your guardianship."

"Make it so," Emma said. "I'm not leaving."

Molly didn't know whether to laugh, or to cry. "Aye aye, captain!"

Emma threw her arms around Molly. "I'll meet him, but I'm not leaving you."

Molly hugged her tight. "I have to call him, Emma. Would you be willing to meet him Sunday?"

Emma pulled back. "That soon? Can't I wait and think about this?"

Molly shook her head. "The sooner the better. Let's get it over with, okay? Hey, he's probably more nervous than you. Maybe you two could have lunch."

"Will you go with me?"

Molly smiled gently. "That wouldn't be fair, now would it? Give him a chance, Emma. He won't bite. In fact, he seems like a nice man."

Emma avoided Molly's look. She fiddled with the hem of her sweatshirt. Letting out a deep sigh, she said, "Okay. But just this one time. And it has to be at Daria's."

"I'll set it up."

# Chapter 24

MOLLY CALLED Marshall Macomber at the Lodge at Pebble Beach before seven the next morning. "I apologize for the early hour, but I wanted to catch you before you went out on the golf course. I've talked to Emma, and she's agreed to meet you." Not waiting for him to respond, she hurried on. "Lunch at Daria's tomorrow at one. Does that fit in with your schedule?"

She heard Macomber's soft chuckle at the other end. "Perfectly, Molly. And many thanks. Will you be joining us?"

"No. I don't think it would be fair to you."

"I appreciate that. Very much. And thank you."

By seven-thirty, Molly and Emma were on their way to Carmel Valley and Bello Lago. Missing her morning espresso and croissants at Tosca's, Molly pulled into the parking lot at Safeway at the mouth of the Valley and made a beeline for the Starbuck's inside. She quickly returned to the van and handed Emma the bag. "I got you a mocha and a cinnamon coffeecake."

Between bites of her coffeecake, Emma asked, "What should I wear to lunch? I'm kinda nervous. I mean, is he an old fudd and expects me to wear a ruffled skirt and cute little shoes?"

Molly laughed. "How about that new yellow turtleneck?"

"Can I wear jeans to Daria's? Would that be okay?"

Molly glanced at Emma. "I don't see why not. Just make sure you wear the new pair."

When they pulled into the Bello Lago driveway, Molly said, "When Michelle gets there, don't go running off. I need you to help me."

Emma laughed. "You just don't want to go in that cave thing alone. You're such a scaredy-cat!"

Molly parked in front of the tasting room. "Yep, that's me. Wait here. I'll see if Carla has arrived." She brushed the crumbs from her jeans, grabbed her tote, and headed for the massive front doors, which were standing open. She was about to enter when she heard loud voices inside. She caught only snatches at first, but it was apparent an argument was in the works. She wasn't sure who the voices belonged to but decided it wasn't a good time to make an appearance. Molly glanced at her watch. She stepped back and was about to return to the van when the voices grew louder. She recognized Dino Horne's voice saying, "Don't give me that bullshit! She damn well knows who killed him! And I wouldn't put it past her to have set it up either!"

When Molly heard the second voice say, "You're outta your mind," she knew it was Reggie Sullivan. "My money is on Giordano," he added. "If Carla wanted out of the marriage, all she had to do was divorce the prick."

"Just because you've always had the hots for her don't mean she's home free," Horne said.

"You're off base, Dino. For all I know, you had him knocked off to save your precious wine and your job."

"Hey, hey! My job wasn't on the line, and you know it. If anyone was gonna get axed, it was you. You were number one on his list. I heard Jessop tell Carla you had to go. So back off, man. Besides, my brother isn't an award-winning skeet shooter."

"What? You bastard! You got a nerve bringing that up. So what if he is?"

"Just saying, okay? So you back off, and I will, too."

"Screw you! You think I'd have my brother knock Jessop off? Oh, man! That's really reaching. Like he'd do it? Sure. Maybe you hired someone?"

"As if I could afford a hit man. Now who's smokin' shit?"

Molly flattened herself against the outside wall. She made a dash for the van and hurried inside. She put her finger to her lips. "There's an argument going on inside between Dino Horne and

Reggie Sullivan. Let's pretend we just got here. Grab those two new auction catalogs in the back. You read one, and I'll read the other." By the time Molly noticed her window was open, it was too late. Both men were out the now closed door and staring at her. Molly took a deep breath, smiled, and opened the van's door. "Hi, just got here. I'm meeting Carla, but I don't see her car. Did she park somewhere else?" Molly knew the corporate offices were in the building next to the tasting room. She decided not to act surprised at seeing them here on a Saturday. "You guys working today?"

"Hey, Molly," Dino said. "Yeah, we've got some work to catch up on. I haven't seen Carla." He turned to Sullivan. "Have you?"

Sullivan's face was flushed. "Uh, no, we just got here, too. We're parked in back, but I didn't see her car. Something we can help you with?"

Molly got out of the van and walked toward them. "No, but thanks. Carla said the furniture had arrived and she wanted me to get it placed." She glanced at her watch. "Guess I'm early. Can you unlock the tasting room for me? I'd like to get in and do some shoving around."

"It's open," Reggie said. "It looks like everything is in place already. I guess Carla was here earlier with some of the guys."

"Oh. Well, maybe she decided not to wait for me. No problem. Emma and I can wait out here for her."

"Yeah, sure, but you're welcome to go in," Dino Horne said.

Molly was positive they'd bought her story of just arriving. At least she hoped so. "Thanks, we'll do that." Molly waved to Emma to follow. Once inside, she was surprised to see that the large refectory table had already been centered and the other furniture positioned exactly as laid out in her drawing. She stood in the center of the room and wondered why Carla hadn't waited for her. She was about to leave when Carla came rushing in. "Sorry I'm late. I was in the cave getting boxes ready for you."

"The furniture has already been placed."

"I got here early so I had some of the guys do it. Some things have come up and I didn't want to waste time in here. Why don't you and Emma follow me and Michelle. I'll pull out in front. It's not far."

Molly followed Carla's Jeep past what seemed like acres of vineyard, but were in fact, less than two city-blocks'-length of vines
planted just for show to the tourists. They drove a short way up a
sloping gravel road to what looked like an old wooden shed built
against a small hill. When they parked and got out, Carla said to
Molly, "It's not really a cave as such. We just call it that. It used to
house equipment before some of the newer buildings went up. Now
it's just for storage and old furniture. It's got stone walls inside, so it's
pretty well weather-resistant. But hold your nose when we go in. It
still smells of wine. We had a spill in there years ago, and it soaked
the wood-planked floors." She pulled out her cell phone. "I'll get
some of the warehousemen here to help us load up."

Molly didn't have to worry about holding her nose. She was too
busy trying not to gag. The musty odor combined with the old wine
spillage was enough to make her wish she hadn't stopped for food
earlier. Emma and Michelle were giggling at Molly. She put on a
brave face for everyone's sake. She hoped to hell whatever Carla had
found was in front and close to the open door.

But that was not to be. Molly held her hand over her mouth as
she and the girls followed Carla farther into the room. From outside,
the size of the building was deceptive. What had appeared to Molly
to be no bigger then twenty feet wide and probably fifteen feet deep,
was, she soon discovered, misleading. The so-called shed was merely
a façade. One would never know it was the entrance to an enormous
cavern built into the hill. "How far in do we have to go?" Molly
asked.

"Oh, maybe a hundred feet," Carla replied.

That was ninety-nine feet farther than Molly would have liked.

Molly followed Carla for a short distance, then stopped when
Carla pulled a rope hanging from the ceiling to turn on a row of
overhead lights. Boxes, old wine barrels, and crates lined the walls,
and the sour wine odor was strong. Molly knew by now they were
heading deeper into the hill than Carla had said, and she was quickly overcome by claustrophobia. It wasn't a basement, but the feeling
was the same. Even the chance of finding something great might not
be a decent payoff for her fears. The finds would have to be at least

nineteenth-century to warrant going farther. And even then, she wasn't sure if she'd go on. Maybe she could talk Carla into having some of her employees take the boxes out to the front of the shed. "Uh, Carla? I've got a problem, remember? I think I told you about my fear of closed-in places. I don't do caves, okay? Could some of your employees get the boxes for us instead?"

Carla looked at Molly and laughed. "Oh, come on. Don't be a ninny."

Stung by Carla's remark, Molly hesitated. There was no reason to embarrass her in front of Emma and Michelle. Bristling, she said, "How much farther?"

Carla shrugged. "Oh, maybe ten feet?"

"Okay. But a quick look, and then I'm out of here." Molly turned to Emma and Michelle. "Do you two want to go back?"

When both girls shook their heads, Molly said, "Thanks. I was hoping you'd say yes and insist I go with you."

Molly followed closely behind Carla. They made one turn to the right and walked into a smaller room piled high with more boxes and wooden crates. Molly could see that some of the large crates had already been opened. She moved to the first one and caught her breath. Sitting on top of a mound of packing straw was a single dish. She picked it up and ran her hand across the surface of the dish and then around the rim. Without saying a word, she turned it over and then carefully placed it back on the straw. "Is this the only one, or are there more? I mean, with this pattern?"

"There's a full set in there. Sixteen, I think. Cups, saucers, soups, the gamut. It's not one of my favorites. Those strutting birds and sprays of flowers are kind of insipid."

"Do you have any idea what these are?" Molly asked. "I mean value-wise?"

Carla's eyes were scanning the room. She seemed to be distracted as she moved from box to box. She turned to Molly and folded her arms impatiently. "No. That's why you're here."

Molly was sympathetic with what Carla was going though, but still that was no reason for her to be short with her. She was no longer interested in attempting to be polite, and decided it was time to let her know. "Well, these *insipid* dishes are eighteenth-century Italian faience. This dish is probably worth about nine hundred bucks. I'd have to check current values, so that's just a guess."

"You're kidding. Just that one dish?"

Molly's voice was brisk. "I don't kid about stuff like this." She took a deep breath. "Okay, let's check another box." She tried hard to ignore the thick, cloying air. She could feel perspiration already running down her back. She focused on what might be in the next box instead of where she was. But she knew, no matter what they might find, she could manage maybe another five minutes in here, and that was the max.

Carla selected a nearby cardboard box. "This old packing tape is really brittle," Carla said. "I should be able to just use a fingernail to start a tear." It only took a moment to get the tape off. Carla was soon pulling out several layers of crumpled newspaper. She unwrapped a small jug and handed it to Molly. The light tone of her voice seemed forced. "This is kind of cute. We could use this in the tasting room."

In spite of her growing anger with Carla's indifference to her problem and her sudden change in attitude, Molly's eyes lit up as she reached for the jug. She heard Emma's quick intake of breath. She looked at Emma and smiled. "Cute? What do you think, Emma?"

Emma moved closer to Molly. Her grin was huge. "I've never heard Bow jugs called cute before. Can I hold it? I might never get the chance again!"

Molly handed Emma the jug. She said to Carla, "Whoever your grandmother bought this from was a collector. This baby is worth a cool two grand, or I'll bite my tongue."

Emma whistled. "Wow! I've only seen these in pictures." She handed it back to Molly. "Here. I don't want to be responsible for it."

Michelle shrugged. "Doesn't look all that special to me."

"Big bucks, Michelle," Emma said. "Really big."

Carla had just pulled out a small wooden box. She looked at Molly. "Wonder what we'll find in this one." She opened it and smiled. "I'll be damned. Old silver wine labels!" She handed Molly the box. "I told you I'd found some great stuff!"

Molly's forehead was damp and her sweatshirt was clinging to her back. She began to hear a ringing in her ears. Great finds or not, she couldn't stay a moment longer. She could actually feel the walls closing in on her. "Great. Uh, look, I really have to get out of here."

Carla was elbow-deep into the large box. Ignoring Molly, she pulled out a silver-mounted clear glass claret jug. "Oh, this is gorgeous!"

"Stunning," Molly said. She put down the box and began to step back. "Looks like it's Victorian. If it's signed, even better."

Carla handed it to Molly. Annoyed, Molly turned it over and squinted. "I'm not sure, but the maker's mark might be Robert Harper. He was a fine silversmith. I'd have to check my marks book to be sure." Molly handed the jug back to Carla.

"Is that good?" Carla asked.

Molly continued to back away. "Very good." She could feel her heart pumping. "Twelve hundred, if it's perfect."

"Wait!" Carla said. "Just take a look at these wine labels and then we'll leave."

Molly picked up the small box again. She took a deep breath, opened it, and gave Carla a weak smile. Some of the chains on the labels were broken. "Nice. We can use these." She set the box down on a table near one of the crates. "If you want to stay, that's fine. I'm leaving, Carla. I really, really have to."

Molly's annoyance with Carla was at the boiling point. How much clearer could she be? It was as if Carla were purposely ignoring her. She motioned to Emma and Michelle to move aside and brushed past them. She was thankful there were no twists and turns to try to remember. Once out of the small side room, it was a straight shot to the shed and she was there in no time. She found an old metal chair and plopped herself down. She could hear her heart hammering in her ears. After a few seconds, she got up and flung the door open. She stepped outside and sucked in as much fresh air as she could.

There are moments of clarity that pop up at the strangest times, and Molly experienced one that moment she'd never forget. Facing your fears was bullshit. She'd just faced hers and lost. Even the lure of treasure hadn't been worth it. She'd succumbed to pride and the curse of greed that drives antiques dealers, and that made her angry. She also decided that once she looked over Carla's finds and gave her the valuation information, she was out of there. Carla Jessop was on her own.

# *Chapter 25*

MOLLY HEADED for her van parked alongside the shed. She opened the door on the driver's side and reached for her tote. Fishing out her cigarettes, she lit one quickly, then leaned against the open door and inhaled deeply. She'd only been outside for a few minutes when two pickups arrived. The first one parked in front of the shed. Two men got out and headed inside. The second pickup seemed to idle, as if waiting for someone, or maybe, Molly thought, to see if he too, was needed. Molly could barely see the driver over the steering wheel. She didn't know if he was slumping down in the seat or just short. It was his cap, however, that made her notice him. Most of the laborers wore baseball caps, but this man wore what appeared to be an old-fashioned shooter's cap with a short, peaked brim. What made her think of a shooter's cap was the gun rack attached to the rear window. Somehow the combination seemed to fit.

Molly quickly lost interest and turned away. She was still seething about Carla's indifference and with herself for not holding her ground in the first place, when she saw the second truck finally pull away. She checked her watch. She hoped Emma at least would have the courtesy to come out and join her. She quickly discounted that thought. Emma had much on her mind. Worrying about Molly's pride wasn't one of them. But, she decided, if Emma wasn't out in five more minutes, she would go in and call her. Molly didn't have to wait much longer. Emma stepped outside, with Michelle still in the open doorway. "We can go back now. Michelle wants to ride with us, okay? She's mad at her mother and doesn't want to ride with her."

Molly nodded, and climbed in the van. "Yeah? Well, I'm a little pissed at Carla, too. What's Michelle's problem?"

Emma shrugged. "They're leaving next week. She doesn't want to go."

Before Molly could reply, Michelle opened the back door to the van and climbed in. "They're coming out with the boxes now," she told Molly. "My mother said to meet her back at the tasting room."

While Molly waited with the two girls for the boxes to arrive, she tried to think of some excuse to leave the van and call Randall. She was itching to tell him about the conversation she'd overheard between Dino Horne and Reggie Sullivan, and thought he might also be interested in Carla's travel plans. She grabbed her cell out of the van. On the pretense of stretching her legs, she said, "I'm going to take a short stroll and check with Bitsy."

Appearing to take her time, Molly punched in Randall's number. When he answered, she quickly said, "Don't interrupt and listen carefully. I don't have much time, and I can't repeat myself." She relayed what she could remember, then added, "An FYI just in case. I've got to go."

"Good work, McGee," Randall said. "Very good work. I'll see you later."

"Let me do the unpacking," Molly said to Carla as the boxes began to arrive. "I get the impression you've got some things to do, so I'll get everything out. Give me a couple of hours, and we should have everything open and arranged. If you can find some trash bags for the packing stuff, we can keep everything neat."

"Great," Carla said. "I've got a few problems in the office I need to handle. Some of our corks from Portugal are defective. I've got to sort it out. I'll have someone come back with the bags."

Molly set up a production line for the unpacking. Emma stood on one side of the table ready to take the packing material, and Michelle held the big plastic trash liners open for Emma. Molly was careful, but relentless. The sooner she was out of there the better. Except for the few good pieces she'd seen in the cave, the majority of the items were nothing to get excited over. But when she was down to the last boxes, all that changed. Molly's eyes popped open when she pulled old newspaper away from two dishes separated only by a thin layer of cardboard. Her hands began to shake as she carefully set them down. She glanced at Emma, and said, "*Montelupo!* Can you believe this? Two of them!"

Emma hurried to Molly's side. "This is new to me. What are they?"

"Uh, only just incredible mid-seventeenth-century pottery! Will you look at the colors! Oh, the ochre and blue are to die for," Molly said.

Michelle joined them. "Just looks like some ancient dudes on horseback to me."

Molly's laugh was nervous. "I've only seen one of these. And that was at a Sotheby auction when I was in London. Don't touch them, okay? I want to see what else is in here." Molly's hands were already sweating from excitement. She wiped them on her jeans, pulled out the next parcel, and unwrapped the old newspaper to find a silver cup with a turned-wood handle. "Oh, this is nice. It's a brandy saucepan." Molly turned it over. "The maker's mark is faint, but I'll guess it's a London silversmith and possibly George the Second."

"How much money are we talking about?" Emma asked.

Molly thought for a moment, then said, "The two dishes are close to ten grand and this little darling could be anywhere between eight and nine hundred." She smiled at Michelle. "I can't wait to tell your mother! Isn't this exciting?"

Michelle shrugged. "I guess so. She could use some good news today. We all could." The young girl turned away and covered her face with her hands. "I'm so sick of all the fighting at home!"

Molly was at her side. She wrapped an arm around Michelle. "Hey, I know this past week has been hard on everyone but try to hang in there, okay? Your mother is under a lot of stress right now."

Michelle threw off Molly's arm. "I hate her! And I hate my brother. All they do is fight over this stupid winery. My grandfather is dying, and now he's changed his will and taken my brother out of it. Nicky stormed out of the house and told my mother he was going to live with our other grandfather. And if we go to Peru for some stupid vintner's conference, we won't be here when my grandfather dies! It's horrible!"

"Your grandfather isn't going to die right away," Molly said. "He's had a stroke, but that doesn't mean—"

"You're wrong! He's going to die. He said so himself."

Molly glanced at Emma. "Maybe you and Michelle need to take a break. Why don't you both go outside for a little while? I can handle what's left. I'll call Carla as soon as I open the last box."

Molly watched the girls leave. She shook her head and turned back to the box she'd been unpacking. She carefully set the two Montelupo dishes and the brandy saucepan aside. The Bristol Delft charger she discovered in the next box should have lit up her eyes. But Michelle's outburst clouded her thoughts. She was only dimly aware of the exquisite colors on the rare and expensive dish and numbly set it down. Why were they leaving for South America? Why wasn't Reggie Sullivan, the marketing director going instead? And why was Carla's father convinced he would die soon? Her mind churning over Michelle's outburst, Carla's rude challenge to her in the cave and the conversation between Dino Horne and Reggie Sullivan clouded her awareness when she lifted more newspaper and found what looked like a two-tiered leather belt with two wide leather rings attached. She pulled it out and set it on the table. Under the belt, she found two strange-looking leather pads with straps and a sharp spike attached at the end.

Molly frowned. Searching her vast store of knowledge, she had no idea what these odd-looking things were, or why they were packed with an expensive Bristol dish. She looked at the belt-things again, then shrugged and put them back in the box. Most likely, she finally decided, they were some sort of farming implements Carla's grandmother had found. The last box yielded a mix of unimpressive pottery, a few photograph frames, and several mismatched cups and saucers.

Molly set about packing up the more mundane items and left the best pieces on the table for Carla to see. She called Carla on her cell and told her she was ready to leave. When Carla arrived a few minutes later, Molly showed her the great finds. She told her what they would bring at auction, but if she wanted to keep them, along with the Bow and claret jugs, and the set of Italian dishes, she suggested they be placed in one of the display cabinets that had locks. "Considering the values here, it might be wise to call your insurance company."

Carla ran her hand over one of them and smiled. "I had no idea a silly little dish could be worth so much. Thanks for being honest with me. You could have—"

"No. I couldn't have and I wouldn't have," Molly said. "I don't operate that way."

Carla gave Molly a quick nod. "Of course not. That's why I hired you." When Carla's cell rang, she stepped a few feet away. Molly saw the tight set of her lips as she listened to the caller. She saw Carla look at her watch, then heard her say, "You're an hour early. I'm not ready for you. I've got someone here. Give me twenty minutes."

Carla snapped the cell against her thigh to close it, then said to Molly, "I don't want any of these expensive things here. We get hundreds of tourists in here every month. God only knows who might recognize what this stuff is worth. How about taking everything back to your shop and selling them?"

Molly thought for a moment. The offer was tempting, and the commission would be delicious. "Let me think about it. I'd have to check my client list."

"Just take them. I'm in no hurry for the money."

"Okay. I'll fax you a list and valuation estimate as soon as I get back to the shop."

Carla squeezed Molly's arm and smiled. "Great. Let me give you a hand packing this up. I've got an appointment showing up early." Carla moved to the table and picked up one of the boxes Molly had set on the floor. "You wrap, and I'll fill the box."

It only took Molly a short time to double-wrap the dishes and the brandy cup. As an afterthought, she picked up the small wooden box that held the silver wine labels. "I'll get the chains on the labels fixed for you. We can set them in a shadow box and hang them in here."

"Great. Whatever," Carla said as she placed the wrapped packages in the box. "I'll help you carry the boxes to the car."

*DEADLY VINTAGE* *201*

"I can manage," Molly said. "You go ahead and get ready for your appointment."

Molly found Emma waiting at the van as she carried out a box. "Open up, would you? Carla wants me to take the pricey stuff to the shop to sell."

"Oh, cool! Wait until Bitsy gets a gander at those dishes! I can't wait to look them up in *Miller's.*"

Molly smiled. "Forget *Miller's.* It's a year old. We need current prices. I'll call Cleo in London. Where's Michelle? We could use her to help us load the rest of the boxes."

"She just took off for those vineyards we passed on the way to the shed. She's still mad at her mother. She said she likes to walk out there sometimes. I figured I should stay here in case you wanted me."

Molly set the box in the back of the van and then pulled out the three old blankets she kept there to protect furniture she might buy at a sale. After the remaining boxes had been loaded, she placed blankets around some of the boxes for a cushion in case she had to hit the brakes. When they were ready to leave, Molly turned to look out the back window as she pulled out. She braked so quickly when she saw who was in the car passing behind her that Emma lurched. She couldn't believe her eyes. Susan Jessop was in the passenger seat and the bothersome TV reporter who had been calling her for an interview was driving. Randall, she quickly realized, had been right. How he knew Susan planned to show up was beyond her, but at the moment, she didn't care. She only cared about getting the hell out of there.

Fat chance of that. It was too late. Susan saw her and waved.

"Crap," Molly said.

Emma turned as the car pulled alongside. "Gulp. I see what you mean. This is *so* not a good place to be right now." She looked at Molly. "Do you think there'll be a cat fight?"

"I don't know what to think, but we're leaving." Molly began to slowly back away, but it was too late again. The TV reporter was out of the car and knocking on Emma's window.

Emma asked, "Should I ignore her?"

Molly stopped the van. "No. Open the window, but let me do the talking."

"What great timing," the TV reporter rushed before Molly could say a word. "Hang on a minute." She turned away and motioned to Susan to get out of the car.

Before Molly could reply, another car parked on the other side of her. A young man jumped out, leaned over the seat, and pulled out a mini-cam. Molly's mouth fell open when Carla came out of the tasting room and threw her arms around Susan.

"Hold that pose," the TV reporter said to Carla and Susan. "Lonnie just got here."

"I'm cool," the camera man said. "This will be a great shot for your voice-over."

Molly slammed her hand on the steering wheel and shook her head. "I don't believe this!" She looked at Emma. "This is...is—"

"Kinda crazy, I'd say. I don't get it. How could they all of a sudden be friends?"

"I don't know," Molly said, "but something stinks and I don't want any part of it."

Molly backed the car away, and said, "We're out of here. Get my cell out of my tote, would you? And call Randall for me?"

Molly had just entered the long drive to the highway when the pickup she'd noticed at the shed earlier drove past her. The same man with the short-brimmed cap was driving. Molly was surprised when he turned his face away from her. At that point, she really didn't care who he was. She just wanted to put distance between her and Carla.

Molly was onto Carmel Valley Road when Randall answered. Emma said, "Aunt Molly needs to talk to you pronto. The weirdest thing just happened, and—"

Molly said, "Let me tell him." She took the phone from Emma and without pausing told Randall what they had just witnessed. "You must have a crystal ball or some damn psychic on the payroll! This is so bizarre, it defies description. Yeah, we're on our way back to the shop now. I wouldn't stay there for all the merch in China. I'll tell you the rest when I see you."

"Whew!" Emma said. "Like, what a goofy family? I'm glad we're—" She paused, then said, "Well, *almost* not as crazy." She gave Molly a smile. "At least so far."

With all the strange developments this morning, Molly couldn't believe she still was thinking of Emma's meeting tomorrow with Marshall Macomber. "Uh, might be a good idea not to let Mr. Macomber know about any of this?"

"Duh?"

Molly laughed. "I figured you'd see it that way."

It was good Molly could find her way home by rote. Her head was spinning from all she had seen and heard this morning. She understood now why Carla had seemed so distracted earlier. If she had a more generous soul, Molly thought, she might even excuse her snarky comment about Molly being a ninny. Carla apparently had been preparing herself for Susan's visit. It was obvious now why she wanted her out of the tasting room so fast. She wondered how Carla was going to explain that little scene to her. Especially since Carla had been so angry with Molly for not telling her about Susan Jessop. Not that Carla owed her an explanation, but then, Molly figured, it would be interesting to see if she offered one.

When Molly pulled into the back alley, she said to Emma, "I'm not going to tell Bitsy about the stuff we brought back yet. I want to call Cleo first and get more info. I have a hunch that I'd be better off convincing Carla to consign everything to Sotheby's. She'd have a huge international exposure and a better opportunity to get top dollar that way."

"Then we'd lose out on the commission. Can we afford to do that?"

Molly smiled. "Not to worry, dear girl. I'll charge Carla a fee. We'll probably make more that way."

"Aha! The devious mind of an antiques dealer is still alive."

"Nothing devious about it. It's called business."

After they'd unloaded the van, and set the boxes in the garage, Molly dropped in to see Bitsy. She was with two men who were looking over a Dutch mahogany floral marquetry washstand. Molly could hear Bitsy's sales pitch, and she almost felt sorry for the men.

They had no idea what they were in for. Once Bitsy Morgan took center stage, she was hard to refuse. It would be a terrific sale. Eighteen hundred bucks for the early-nineteenth-century piece was a good price, and it would help make up for the day the shop had been closed.

Molly backed out slowly and took the back stairs in the courtyard up to the apartment. She called Daria, made a reservation for Emma and Macomber for tomorrow, and then, on a whim and a need to fill the rest of the day, Molly said to Emma, "Hey! How about doing a little shopping and then maybe a movie? We haven't done that for a while."

Emma gave Molly a sly smile. "Like, maybe the yellow turtleneck and jeans might not be too cool to wear tomorrow?"

Molly laughed. "Like, maybe one of those cotton matchstick skirts you were looking at in that Macy's ad might be better? And maybe with a new T-shirt to go with it?"

"And, like, maybe that new Orlando Bloom movie after?"

Mimicking Emma, Molly laughed. "Oh, that *so* works for me."

# Chapter 26

MOLLY AND EMMA were on the way home from the movie when Molly's cell phone rang. "Wanna bet it's Randall?" Emma said.

Molly rolled her eyes. "No. I'd probably lose. Let's hope it's Bitsy telling me about another fabulous sale." When Molly answered, she looked at Emma and grinned. "Yes, Randall, what a pleasure to hear from you."

"How's pizza with the evening news?" Randall said. "You might need moral support, so I thought I'd lend mine."

"The pizza sounds good, but if you're referring to Carla and Susan and that thing this morning, I wasn't involved, remember? And besides, how do you know what's on the news?"

"I told you before that I know everything. I haven't seen the tape yet, but I understand they got you leaving Bello Lago."

"Damn it! Why waste film on me leaving?"

"Good question. So let's find out, okay? I'll bring the pizza."

Molly snapped her cell shut with such ire, that Emma blinked at the sound. "Oh, oh. Now what?"

Molly told Emma what Randall had said, then added, "Let's just hope Mr. Macomber misses the news."

"I don't care. I'm just having lunch, and that's all."

But Molly did care. She didn't need to offer him more fuel for any fire he might want to keep burning. Molly checked the time on the dashboard clock. They had fifteen minutes to get home before the news came on. The time to get from Del Monte Center in Monterey to the apartment was ten minutes max. She wouldn't have time to stop in and see Bitsy. She picked up her cell and called her. "Bitsy? Hi, how's it going? Really? The washstand, too? Great!

Listen, I'm running late for something, so I won't stop to see you, okay? I'm waiting on a call from Cleo. I know it's an odd time for her to call, but what can I say? We'll chat tomorrow. 'Bye."

"Uh, that was a fib, wasn't it?" Emma said.

"Sort of. I left Cleo a message to call me when you were trying on clothes, so it's not a total lie. We just don't have enough time to explain to Bitsy what's going on and still catch the news. I hope Randall comes up the back stairs. Besides, she'll see it later and call me."

Emma laughed. "That's a given."

Molly took the Carpenter Street turnoff a little too fast. She slowed down and tried to concentrate on her driving. "Speaking of fibs, there's something I need to talk to you about."

"Are there more things I don't know about?"

"If you're referring to Mr. Macomber, I haven't lied to you. There really isn't much of a distinction between lying and fibbing. It's a character flaw most of us are not immune to. And that's what I really want to discuss. Pride is one of them, too. Which I know happens to be one of my worst flaws. You got a front-row seat this morning in the cave. I should have held my ground and not gone along with Carla."

"She was rude, pushing you like that."

"Yes, she was. But the point is—"

"How easy it is to not stick to your guns and cave into peer pressure?"

Molly gave Emma a big smile. "I should have known you figured that out right away. But I want you to remember that tomorrow, okay? No one can put any pressure on you. But give Mr. Macomber a chance."

Emma looked out the window. She was silent until they reached Ocean Avenue. When they parked in the alley, she said, "I'll keep an open mind tomorrow."

Randall was waiting at the top of the stairs. He held a big box of pizza. "Good timing. We've got four minutes until show time."

They didn't have to hurry. The top news covered an earthquake in Santa Cruz that had set buildings swaying, and the latest political scandal in Sacramento. The segment showing Carla and Susan ran at the end of the news. It was apparent the piece had been trimmed, and a live interview with the two women had been cut. Only the brief voice-over by the reporter, offered viewers a clue to the meeting of the so-called widows.

After a quick reminder of who they were and their ties to Todd Jessop, the reporter went on to say: "A true example of compassion was witnessed today between two remarkable women, who by all expectations should be opponents. It was touching to see how they have banded together to help each other in their time of need. An in-depth interview with Susan Jessop and Carla Jessop will be aired later in the week."

Molly clicked off the TV and looked at Randall. With much relief, she said, "I think your source was misinformed. I thankfully wasn't part of that Kodak moment."

Emma said, "Maybe you're in the next installment?"

Molly pretended to shiver. "Let's hope not! I've had enough TV exposure for a lifetime."

"Guess we'll have to stay tuned," Randall said.

Emma jumped up from the sofa. "I'll clear this pizza stuff up, and then I've got some homework to do." She looked at Molly, then bit her lower lip. "I might not have time tomorrow."

"I'll take care of the mess," Molly said. "You go on ahead."

"Okay, but why don't you show Randall those cool dishes Mrs. Jessop wants you to sell? Bet he's never seen those Montelupo thingies."

"I've got a meeting with Loomis and Lucero in an hour. This won't take long will it? I mean, no lectures or anything, okay?" Randall winked at Molly.

Molly headed for the French doors. "I think we can manage to accomplish a quick history in about three minutes."

When they entered the garage, Molly told Randall about Carla's plans to go to Peru for a vintner's conference. "What I don't get is, if Carla is so worried about her father's health, why leave for a conference now? It doesn't make sense."

"This trip to Peru sounds snaky. And why take Michelle with her? What the hell is a kid gonna do there when her mother is tied up in meetings? I agree it would be more up Reggie's alley. I'll pass the info on to Stuart. I don't know if he's cautioned her to stick around or not."

When Molly stopped at the box where the dishes were stored, Randall said, "Hold up here. That's a big box. I don't have a lot of time."

"Calm down. Carla pulled this box out for me when I was wrapping the dishes. The good stuff is on top of whatever else is in there. Probably some of the lesser pieces."

When Molly pulled the wrapping from the Montelupo dishes, she was delighted to see the appreciative glimmer in Randall's eyes. Most people didn't know he collected Directoire furniture from the late eighteenth century, and was more astute about the period than many dealers Molly had known. She gave him a quick rundown on their history. "Aren't they gorgeous?"

"They're beauts. Big bucks, huh?"

"Very big. We're talking about an easy five figures for all."

"Okay, you got my attention. Let's see what else is in the box."

Molly removed the rest of the paper, and then said, "Nothing exciting. Just some old farming stuff. I'm not sure what it was used for."

Randall peered over her shoulder. He quickly pulled her hands from the box. "Don't touch that!" Gently easing Molly away, he reached in his pocket for a pen, then lifted the leather pads with the straps and attached spike, and set them on the table. Very slowly, he pulled out the rest of the old newspaper and then blew out his breath. "Jesus, Mary, and Joseph!"

"Are there spiders in there?"

Randall shook his head as he opened his cell. "Don't talk and don't touch anything." He punched in a number, waited for a moment, and then said, "Dan? I'm in Molly's garage. Get Stuart on the phone and tell him to get his ass over here on the double and bring a crime-scene tech with him. No...no, Molly is fine. I think I've found something connected to Jessop's shooter. Tell Stuart to come in an unmarked. Low profile, okay?"

When Molly heard Randall go on to tell Lucero that what she thought were old farming tools were, in fact, tree-climbing apparatus, she sank into a chair, and said, "Holy moley."

Randall hung up, looked at Molly, and added, "And then some. Tell me when you first saw these and where."

Molly told him about the shed that was really an old wine cave, and how Carla had some of her employees take the boxes back to the tasting room. "I was unpacking and saw them in one of the boxes. Like I said, I thought they were farm things. I just threw newspaper back on top, and then went on to the next box."

"Did Carla see them?"

"No. And I didn't mention them. I mean, they didn't mean anything."

"Did you handle them?"

Molly thought for a moment. "I think I did. I'll have to tell the sheriff's guy. The employees who brought the boxes over to the tasting room wouldn't have. These things are used to climb trees?"

"Yeah. The thing with the double belt is called a saddle, and the other pieces are tree climbing spurs."

"Who uses this stuff besides utility men when the power goes out?"

"Foresters use them, and loggers, and hunters setting up blinds." Randall began pacing the room. He shoved his hands into his pockets, searching for his cigar case. "Funny place," he said, "to stash this stuff. Why keep it? Why not dump it somewhere or bury it? And where's the rest of the climbing gear?"

"Maybe he planned to, but hasn't had time," Molly said.

Randall shook his head. "He had the time. And he knew about the old wine cave and the boxes of family stuff. He felt safe stashing it there. The killer isn't a stranger or a hired hit. Big thing is, we've finally got something tangible. Stuart can get some mileage from this find."

"My mind is rewinding a few things," Molly said.

Randall found a chair and pulled it next to her. "Such as?"

She thought for a moment. "First of all, that conversation I overheard between Dino Horne and Reggie Sullivan. Reggie's brother?

The skeet shooter? And then this surprise *simpático* act between Susan and Carla. I mean, come on! I just don't buy it. Do you?"

Randall threw up his hands. "Hey, at the risk of being accused of being a misogynist again? No."

"So what do you think?" Molly asked.

"I'm not sure yet. But it ain't charitable."

It was after eight that evening, and Molly was worn out. Lieutenant Stuart, from the sheriff's department, had at least been a gentleman and had only asked Molly twice how she'd happened to be in possession of the tree-climbing gear. He'd read her file earlier, he'd said, and didn't feel it necessary for her to go into the office yet to make a statement. Randall said Molly's prints were on file, and he'd send them over. Molly, however, almost lost it when the crime-scene tech who had accompanied Stuart wanted to include the Montelupo dishes along with the tree-climbing gear. Randall stepped in and explained to Stuart what they were and that they had no connection to Jessop's homicide. "I don't think," Randall had said, "the department wants to be responsible for a couple of dishes worth maybe ten grand." Stuart quickly agreed. He made a few notes, and then left with the crime-scene tech.

The discovery interrupted Randall's meeting with Lucero and Loomis, so they decided to just hold it in Molly's garage. Molly offered to make coffee in the storage room, and as she was about to leave, she said, "By the way, Emma is having lunch tomorrow with Marshall Macomber." She saw the surprise on their faces. "It's the right thing to do, guys." When no one replied, she nodded. "Good. I knew you'd all agree."

Molly set up the coffeepot, then checked to see how Emma was doing. She'd gone up earlier to let her know that she was chatting with Randall about antiques and would be in the garage for a while. She didn't want Emma to walk in on the discussion. The less Emma knew, the better. Besides not wanting her involved in the solving of the homicide, she feared Emma might innocently slip and tell Michelle something. When Emma asked if Randall's meeting had been cancelled, she'd lied and said they'd decided to meet later.

She found Emma in her room. She was propped up on her bed, reading. "Hey, I just wanted to let you know that Loomis and Dan decided to drop by. We're having coffee in the garage."

"The garage? Why don't they come upstairs?"

"They're having fun looking over all the merch we haven't inventoried. And you know, just 'hangar flying.' So, what are you reading?"

Emma showed Molly the book. "I've decided to be a mystery writer. I got this at the library. It's a 'How-to' by a lady named Carolyn Wheat."

Molly sat next to Emma. She laughed. "Uh, I think you'd best wait until you're a little older. Murder and mayhem is, well, not something we want as a steady diet, right? I think we've had just about enough of that around here."

"Well, they say, write what you know. I figure I've got a head start."

"I thought you wanted to be an antiques dealer."

"Oh, I do. But just think about how the two professions seem to work together."

"You *are* kidding, aren't you?"

Emma laughed. "Yeah, I am. I have to do a report on how a book is constructed. I figured this one would be fun to use."

Relieved, Molly said, "Don't stay up too late. You've got a busy day tomorrow."

Emma nodded but said only, "Night, Aunt Molly."

Molly whispered, "Night, Emma."

# Chapter 27

WHEN MOLLY returned to the garage with a fresh pot of coffee, she was surprised to see Lieutenant Stuart was back. He rose when Molly entered. "Hope you don't mind my returning, Molly," he said. "Randall asked me to come back and sit in on the confab."

Molly had decided she liked Stuart. He'd been courteous to her and appreciated her contributions. And, she had noticed, he wasn't hard on the eyes. Not quite as tall as Randall or as broad in the chest, he was also a good fifteen years younger. Molly guessed him to be around thirty-five. His brown hair was razor-cut close to his skull, and his rather large brown eyes reminded her of a basset hound. It was nice to see he was one of the few men these days who wore a wedding ring.

"Not at all," she smiled. And then she laughed. "I guess Randall thought it was time you got used to these little gatherings. We usually have them in Daria's private room at her restaurant when…well, when things pop up."

"So I hear. A nice place to have a command center." He looked at Loomis, Lucero, and Randall. "We all know it's not in the handbook, but I've got to say I kind of like this roundtable idea. I'm not opposed to it at all. The more info I get, the sooner we'll nail this killer. By the way, I want to thank you again for your cooperation and offer an apology for the rude way you've been treated. You know it's not our policy to harass witnesses."

"Thank you," Molly said. She set the coffeepot on the table and found a chair. "So, what have I missed?"

Loomis cleared his throat. "Some interesting news, Molly. Apparently Susan Jessop and Carla Jessop have been in communication for some weeks."

Molly shot a look at Randall. "You knew this all along? Is that why you told me to stay away from the winery? Damn. I was right. The meeting this morning was a phony!"

Randall nodded. "There's more."

Loomis went on. "Maili Montgomery and I have been coordinating our research. Man, she's a whiz on that computer. What she can sneak into makes me ready to give up my e-mail address. Anyway, there's a good dozen e-mails between them, and we've got cell phone records showing calls going back and forth. The e-mails are worthless. They're cryptic. It only proves they've been in contact. But it's a link of sorts if we need it down the road.

"Randall called me about Sullivan's brother. The skeet shooter? I did some quick checking on him right away. He lives in Redding, and his leg has been in a cast for over a month. He broke it skateboarding with his son. But that doesn't let Horne and Sullivan off the hook. I'm still digging on those two."

"I don't get the Carla-and-Susan thing," Molly said. "It's just too bizarre. I mean, it's so unlikely that they would become friends." She thought for a moment, then yelped, "Oh, wait! Wait just a damn minute! They both have access to belladonna!" Molly's eyes flew to Randall. "Am I out of my mind thinking what I'm thinking?"

Lucero laughed. "If you are, then so are we."

Randall grinned. "Bingo. Molly Doyle hits the mark once again."

"Sounds like all of you are a few steps ahead of me for once," Molly said. "But that still doesn't tell us who shot Jessop."

"That," Stuart said, "is the jackpot question. Your coming across the tree-climbing gear might give us a winning ticket." He turned to Lucero. "If we can come up with prints that make sense."

Lucero shifted in his chair. "I'd bet my next election the shooter wore gloves. Anyone familiar with that gear would know he'd have to. The rope pulleys would tear up his hands. He'd never get more than a few feet off the ground without them."

"The only good news is that the discovery will help narrow the suspect list somewhat," Randall said. "Not many people know how to use that stuff. Including Mafia hit men."

"What about those rumors that Mr. Mattucci was responsible for

Carla's first husband's death?" Loomis asked. "I don't know the history around here, but could there be something there that might connect?" Loomis put up his hands. "Before you remind me that Mattucci is in a wheelchair, just think about it." He looked at Lucero. "Let's do an out-of-the-box exercise here."

Lucero shrugged. "It was a chopper accident. I don't remember the details."

"No offense, boss," Loomis said. "I know the Mattuccis are old family friends, but—"

"Whoa," Lucero snapped. "I won't take offense, but don't think for one minute I'd hesitate to check on anybody or anything. Friends or not. If Stuart thinks looking into the accident report merits attention, then I'll do it. In fact—" Lucero pulled out his cell phone. "Hang on."

He waited for a moment, then said, "Hey, Dad! How you doing? Good, good. Listen, put on your thinking cap for a minute for me. Remember when Tony Giordano's chopper went down? Yeah, way back, I know. Do you remember where it happened? Was he dusting crops, or joy riding?" Lucero listened, then shoved his hand in his pocket and began to jiggle some loose change. "No kidding?" he said. "Where? Do you remember who was there? I mean, in the party?" He nodded a few times, then said, "Hey, thanks, huh? No, no...just doing some jawing about a similar case. Yeah, keep it between us. Give Mom a kiss. See you later."

All eyes were on Dan Lucero as he set his cell phone on the table, then poured cold coffee into his cup. He took a sip, then said, "It happened at a hunting party near Reno. Dad said he remembered that Mattucci was there, old man Giordano, and some ranchers from Salinas and Stockton. Maybe some others, but he hadn't gone that trip, so he's not sure who else went. Tony Giordano flew his chopper up to use for spotting elk. He went down the third day they were out. My dad said they chalked it up to mechanical failure or pilot error. He's not sure which."

"I can get the details from the Washoe County Sheriff's Department in Reno," Stuart said. He looked at Loomis. "I like out-of-the-box thinking, and I like this group."

Randall rose, and picked up the now-empty coffeepot. He turned to Molly and said, "I think we're going to need more fuel. Do you mind?"

Molly took the coffeepot. "Not in the least."

She stopped when Randall asked Stuart, "Are you a hunter?"

"No, never saw the attraction."

"We should know who were their camp people," Randall said. "Who they hired for the setup, and who the guides were. That gear is used by hunters to make shooting blinds."

"You gotta be kidding," Lucero said. "It was years ago."

Randall's smile was slow, but tight. "I never kid."

Molly said, "I think the killer is someone who works at the winery." She looked at Randall. "Did you tell them about that man in the truck? The one who stopped at the cave, and then later passed by the tasting room when Susan showed up with the reporter?"

"Yeah, I did. Probably just a supervisor checking up on the laborers."

Molly didn't agree, but didn't reply. She left for the storage room and pulled back the memory of the man in the truck. She hadn't seen enough of him to offer a description. Still, it bothered her. She remembered a creepy feeling when he stopped at the cave. It was his utter stillness as he sat in the truck. Add to that, it seemed strange that he would turn his face away when he passed her leaving the tasting room. She thought she could describe the truck, but then realized it was probably a company truck and would be available to many of the employees. She began to think Randall was right and that she was reading too much into too little.

While she made the coffee, her thoughts wandered to Emma's meeting with Marshall Macomber tomorrow. She would take her to Daria's and make the introductions. She didn't relish sitting in Daria's back room twiddling her thumbs, but she knew she had to stay. She had no idea what the girl's mood might be after lunch, and she wouldn't think of letting a confused Emma walk home alone. The thought of it tore at her heart. She knew she had to stop dwelling on tomorrow. God willing, Macomber would realize that Emma was happy here, and would leave.

On her way back into the garage, Molly paused. She couldn't help but grin when she took in the scene before her. Amid tables filled with antique objets d'art, china, lamps, old books, and odds-and-ends of flatware, Carmel's chief of police, a sheriff's homicide detective, the district attorney, and his private investigator sat on folding chairs eating stale cookies as they analyzed and dissected the murder of Todd Jessop. She wondered what the villagers would think if they knew what was going on here.

Molly's thoughts moved in another direction. She made a quick vow to be more careful in the future when taking on outside commissions. Her last one with Frances O'Brien had been nothing but trouble. And now she was in the middle of another mess. Maybe, she thought, it would be better to avoid freelance work, period. She didn't need the grief. Frances had been bad enough, and now she had Carla and Susan messing up her life. As Armand, her cousin Angela's husband, always said when the shit hit the fan, *"Cherchez la femme!"* Look for the woman!

Molly was about to offer fresh coffee to Loomis when her hand halted in midair. "Wait a minute, a crazy thought just skittered through my brain. As in *cherchez la femme?"* She handed Loomis the pot, then said to Randall, "Remember me telling you about the day Susan Jessop came in the shop? And how she wanted to hire me to find out about Carla?"

Stuart broke in, "Hire you? Sorry, Molly, but I don't get the connection."

"I know, I know!" Molly said. She quickly filled him in and then added, "So in comes Susan pretending not to know Carla, then add Carla giving me hell for not telling her about Susan." She looked around the room. "We all know now that Susan had a PI following Todd for at least a year and obviously knew about Carla. I'm convinced now this whole thing is an elaborate ruse to cover up the fact that they're in this together. I still think they were *both* poisoning Todd." Molly saw thoughtful faces. No one said a word. "Maybe the reason Carla has been in a hurry to get the tasting room ready is because the poison wasn't working fast enough. He probably wasn't experiencing any symptoms, so they hired a killer. And her excuse for taking over running the winery isn't because of her father's health. I think she expected Todd to keep interfering, and *wanted* him to so there would be other suspects for the cops to look at." Molly took a breath. She looked at Randall. "If, like she reminds us, her father 'hasn't much time,' why the hell is she going to Peru for a vintner's conference? Why not send someone else? Something stinks."

When no one replied, she held up her hand. "Try this on for size. Peru is just a hop, skip, and a jump to Brazil. They don't extradite, right?"

"Generally, you're right," Lucero said. "Brazil won't extradite a U.S. citizen facing a murder charge if that citizen lives in a state that has a death penalty. But the death penalty is only used if the crime is attached to special circumstances: more than one murder or in conjunction with a robbery or sex crime. In this case, we've got only one homicide. So unless Carla doesn't fully know the law, her trip won't do her any good."

"Hmm. I wonder if Susan Jessop knows she's going?" Molly asked.

Randall laughed. "Maybe not. Like you said, Molly, *cherchez la femme.*"

It was near midnight by the time everyone left. Molly gathered the mugs in the garage and took them upstairs to wash. Her weary brain was filled with umpteen snatches of the thoughts and theories tossed around earlier. On her way to bed, she checked on Emma. The light next to her bed was still on. Tiger and both kittens were snuggled against her back. Molly turned off the light and watched her for a moment. She didn't look forward to tomorrow. She almost wished she could make time stand still. She also knew she had to stop putting off telling Bitsy about Marshall Macomber, and best do it tomorrow in case Emma… No, she quickly thought, erase that line of thinking.

Molly fell into bed and almost forgot her nightly prayers. She opened her eyes and glanced at her father's photo on the nightstand. It had been a while since she had found a need to tell him the latest news. She wondered if it was a sign of maturity, or just a dose of reality. Happy people didn't talk to photos, even those of loved ones. Molly had been happy for quite a few months. But once again, events were piling up around her. The solace of speaking freely and from deep within her heart weakened her resolve to act with some semblance of normality.

"Carrie's at it again," she murmured. "Will she never leave me in peace? Why does she have this need to bedevil me? Why?" She turned away from her father's photo, closed her eyes, and said her prayers. Since she was in a talkative mood, she decided her best bet was a chat with the Big Guy. *It's me, Molly Doyle. You busy?* She hesitated for a moment. She punched her pillow into submission, then fussed with the duvet. She wanted to word her plea carefully. She didn't want to sound whiny or ungrateful. The words would not form. She had so much to be thankful for already. With all the sorrow in the world, asking for anything would sound greedy. *Never mind. You already know what's on my mind. You've already got a plan. Whatever you decide is fine. I can handle it. Just thought I'd drop in and say hello.*

While trying to zip her mind shut and nod off, Molly thought she heard a noise outside on the balcony. She turned over to squint at the French doors and pulled off the duvet covering most of her head. Her brain tried to label the sound. She settled on wrought iron scraping on the terra-cotta tiles. A cat, no doubt jumping off one of the small bistro chairs she and Emma had found a few months ago at a garage sale. Carmel, the locals liked to boast, had more cats per capita than any city in California. It might even have been one of those pesky raccoons. She was about to accept that scenario, when the next noise she heard was a loud thud.

Molly threw off the duvet and tiptoed to the French doors. She carefully pulled the drapery aside. She didn't have time to have hysterics, or to worry about stepping outside in the long, ratty T-shirt she wore to bed. She unlocked the door, yanked it open, then tried to help Susan Jessop up. "Oh, God, what now?" Molly wrapped an arm around Susan's waist and helped her into the bedroom. Susan was mumbling, but Molly couldn't understand a word. She managed to sit Susan on the bed, then waved her hand in front of her face. "Hello? Susan? What happened?"

Susan's eyelids fluttered. She took in deep breaths and finally managed to speak. "I didn't know where else to go." She grabbed Molly's hands. "Someone...someone tried to kill me, Molly! He was in the apartment when I got home. I...I walked in and that's the last thing I remember until I woke up. My head hurts."

"Let's get you to the living room. We need to call Chief Randall."

"No!" Susan blurted. "No cops. I just needed a place to feel safe. I thought of you first. Please, Molly, if I could rest on your sofa for a little while. I...I won't keep you up all night."

Molly helped Susan to the living room and eased her gently onto the sofa. "I'll get you some water. I'd offer something stronger, but it might not be a good idea if you have a concussion. You need to get checked out, Susan. At least let me take you to Emergency."

"Just some water. I'll be okay."

When Molly returned to the living room with Susan's water, she found Susan trying to comb her hair with her hands. She kept her voice low so Emma wouldn't hear them. "What makes you think someone tried to kill you? It could have been a burglar or even a rapist."

Susan took a long sip of water before replying. "Nothing is missing." Her voice became harsher. "And if I'd been raped, I think I'd know it."

Molly saw the fear in her expression and wondered why she refused to report this to the police. "Let me get you a blanket. Stay the night. But I have to tell you that if we don't call Randall right now, it's going to be tough for him to find whoever did this to you. If I don't call him, then I'm in hot water." Molly reached for the box on the coffee table and pulled out a cigarette. "I get into enough trouble on my own. I don't need your problems adding to my ledger." She lit the cigarette and stared at Susan. "Well? What's it going to be?"

When Susan looked away and didn't answer, Molly said, "You've already lied to me once, Susan. How do I know you're telling the truth now?"

Susan's head jerked back. "I've never lied to you."

Molly could have slit her own throat for that slip-up. "Okay, I'll take that back. Let's amend that to, what the hell is going on between you and Carla? I'm not buying into that commiserating act I saw at the tasting room."

Molly watched Susan's face for those tell-tale signs Randall had once told her about. He said liars usually furrowed their brows, avoided eye contact, fiddled with something in their hands. However, the really good ones, he'd said, gave you full eye contact: wide open with a hint of calm and sincerity. Susan leaned in and crossed her arms on her knees, as if narrowing the distance between them. She appeared to be moving closer, trying to establish a heartfelt connection. Her eyes were open and clear. "I called Carla a day or so after I saw you. I…well, I realized she had been fooled by Todd as badly as I was. He was dead, but we were victims as well. I thought if we showed a united front, well, it would be an inspiration to other women with rats for husbands."

Molly took in every inch of her body language. She didn't buy the story anyway, but she nodded sympathetically. "That's awfully generous of you two."

Susan sniffed. "We both agreed it was time to let women know they didn't have to be adversaries in situations such as this." Tears welled up, and she sniffled again. She looked around the living room. "My bag? Did you bring it in with you? I must have dropped it. I really need to blow my nose."

Molly said, "I only brought you in. Are you sure you had it with you?"

"Of course."

Molly rose. "Stay put. I'll get it for you."

She turned on the light on the balcony and saw Susan's purse under the small round bistro table. Susan must have dropped it when she fell over the cat dish. Molly picked up the wallet and keys, put them in the bag, and then reached for a small notebook and several business cards. She was about to add them, when her eyes zeroed in on one of the cards. Molly bit her lip when she read the heading on the card. The *Enquirer*? She shoved everything into the bag and hurried back to the living room. "I found it. It was under the table." She handed the bag to Susan. "I'll get a blanket and pillow for you."

Susan reached into her bag and pulled out a small packet of

Kleenex. She smiled at Molly. "You've been so kind to take me in like this, but I can't impose. I think I'll go across the street to the Pine Inn and check in there for the night. I had a moment to think about things while you were gone. You're right, I should call the police. It probably was a burglar. They should know in case that person comes back. I'm sure I surprised him and he panicked when he hit me." She rose from the sofa. "If you could just walk me out?" She gave Molly a tiny smile. "Maybe watch me cross the street?"

Molly wasn't that anxious to have Susan Jessop on her sofa, and she quickly agreed. "If you'll be more comfortable, I'd be happy to walk over with you."

"No, you've done enough."

When Molly got back to the apartment, she was so revved up by this new discovery, she almost called Randall. She looked at the cat clock in the kitchen and was shocked to see it was almost two A.M. Her news would have to wait until morning. She climbed into bed but could not sleep. A cavalcade of events danced through her mind, teasing with possibilities so crazy they could possibly be true. Was Susan Jessop planning on selling her story to the *Enquirer*? Had they contacted her, or the other way around? Could the "Larry King Live" show be far behind? Was this act with Carla the beginning of a talk-show circuit and lecture series for discarded wives? The other thing that tugged at her brain was Susan's makeup. It was perfect. At this time of the night? After a long, emotional day and an evening out? Had she stopped to freshen her lipstick after she'd been hit over the head? And why was she so reluctant to call Randall? Maybe because she was lying?

# Chapter 28

MOLLY CALLED Randall and told him about Susan's visit the next morning while Emma was in the shower. "I don't believe a word of it," she snapped, "and I hate being taken for a fool!"

"Sounds fishy to me, too. Okay, sit on it. Don't let on I know. What time are you going to Mass?"

"I'm shooting for eleven."

"I won't see you then. I'm going up to San Jose with Loomis. We've got some leads to check out."

Molly's eyes lit up. "Oh? Anything you can tell me?"

"Not yet."

"That's not fair! Damn it! I tell *you* everything!"

Randall chuckled. "You're supposed to. Later, okay? I'll call you when I get back."

Molly was no sooner off the telephone than it rang. It was Marshall Macomber.

"Would it be possible," Macomber asked, "to move lunch up to noon? Some things have come up at my office, and I'll have to return home later today."

"Not a problem. I'll change the reservation."

Molly checked her watch when she hung up. It was already ten-thirty. The Mission San Carlos Borromeo de Carmelo that she and Emma attended each Sunday was only five minutes away. Emma would have to change into her new clothes right away. Molly found her on the balcony. "Lunch has been moved to noon. Come in and change pronto, okay? We won't have time after Mass. Call me when you're ready to go. I'll be downstairs with Bitsy."

Molly had been dreading telling Bitsy about Macomber. She

knew she couldn't sit on the problem any longer. Bitsy adored Emma, and Molly was worried that she would be heartbroken if they lost her. Nonetheless, it was time to bite the bullet.

The shop had been open for a half hour and Bitsy was showing a customer the intricacies of an American Victorian burr walnut dressing table. It was a lovely piece with an arched beveled mirror, fitted with six small drawers and one secret compartment. Molly knew it was worth more than the eight hundred she marked on the tag, but as handsome as it was, the piece didn't mix well with the English and French furniture Molly preferred to stock. She decided she would talk to Bitsy after dropping Emma off for lunch.

Mass was later a hazy dream for Molly. She hardly remembered when to stand, kneel, or sit. She barely heard the priest, and it almost bothered her to see how calm Emma was. Her gaze wandered around the simple, yet somehow elegant church. Emma was so taken after her first visit, she made it a point to learn the history of this second mission built in California. She had checked out a book from the library and given Molly the full rundown.

The several restorations over the years of the Moorish buildings and the now-beautiful grounds made it unlike the other missions up and down the coast of California. She remembered Emma excitedly telling her that even the walls inside this church were different from the other missions. Tapering inward, they formed a catenary (like the St. Louis Gateway Arch) instead of a flat ceiling. Molly had been surprised to learn the mission had originally been built in 1770 in Monterey, and was moved to Carmel in 1771. Molly knew it was the resting place of Junípero Serra, the founder of the long string of California missions, but she pretended to be surprised. What she did know, she'd proudly told Emma, was that it is one of the most important in California, and is one of three basilicas on the West Coast.

Molly closed her eyes and ignored what the priest was saying. She had only one thing on her mind, and that was whether Emma would be swayed by Marshall Macomber. Time and again, Emma had said how much she loved living in Carmel. Molly prayed she would remember that.

Emma had barely said a word on the way to Mass or on the trip back downtown, which unnerved Molly no end. Her hands were clammy as she gripped the steering wheel. She turned off Ocean Avenue onto Dolores Street searching for a parking place. "Damn, town is loaded today. Maybe we can find something around the block on Lincoln."

"Just let me off in front of Daria's," Emma said. "I can go in by myself. You don't have to come with me."

"I wouldn't think of doing that. That would be rude. Besides, what would Mr. Macomber think? And you don't know what he looks like."

Emma turned away from Molly. "I remember him from the beach. I'll tell him I insisted you didn't come with me."

Molly was stunned by the flat tone of Emma's voice. She double-parked in front of Daria's, then touched Emma's arm. "I'll be in the back room with Daria. Meet me there, okay?"

Emma opened the van's door. "Have you told Bitsy yet?"

Molly sighed. "Have you been peeking into my mind? Not yet."

Emma stepped out. She didn't turn around but said over her shoulder, "Maybe you should do that first. When I go in, I'll find Daria and tell her you'll be back later."

Molly wasn't sure who the adult was here. She knew Emma was right, but it rankled her a bit to think she was being given a slight scolding for not doing her duty. "Good idea," she finally said. "I'll see you later."

Molly watched Emma enter Daria's, then drove back to the shop. When she pulled into the alley, she called Daria on her cell and told her about Emma's decision. "Yeah, cool as a cucumber. Keep an eye, okay? I'll be over shortly. I'll come in the back way."

Molly found Bitsy at the desk with a customer. She appeared to be having a serious conversation. Her usual sales smile was missing, and Molly could see how rigidly her shoulders were set. "Hi, I see you're busy. I'll be in the storage room for a few minutes."

Bitsy waved. "Come back. I want you to meet someone." Bitsy rose and motioned to the woman to stand. When the woman turned to face her, Molly was surprised by her beauty. Her frame was so tiny, Molly thought she must wear a size two. Her short, raven hair framed an exquisite doll-like face. The young woman held out her hand. "You must be Molly Doyle. I'm Coco Ihle. Del Tinsley sent me down to see you."

Molly took her hand. "I'm plumb out of the type of chairs Del's looking for now. I should have returned her call. It's been a crazy week."

"I'm not here for chairs," Coco said. She picked up a large manila envelope from Molly's desk. "Del thought you should see these. I think you'd best sit down, though."

Molly took the envelope, pulled a chair away from a display, moved it to the desk, and sat down uneasily. She stared at the envelope for a moment. "Oh, God. I'm getting tired of saying, 'What now.'" She looked at Bitsy. "Do you know what's in here?"

"Unfortunately, yes," Bitsy said.

Molly opened the envelope and found two large, glossy photos. Her eyelids barely flickered when she saw Todd Jessop in the first photo. She looked at Coco. "Looks like he's at one of your, uh, evenings. He seems to be enjoying your attention."

"I'm good at what I do." Coco smiled almost shyly. "That first one isn't important. Look at the other one."

Molly set the first photo on her lap and glanced at the next one. It was Todd again, in the same chair as before, but this time, besides Coco, there was another woman with him. Both women appeared to be actually on his lap. From the angle of Coco's head, it was apparent she was moving seductively. But it was the second woman, back-to-back with Coco, who made Molly's jaw drop. "It's Carla!"

"I think," Bitsy said, "you need to show them to Randall."

Molly was nearly speechless. But, she quickly thought, she had no right to judge. "I don't see how this means anything. I mean, so Carla and Todd liked to, well, spice up their lives. That's their business, not ours."

"Susan Jessop has copies as well," Coco said. "Before you jump to conclusions, let me explain why."

Molly handed Coco back the photos. "Oh, please do. This is really getting convoluted." Molly rose. "But first, I'm putting the 'closed' sign in the window. I don't want anyone walking in on this. We'll move to the back of the shop so we can't be seen."

After they were settled by the fireplace, Coco said, "Del makes it a practice to, well, keep a record of guests who misbehave. The first time someone gets out of hand, she warns them. But still, we have cameras all over just in case things get out of hand. You might call it an insurance policy. If there is a second time, then that person is no longer allowed back. Todd Jessop was a pig, and Del finally had to bar him."

"That doesn't explain why Susan has a copy. If he was barred, then that should have been the end of it," Molly said.

"Normally, it would have, except I got one of our techs to make me a copy." Coco moved back against the chair cushion and tugged at the hem of her skirt. "I'm really good at sales, Molly. Don't laugh, I'm serious. I wanted a job at the software company the Jessops had recently sold. They have a great employee package, and I wanted to give up my night job. I went to see Susan Jessop, and showed her the photos. I was hoping she might exert some influence with the new owners to take me on."

Molly shook her head. "I think that's called blackmail?"

"I'm like Del. I think of it as insurance," Coco said.

"What happened? Did Susan bite?" Bitsy asked.

"Totally," Coco said. "I've been with the company now for four months, and I'm already in the top ten of sales."

"I still don't see why Del thought you should bring this to me. I mean, you got what you were after."

"When I read about Jessop being murdered, and then saw Carla and Susan in the paper, hugging like long-lost sisters, I almost fainted. See, I didn't know Carla was Todd's wife when they came to one of our evenings. I thought she was just a girlfriend or some bimbo he picked up at a bar."

"I still think," Bitsy said to Molly, "you should hand these over to Randall. We have no idea if they mean anything, but he might feel differently."

Molly looked at her watch. It was already half-past noon. Emma and Macomber would be in the middle of lunch. "He's out of town today. I guess I'll see him later. Okay, I'll give them to him, but if he wants to talk to you, I'll need to give him your telephone number."

Coco pulled a business card from her bag. "I'm going right back to Palo Alto. I should be home in a couple of hours." She rose from the chair and gave Molly a half smile. "Just remember when you talk to the cop, it wasn't blackmail. I was desperate for that job, Molly. Besides, a wife needs to know when she's married to a piece of shit. I wasn't asking for money, I just wanted out of the dancing."

"I know, Coco. You don't have to explain." Molly shook her hand.

She returned to her desk and put the manila envelope in the drawer. She wondered if Susan had copies of the photos with her. If so, then could that have been what her attacker was after? And if that were all true, she realized, the finger pointed in a straight line to Carla Jessop. What was it Bennie had told Molly about? She couldn't remember the word in Italian, but she did remember it had to do with appearances. "Face," that was it.

When Bitsy returned from seeing Coco out, she collapsed in a chair. "What a turn of events! What next?" she sighed.

"I'll tell you what's next. You might want a shot of Jack Daniel's after I'm through." Molly proceeded to tell Bitsy about her encounter with Marshall Macomber, and her later talk with Emma. To Bitsy's credit, she didn't interrupt or utter a word. When Molly was finished, she felt the same lump in her throat she was sure Bitsy felt. Bitsy's eyes were misty, and Molly had a sudden urge to throw her arms around her and break out in a good old women's crying fest. Instead, she squared her shoulders and said, "I've got to get over to Daria's. They should be on dessert by now."

Bitsy remained in her chair. "You'll be coming back here, won't you?"

"I'm not sure. It depends on what kind of mood Emma is in. She might want to spend the rest of the day with Macomber. Hell, I don't know. Besides, I still have a box of silver I need to give to Daria. Either way, I'll call you."

"By the way," Bitsy said, "those Foo Dogs in the window? From Max? They're repros. Max's eyesight must be going. I assume you went by his inventory list when you made up the tags. They're not nineteenth-century. Early nineteen-fifties, I'd guess."

Molly rolled her eyes. "Great. That's just great. And you're right, I didn't check them out. I assumed he was correct. Okay, I'll take care of it later."

Molly loaded the box of silver in the van, pulled out of the alley, and headed for Daria's. Carmel was packed with tourists, and there still wasn't a parking place to be had. She circled the block three times, then decided to park in the alley. She could always move the van later. Going in the back way through the kitchen, Molly struggled with the box and almost ran into one of the kitchen staff coming out of the walk-in freezer carrying a container filled with poultry of some kind. She knew most of Daria's employees, but didn't recognize him, and thought it strange he was wearing sunglasses. She almost laughed when she saw the cap he was wearing. It looked like a tea cozy. She gave him an apologetic smile, moved out of his way, and almost ran into a waiter before she made it into Daria's back room. Daria was on the phone and motioned her in. Molly set the box on the table and began removing the silver.

Daria handed the phone to Molly. "It's Randall. He wants us to have dinner here tonight."

"Any news about Emma's lunch?" Randall asked Molly.

"She isn't back yet. But listen, I've got to tell you…"

"Save it for later, okay? Loomis and I just pulled up to meet our appointment."

Daria took the phone from Molly. "You look like you're ready to fall apart at the seams," Daria said. "Calm down, would you?"

"I'm trying… Hey, who's the guy in the kitchen with the sunglasses? Someone new? I had to bite my tongue not to laugh at that goofy hat he's wearing."

Daria grinned. "That's Dando Osa, Mr. Mattucci's cook. He comes in now and then. He and Julio, my head chef, are old friends. I buy my pheasants from him. He raises them out at the ranch."

"So he's not so mysterious after all. I only got a glimpse of him at that dinner at the tasting room. He stuck his head in the room to wave to everyone, but he had a chef's toque on then. That was before Todd Jessop showed up. I guess I was too busy wondering what the hell I was going to say to him to notice Dando."

"He's just kind of private," Daria said. He's been with the family for years. He and Domenico are very close." Reaching for one of the silver trays, Daria said, "This stuff is fantastic! But this is too much for our deal. I want to pay you this time."

"Forget it. I don't think I spent more than fifty bucks. The way you feed us, that hardly pays for one dinner for Emma and me. Plus, we're back again tonight."

Daria picked up another heavily chased tray. "I just can't fathom people not wanting to keep beautiful silver like this. But they love coming here for dinner and being served with all this elegant stuff."

Daria saw the blank look on Molly's face. She knew she hadn't heard a word. "Why don't I take a walk out front and see how Emma's doing. Maybe I could stop by, and—"

Before Molly could reply, the door opened and Emma walked in. Molly's hands fell to her lap. She clasped them tightly. "Hey, good timing. I just got here a few minutes ago."

When Emma took a seat at the end of the table, instead of her usual place next to Molly, it was apparent to Daria and Molly that this act had meaning.

Emma set her hands on the table and then folded them. She cleared her throat. She licked her lips, pushed her glasses back, and wiggled just slightly in the chair. She looked as if she were about to give a book report. "Mr. Macomber seems to be a nice man," Emma began. "He said to tell you, Daria, that his lunch was excellent. It was, too. I had the Cobb Salad."

Daria smiled her thanks, and Molly pretended to be calm.

Emma looked down at her hands. She meshed her fingers together as if in deep thought. "Well, uh, let's see. He said he wants to get to know me. He knows I'm happy here, and that I'm lucky to have landed here with you, Aunt Molly. He said he wished he'd known about me sooner though." She looked at Molly. Her words seemed to rush out. "He wants to talk to you about taking me to Europe this summer. He said I'm old enough to appreciate the trip. And that I should see some of the world."

Molly hadn't been ready for that. She wasn't sure what she had expected. Maybe a short summer break to visit him in Vancouver, but certainly not a trip to Europe. It killed Molly, but she knew she should ask Emma how she felt about the invitation. "Well, that's awfully generous of him. What a great opportunity. What did you say?"

Emma's eyebrows slowly rose. Her eyes seemed to offer an apology for what she was about to say. "I told him that I would so love to go, if you'd let me. Who'd turn down a whole summer in Europe?"

Molly hoped her smile looked genuine. It was only a trip. It wasn't as if Emma were leaving her for good. "How soon does he want to leave?"

"The day after school is out."

"That soon?"

The flash of disappointment on Emma's face didn't go unnoticed. Molly waved her hand. "It's okay, I mean, that makes sense. Of course you can go. How could I let you pass that up?"

Molly felt a tiny stab in her heart when she saw Emma's excited face. She pasted a big smile on her face when Emma jumped up and rushed to hug her. "Awesome! Thank you, Aunt Molly!"

Molly laughed. "You didn't really expect me to say no, did you?"

Emma grinned at Daria, then plopped down next to Molly. "Nope. But there was always a chance. You've told me about old Murphy and his Law, so I wasn't sure. I can't wait to tell Michelle! She'll be, like, so jealous!"

"When does Mr. Macomber plan to talk to me about this?"

"He's waiting at the table. I told him you would go out and talk to him. That was okay, wasn't it?"

Molly's eyes darted to Daria. She was being put on the spot, and she wasn't thrilled. "Sure. I'll go right out."

"Oh, and he wants to take me to a movie and then dinner after that so we can talk about the trip. Is that okay, too?"

Molly was at the door. Her grasp on the doorknob was so tight, it was in danger of being ripped off. She smiled over her shoulder. "Sure. Fine. Great idea."

There was danger in Molly Doyle's stride as she marched down the hall to the dining room. She spotted Macomber right away. The temptation to grab one of the waiter's trays and dump it on the elegantly dressed man was almost overwhelming. She wondered how a few plates of pasta would look on the tan cashmere sport coat he wore. Molly reached his table, leaned on the back of a chair, and said, "That was a pretty nifty trick inviting Emma to Europe. You knew damn well I wouldn't refuse her, didn't you!"

Marshall Macomber motioned to the empty chair. "Please sit with me, Molly."

Molly didn't want to sit; she wanted to wiggle her nose and make him disappear. She hesitated, then pulled out the chair and reluctantly sat. "I told Emma she could go."

Molly always thought the description of someone's face "lighting up" was really dumb. It was physically impossible. But it was the first thing that came to mind when she saw Macomber's wide smile nearly split his face in two. She felt a twinge of guilt for being so hard on the man.

"Thank you, Molly." He paused for a moment, then said, "I grew up poor. I worked two jobs in high school and in college. I was determined, Molly, much like you, to shake off the smell of poverty and make something of myself. I worked like a dervish for twenty years building a law firm that became significant. In the process, I ruined a childless marriage. I gave my wife everything, except myself. She traveled all over the world. I never had the time. I have few hobbies, and few friends. I finally saw Europe two years ago. Alone. Sad, isn't it? I need to make amends for a selfish life, Molly. I'd like to start with Emma. I want to give her the chances I never had, a head start, if you will. Opportunities I imagine you didn't have either."

Molly was surprised by his candor. She had him pegged as a WASP from a patrician family whose success was a given. He'd reminded her at first of clients she'd had in New York. Trust-fund men and women who filled their many homes with antiques, then soon forgot them until it was time to redecorate and start again. "Ex-cop's kids, whose fathers scramble to feed them, learn to be self-sufficient pretty damn fast. But we had love," she said. "Will you be able to offer Emma that?"

"Yes, if you'll give me the chance."

The sincerity in his voice was hard to ignore. Molly realized how selfish and wrong it would be to deny him, and Emma, the prospect of building a relationship they both obviously wanted to explore. But he was a successful lawyer, trained to sway people with his golden tongue. She didn't want him to think she'd been won over too easily. It was important for him to know that.

"You've got your chance. But I'm warning you, don't ever pull another preemptive strike like this again. Next time you want to offer her the moon, you talk to me first. I don't care if you're her natural father. Understand?" Molly hadn't meant to sound quite that harsh, but it was too late now.

"Fully. Can I have the waiter bring you something?"

"No, thank you." She tried to soften her earlier demand by smiling when she said, "Now tell me where you're taking her and how long you'll be gone. It better damn well be first class all the way."

# Chapter 29

BITSY WAS PACING the center aisle of the shop. She stopped every few steps to adjust a lampshade, move a stature, or examine a sales tag. "Bastard. He dangled that trip knowing you'd never make her stay home. Sneaky lawyer bastard."

Molly was slumped in a wing chair. "He knew which button to push, that's all. So he won the first contest. How many more does he have up his sleeve?"

With an imperious lift of her chin, Bitsy said, "I'm taking Emma to the City tomorrow. We're going to buy clothes for her trip, and don't you dare refuse me this time. I'll be damned if she leaves here without the best of everything. In fact, I'll call my personal buyer at Saks tonight at home and tell her to have a full wardrobe ready, luggage and all."

Molly couldn't help but laugh. "You're incredible. Okay, I won't argue this time. But, uh, Emma has school tomorrow, remember?"

Bitsy's eyes were sparking. "The hell with school. Besides, with finals over, they don't do much of anything the last week."

Molly's solitary walk to Daria's for dinner left her feeling glum. When she stood outside the restaurant, she wondered how she was going to get through so many weeks without Emma. She began to understand how parents felt when their children left home. She knew she was being a bit melodramatic, but the little scamp had a tight hold on her heart. Even the possibility of giving Randall an important lead couldn't give Molly the jolt she needed to perk up.

Everyone was already at the table when Molly walked in. She was more than surprised to see Lieutenant Stuart there. Loomis was holding court, telling cop jokes, and Dan Lucero was on his cell phone waving at Randall and Stuart to hold down the laughter. Daria came in just behind Molly with a large platter of bruschetta and an assortment of other finger foods. "I've got an oven down," Daria said. "It's a zoo in my kitchen. We're going to eat whatever I can get my hands on."

"Can I help?" Molly asked. "I can order pizza."

"Funny, I was thinking the same thing. No, we'll be fine. Grab a seat. You okay?"

After Emma had left with Marshall Macomber, Molly had stayed for a short time and told Daria about her conversation with him. "I'm fine now. Bitsy took it well, considering her temper. She's taking Emma up to the City tomorrow for a grand-tour wardrobe."

Daria laughed. "Good for Bitsy. She'll show 'em a thing or two."

Randall turned in his chair and saw Molly. "What grand tour?"

"Emma is going to Europe with Marshall Macomber next week when school is out," Molly said.

The conversation came to a halt. All eyes were on Molly. Lucero was the first to speak. "You're letting her go?"

Molly put her hands up to stop him. "Yes, I am. He *is* her father. Emma had lunch with him today, and she liked him. She wants to go. How could I say no? End of discussion." She pulled the manila envelope from her tote and set it on the table in front of Randall. "Here. Chew over this instead of telling me I caved in, okay?"

Randall picked up the envelope. "What's this?"

Molly sat down. She pulled off her jacket and said, "Just open it. There's a business card in there too. She said she's available anytime you want to talk. I'll tell you how I got it after you've all looked it over."

Randall pulled out the photos and examined them. His face was like a block of concrete. Nothing moved. Without a word, he passed them on to Stuart. The room was as quiet as an abandoned crypt while Stuart looked at them, and in turn, passed one each to Lucero and Loomis.

Lucero finally broke the silence. "Pass this down to Daria," he said to Loomis. "She might as well see it."

Daria took the photo. She looked at it and then threw it on the table. "So? Not my choice of entertainment, but what does it prove?"

Lucero said to Stuart, "I'm going to bring Daria up to date here. She's known Carla for some years. In fact, both of us have. You might say, our little group here is, well—"

"Pretty damn unusual," Stuart broke in. His smile made it obvious he was accepting the lay of the land. "I can't say I've ever worked a homicide like this before. I mean, with civilians." He looked around the room. "No offense, Molly, but your garage was drafty. The atmosphere here beats a squad room, too. Oriental carpets, original art work, and dinner at one of Carmel's best restaurants." To Lucero, he added, "You're the D.A. here. If it's kosher with you, who am I to argue." He turned to Randall next. "Your close-rate is pretty damn impressive." He threw up his hands in mock surrender. "So, hey, go for it. Deal me in."

"Okay," Lucero said. "I'm going to cover all that we know. So consider it a mini-refresher course for all of us. These photos, by the way, might open up some new ideas."

After recounting the major events and discoveries, Lucero said, "I think we're all agreed that Carla's son, Nicky, can be eliminated. He's too big a kid to have used that tree saddle. Even though it's adjustable, he'd never have made it past two feet. The person we're looking for is slim, agile, and has some experience with the gear. Stuart was in touch with the sheriff's in Washoe County, and Tony Giordano's chopper accident was legit. The FAA did a thorough investigation and they determined that the cause was pilot error. We all knew Tony was a show-off. He was probably flying too low, maybe buzzing the hunting group for kicks. Anyway, the postmortem found a high concentration of alcohol in his blood. Old man Giordano didn't want to believe it then, and still doesn't." Lucero shrugged. "Don't ask. It's just the way it is."

"Some of the old-timer Italians are like that," Daria said. "Tony was an only son. I guess it's been hard for Giordano to accept that he was a jerk-off."

"*Face!*" Molly said. "He didn't want people to think—"

Lucero slapped his forehead. "Shit!"

Randall grabbed one of the photos and waved it in the air. "And then some." He turned to Molly and hugged her. "That's it! You just uttered the magic word. You want a motive? I think Molly just gave it to us."

Stuart looked at Loomis. "You getting any of this?"

"More or less. But I think I'm following Molly's train of thought," Loomis replied.

"Okay, Molly," Lucero said, "what's bubbling in that mind of yours? Let's see if we're on the same page here."

Molly explained how she got the photos and gave them a brief rundown on her connection to the woman. "It might sound crazy, but I think Susan Jessop is after the proverbial fifteen-minutes-of-fame trip and is setting up a plan to hit the talk shows. I mean, apparently she's known about Carla for at least a year, so she's had plenty of time to get over her anger and decide how to make the most out of being a wronged wife. I haven't given this a ton of thought, but Susan strikes me as a plotter. I don't think she's impulsive like Carla. So, when Jessop is killed, she knows it's time to make her move. I have to say, when she came into the shop that day, I didn't get the feeling she was very bereaved.

"If Susan and Carla didn't hire a killer, then I think Susan showed Carla the photos and sort of blackmailed her into doing the 'us poor women have to stick together' thing. I'm thinking this, because of the business card she had in her purse from a reporter at the *Enquirer*." Molly turned to Randall. "You told them about all of that?" When Randall nodded that he had, Molly went on, "Well, that's what I think."

"For not giving this much thought," Stuart said, "I think you've done a damn good job. But you're right, it doesn't lead us to the shooter."

"Unless it was Susan Jessop," Daria said. "I mean, let's face it. She wasn't at the party."

"She'd fit that tree saddle," Loomis said.

"No. She's not our killer," Randall said as he reached for a bottle of wine. "Our killer is a man strong enough to haul himself up the tree a good twenty feet. But I think we're closer now than an hour ago. Now we just have to figure out whose *face* would be ruined the most."

Pleased that her idea was being taken seriously, Molly put aside her dismal mood for a moment. She lifted her wineglass to Randall. "I'll join you. *In vino veritas?* Isn't that how it goes? In wine there is truth. Maybe I can have a chat with Susan and a lovely bottle of wine. I can tell her I know about the photos. And maybe that was what someone was after the other night. Or, maybe it was Carla instead? It'd be nice to know if and when Carla first saw them. Kind of like establishing a timeline? If I'm right, that is."

"No way," Stuart firmly said. "I can bend the rules and talk openly here, but I won't allow you to put yourself in danger."

Randall burst out laughing. "Oh, sure. I'd love to see you pull that one off. If you can keep Molly Doyle out of this now, you're a better man than I thought."

Molly winked at Daria. "Maybe a girls' night out, like last year? Us and Susan? Or Carla?"

"You're nuts, Molly. No way." Daria looked at Lucero. "Don't let her do this."

"You heard Randall. If she won't listen to him, what makes you think she'll listen to me?"

Daria rose and reached for the empty platter, "We need more food. I'll see what I can scare up." She looked at Molly. "I'd do anything for you, except this. Leave it alone."

Molly reached for her wineglass. She stared at it, then lifted it to her lips. "You're right." She drained the half-full glass, then nudged it toward Randall.

Randall filled it to the brim. "Let us take it from here."

Molly's voice was just above a whisper. "It's all yours."

Daria stopped by the door. "I hope to hell you mean that, Molly."

Molly looked up and smiled. "Of course I do."

While Randall explained to Stuart and Loomis what Molly had meant by *face*, and while Lucero interrupted to offer the many different terms in Italian and each meaning, Molly listened and recalled the same variations Bennie had offered. She remained silent throughout the conversation, but her mind was rewinding back to the night Carla came into the shop with the bruised cheek. She remembered Carla saying, "He won't get away with this. I'm Italian, remember?"

"Come on, you guys," Stuart said. "This isn't New Jersey. We're not dealing with the Mob or Tony Soprano here."

Randall laughed. He looked at Lucero. "Give him the facts of life, willya?"

Before Lucero could speak, Stuart said, "Okay, okay. I get it. The old man, Mattucci, right? The rumors of him being connected? I checked that out with my Nevada counterparts. He was suspected of being a bag man at the tables in Reno, that's all. Running hot dough through the tables. He won just enough to make it look good. They never made a case on him. He and some sheep rancher friend out of Reno were watched for months. When they couldn't get any hard evidence where the money they gambled with came from, they dropped it. Both men claimed the dough they threw around came from winnings at other casinos. Mostly in Vegas. In those days, things were a little looser. Especially in Vegas."

"But what if Susan has shown those photos to Carla? And Carla is spooked?" Molly broke in. "She'd hardly want her kids, or her father to see her...well, like that. And if Mr. Mattucci had those kind of friends, couldn't he have—?"

Daria was back with a platter of panini. "Are you still at this, Molly? I'm going to hijack you out to the kitchen to wash dishes if you don't—"

"No, wait," Lucero said. "Leave her alone. Go on, Molly."

"That's all I had to say. It was just a thought. I was just thinking about the night Carla came into the shop to see the portfolio I'd made for the tasting room. The night Todd came in and got into it with Randall. She admitted to me that Todd had hit her. Randall urged her to file a complaint, but she refused. When she left, she made a comment that I just remembered."

Randall said, "You're right. Hell, I forgot all about that."

"What did she say?" Stuart asked. "I'd like to hang my hat on something with this damn case."

"When Carla was leaving, I told her to call me if she needed me. She said, 'He won't get away with this. I'm Italian, remember?' I think those were her exact words."

"So," Stuart said, "you never told Reynolds any of this?"

Molly shook her head. "I'd forgotten until now. Besides, I never really thought Carla might be involved."

"Well, she's still top of the list, but hell, we all know how that works," Lucero said. "I just can't figure her having the connections to hire out."

"I'd like to do more checking on Dino Horne and Reggie Sullivan," Loomis added. "After Molly telling Randall what she'd overheard at the winery, I'd say there's some reason to look at them a little harder."

"Agreed. I've got people on them, too, but anything you can find is welcome. Look," Stuart said, "our window is closing. Time is running out if Carla is planning on leaving the country. I'm going to bring both women in again. It's time to take off the gloves. I have to be honest. This 'face' thing is not something I'm putting much store in for a motive." Stuart laughed. "It's too medieval to be valid."

"Medieval?" Randall spit out. "Yeah, sure it is. But it still exists. When a Muslim woman is raped, her family kills her for the same reason. Shame, *face*—it's the same thing, pal. Not everyone has left the Dark Ages." He looked at Lucero. "Right?"

"Can't argue with that. The same mentality still runs deep in Italian families."

Randall picked up a bottle of Bello Lago wine. He turned the label face-out. "See this Latin phrase under the picture of the lake? Anyone know what it means?" When no one answered, he said, "*Non nobis solum nati sumus.*" When the silence remained, he said, "It's something Cicero wrote, 'We are not born for ourselves alone.' That tell you anything? I put my money on the old man early on. Family first, and *face*. It's all there. I figured he knew he was on his way out, and wanted Carla free of that prick so she could take over after he was gone without Jessop's constant meddling. Divorce would have been the normal move. But Jessop had to be eliminated, not by some piece of paper, but permanently." He picked up one of the photos.

"With no forensics, or real leads, you might be able to use these to sweat something out of the two women."

"Wait," Molly said. "Let me see if I've got this straight. Randall thinks Mr. Mattucci had Todd killed just to save face. And we're assuming Susan and Carla were working together, too. Talk about a mess! I wonder how they come up with the plan to poison him? Get together for drinks and one of them says, 'Hey, I've got an idea! Let's poison Todd.' Huh?"

"You're looking for logic, Molly," Lucero said. "If people always used logic, we'd all be out of a job."

There was mischief in Molly's voice when she said, "I wonder if Susan knows Carla is leaving the country next week." When no one commented, Molly added, "I could ask her, couldn't I?" She waited for that to sink in. "With your blessings, of course."

# Chapter 30

IT WAS AFTER NINE when Randall walked Molly home from Daria's. They stopped in front of the Carmel Art Association building and sat on the broad stone steps leading to its beautiful sculpture garden. "Did you know," Randall said, "this was built in nineteen-twenty-seven to showcase local artists, and it's the second oldest nonprofit artist co-op in the country?"

"No, but I should since I sell art. Don't tell anyone. I'm supposed to know stuff like that."

"Our secret. I like to sit here at night when I take my walks. When I have things to think about. Like now. Like this meeting with Susan Jessop, for instance. We're letting you do this on one condition," he said. "You have a lunch, or a maybe a coffee, somewhere public so Loomis and I can keep an eye on you. Understand?"

"You've told me that. Maybe you might want to pick the place?"

"Don't get snarky. I'm against this, but I'm willing to go along with it because I know you'll do it anyway."

"How's the Village Corner? We can sit in the patio and you and Loomis can watch us from inside. I still don't know why you have to be around. What's she going to do? Pull a gun on me or something?"

"See? There you go again. You don't listen. Loomis is going to tail her when she leaves you. We're hoping she makes a beeline to Carla and stirs up some dust. We need to know, okay?"

Molly laughed. "Right, I got it. By the way, do you really think Dino Horne or Reggie Sullivan are involved?"

"Personally? No. They should be knocked off the list. Sure, Jessop was a pain in the ass for both of them, but they weren't really worried about losing their jobs. According to some of my pals up in Sonoma,

Horne and Sullivan have had offers from vintners all over the country. More money, perks, and what have you. They stay because they're home boys and would rather raise their kids here. The personal background checks Loomis did came up with nothing. No big debts, no hanky-panky, nothing Jessop could have held over them."

"I'm glad," Molly said. "I like both of them. So, we're down to Susan and Carla, I guess. Oh, and Mr. Mattucci, according to you."

Randall didn't say anything. He got up. "Come on. These steps are like ice."

They walked on in silence for a few more blocks. When they reached the library, Randall said, "Feel like a nightcap? Maybe the Pine Inn?"

"I think I'll pass," Molly said. "I'm wiped out. Emma's probably home by now, too. Do you mind?"

"Nah. I just thought you might want to, that's all."

"Can I take a rain check? Maybe we could make an evening out of it. You know, drown my sorrows when Emma leaves."

"Hey, stop feeling guilty about feeling guilty. So you're a little possessive about her and maybe jealous of what Macomber can give her. It's natural."

"Possessive? Jealous? You're nuts. Whatever gave you that idea?"

"Come on, Molly. Like I said, it's natural. The mother instinct thing. It doesn't matter that she's not your kid. It matters that you've come to look at her that way. But you have to learn to let go. It happens to all of us."

Molly folded her arms and sighed. "I don't like the way you manage to see inside my head. I confess. I *am* being possessive and jealous. I'm afraid she'll want to stay with him after the trip. And how selfish I am to even think that way."

"Okay, she might. But I don't think so. She loves you, Molly." He wrapped an arm around her. "We all do."

The strength and comfort of Randall's arm nearly brought tears to Molly's eyes. An overwhelming feeling of wanting never to leave his affectionate embrace filled her. She leaned in and rested her head against his chest. "I've never known friends like all of you." She looked up at him. "Especially you."

The surprised grin on Randall's face made her smile. "I shocked you for once, huh?"

"I always look goofy when I'm touched."

"I'll remember that."

"Yeah, do that." He kept his arm around her and said, "Come on, let's get you home before Emma gets worried and calls the cops."

They crossed Ocean Avenue, then walked up the block to the shop. Randall hesitated. "You no doubt haven't changed the light-bulb over the stairs." He didn't wait for an answer. He steered Molly under the arcade to the courtyard. At the foot of the back stairs, he said, "Call me after you talk to Susan Jessop so I can liaise with Loomis. Make it first thing, okay?"

"I know. Time is of the essence. I have an idea she's an early riser. The leftover vestiges of the corporate woman. I'll give her a buzz at seven-thirty, ask her to meet me for coffee at eight."

"Works for me." He leaned over and gave Molly a quick peck on the cheek. "Get some sleep. Stop worrying. Life is good." He watched her smile. "It really is, if you let it."

When Molly reached the top of the stairs, she pulled out her key, then turned and waved. "I'll give that some thought."

"Yeah, do that, why don't you."

Molly was grinning when she unlocked the door and entered the living room. "I just might do that," she mumbled. She pulled off her jacket, dropped it on a chair, and headed for Emma's room. The door was open, and the lights were on. She found Emma sitting on the bed, hunched over her laptop.

Emma looked up. "Hey, have a nice time at Daria's?" Before Molly could answer, she said, "We saw a great new English movie. It reminded me of *Gosford Park*, the one we watched last week on TV? Oh, it was super. Marshall said we would be visiting grand houses like that when we go to England. He said I should make up a list of places I want to see, so I'm surfing the Net. I just left France."

"Marshall?" Molly said.

Emma's eyes had already moved back to the computer screen. "Hmm? Oh, he told me to call him that. He said I didn't have to call him Dad until I was ready. And Bitsy called. She said to tell you that she's taken care of my absence at school. Sister Phil is back from her trip, and she'll see my counselor tomorrow. Charles will pick me up at seven tomorrow morning. Isn't this exciting? New clothes and a trip to Europe? Awesome. I am so ready to explode!"

Molly had a sudden feeling of being asked to step into the waiting room while others decided the agenda. She should be grateful, but she still felt as if she were no longer relevant. She leaned over and kissed Emma on her forehead. "Don't stay up too late. You've got a long day ahead of you."

Emma looked up. "Oh, I guess Bitsy didn't tell you we're staying overnight in the City. She booked a suite for us at the Saint Francis. Did you know it was built in nineteen-hundred and four? Before that humongous earthquake? And they serve tea in the Compass Rose Lounge, and Bitsy said—"

"That's great, Emma. You'll love staying there, it's gorgeous," Molly said rather quickly. "I'm beat. See you in the morning. Oh, better set your alarm."

"Two steps ahead of you. I set it for six A.M. I'll try not to wake you."

Two steps ahead of me? It seems everyone else is, too! "I'll be up."

"Thanks for letting me go, Aunt Molly."

Molly stopped at the door. She was glad her back was to Emma, and she couldn't see the tear. *Letting go.* Yes, that's exactly what she was doing. In her heart, she knew she had to. No matter what. She turned back and smiled. "How could I not?" She blew Emma a kiss. "Sleep tight."

Molly also set her alarm clock for six A.M. She wouldn't dream of not being up and about when Bitsy and Charles arrived. She might even hit the beach until it was time to call Susan Jessop. She sure as hell wasn't going to mope around the apartment or search for imaginary dust in the shop.

After seeing Emma and Bitsy off, Molly headed for the beach. It was freezing, rain was threatening, and Molly gave up after ten minutes. She was out of breath by the time she'd trudged up the hill to Ocean

Avenue. She knew she'd been foolish to walk nonstop. Her legs ached and her lungs felt raw. Being out of shape was no excuse. She was overweight by more than ten pounds, and she still smoked. It was time to do something about both problems. In a few days, after Emma left, she would be back to frozen dinners and solitary nights in front of the TV. The twice-a-week dinners at Daria's would be a challenge. But she knew she could handle that. The weight situation could be remedied. The killer was trying to quit smoking. She laughed as that ran past her brain. It was a killer either way.

When Molly got back, she looked for Susan Jessop's telephone number. She hadn't given much thought to her excuse for calling. In fact, now that she thought about it, no one had offered any suggestions last night at Daria's. Because it had been her idea, she guessed they'd decided to leave it up to her.

Susan answered on the first ring. "Hi, Molly Doyle here. Have I caught you at a bad time?"

Molly could hear the surprise in Susan's voice. "Oh, Molly, hello. No. I was just leaving, but how nice to hear from you."

"I won't keep you, but I wondered if you had time for coffee this morning? I…well, I've been worried about you. The other night, and all?"

"That's so nice of you, but it really isn't necessary."

"Please," Molly said. "It would make me feel better."

"Why, thank you, Molly. Look, I've got some wiggle room in my schedule. When do you want to meet, and where?"

"How's the Village Corner at eight?"

"Perfect. See you then."

Molly hung up and then called Randall. "We're on. Eight at the Village Corner."

Susan Jessop found Molly in the patio of the small restaurant and sat down at precisely eight A.M. Molly looked at her watch, and laughed. "To the minute exactly. I wish I could be that organized. I'm usually late for things, especially opening the shop. The only way I can be on time is to be someplace early."

"My first husband," Susan said, "was a stickler for promptness. I guess it's ingrained in me now. But I like to be well organized, so it was easy for me." Susan looked around at the early morning crowd. "This must be a favorite local hangout. I can't say that I blame people. It's really quaint and quite charming."

"I agree. I usually stop at Tosca's in the morning, but I thought you'd enjoy coming here. So, Susan, how are you holding up? This ordeal must be taking its toll. I think it's just so awe-inspiring the way you've conducted yourself. I don't know if I would be as charitable if I were in your place."

Molly thought Susan almost preened. Her shoulders actually seemed to move like a peacock ready to unfurl his tail. "I have to admit it wasn't easy at first. But when I realized how difficult it was for Carla, too, I just couldn't hold a grudge."

After they gave their order to the waitress, Molly said, "You know, you should think about getting away. I mean, there's no reason for you to stay, is there?"

"I don't think that new sheriff's detective on the case would want me to leave. He called just before you did this morning and wants to see me later today. I don't know how many times I'm going to be interviewed, but I must admit, I'm growing weary."

"Well, I'd certainly ask him, if I were you," Molly said. "They can't keep you here forever, you know." Molly was just about to mention Carla's trip when the waitress appeared with their order. She decided not to rush into it yet. She knew Susan wasn't a fool, and the last thing she needed was for her to realize this so-called get-together was a setup. They had each ordered croissants. When Molly had two bites left, she said, "If Carla can take off, why can't you?"

Molly winced when she heard Susan's knife clang against her dish. "Really? Where is she going?" Susan asked.

"South America. A vintner's convention, or something. She didn't tell you?"

Molly watched Susan slowly pick up her cup. She knew Susan needed time to come up with an answer. The peacock image had morphed into a cheetah ready to pounce. Susan's shoulders turned stiff, rising a half inch. Molly could see the tension in her neck.

"Oh, now that I think of it," Susan finally said, "she may have.

With all that's been going on, I probably missed it. When is she leaving?"

Molly pretended to think. "Hmm. I think it's the end of the week, when school is out. Michelle told Emma, that's how I know."

"But South America? Just for a wine conference? I'd think she'd send her winemaker or marketing man. What on earth does she really know about wine?"

Molly shrugged. "Beats me. She's taking Michelle with her, so maybe she plans to make it a time to reflect?" Molly saw Susan sit up straighter in her chair, getting in position to bolt. She didn't dare try to see if Randall had managed to get a table by the windows.

Susan pulled her cell phone from her jacket pocket. "Excuse me, Molly. I've got this on vibrate and a call is coming in." Susan smiled at Molly as she listened to the caller. "Of course not, I'm just having coffee with a friend. I can come right over. No, she won't mind. Wonderful, give me about fifteen minutes." Susan closed her cell, and said, "My realtor. She's found a condo in Pebble Beach she thinks I'll like, but I've got to move on it quick if I want it." She gave Molly a wide smile, "You don't mind, do you? Maybe we can do this again?"

"Of course not. I know what this real estate climate is like here." Molly waved her hands. "Go, go!"

When Susan reached in her bag for her wallet, Molly said, "Don't be silly. My treat. You get the next one."

Susan rose quickly. "I'll take you up on that."

Molly watched Susan weave her way through the tables out of the patio, and saw Loomis exit at the same time. She wondered if the call was legit, or a ruse to leave. She knew Susan was fuming. Her eyes had gone dead when Molly mentioned South America. She purposely hadn't said Peru. She was banking on Susan thinking it was Brazil or Argentina, or whatever country it was that didn't extradite. Molly couldn't remember and didn't really care. All she did care about was that Susan fell for it.

Randall was at her table. He took Susan's chair and signaled the waitress. "Looks like it worked. She got out of here fast. I saw her pull out her cell. Who called her, do you know?"

"I'm not sure if there was a call. She said she had it on vibrate. She said it was her realtor and had to leave to see a condo real quick."

"Plausible, but probably a lie. We'll know when Loomis calls. So, did she spill her coffee when you told her about Carla leaving?"

"No, but she was surprised. She tried to hide it, but I could tell."

When the waitress appeared, Randall handed her a twenty. "My tab inside, and this one, too." He looked at Molly and grinned. "Courtesy of the Carmel Police Department." He pushed back from the table. "Gotta run. I'll stop by the shop later. Good job, Molly Doyle."

Molly watched him leave. After a moment, she left the small café with a grin on her face. That's it, she thought, use me up and leave. Seems to be my role in life these days. What the hell, she thought, I'm a big girl. I can take the knocks. She stopped at the corner and looked around. She really couldn't remember being this happy anywhere. And suddenly, she *was* happy. Her grin grew as she stepped off the curb. She was surrounded by people who cared for her. Emma had discovered her father was alive, and he not only wanted to know her, he was ready to give her the damn moon. If Emma decided to live with him, then Molly knew she would have to accept it. She'd known that from the start. It was Emma's life after all.

Besides, she mused, I may have helped solve another case, and that was something to be happy about. Even more, she wasn't in the middle of it this time. Well, close to the middle, but not the same as the other times. That alone was cause for celebration. That sudden relief vanished as quickly as it had appeared, and stopped Molly in her tracks. What if Susan were telling the truth, and she really was meeting a realtor? The impetus they had been hoping for might not happen. Suppose Susan took the news of Carla leaving for South America as a good idea. She might also think it's time to hit the road. With both of them gone, out of reach of the long arm of the law, what then?

Molly hurried back to the shop. She hoped Randall had called to let her know if they had been right and Susan had high-tailed it to Bello Lago. There were no calls on the answering machine. She called Randall on his cell and got his voice mail. She sat at her desk and tried to figure out some way to get the ball rolling, just in case. And then she remembered the Montelupo dishes. She felt like slapping her forehead and shouting, Dolt! She'd forgotten to fax Carla an evaluation estimate. She hadn't even looked them up in her books or checked her favorite Internet data site for auction results.

It took her an hour to get the information she needed. She pulled out the auction consignment agreement that Max's attorney had made for her, and filled it out. She listed the dishes, and the current fair market value and entered all of Carla's information. The agreement would give Molly the authority to consign the dishes at the auction of her choice, to insure and ship them, and to agree to the auction company's low and high estimate. She signed her name with a flourish. All that was needed was Carla's signature.

When she was ready to leave, she left the CLOSED sign in the front window. She had no idea how long she'd be gone. Stirring up some action between Susan and Carla was worth losing a sale or two. Bitsy had had a good weekend, and besides, Monday was always slow. She tried Randall again with no success. Damn him. He promised to call her. He should know how curious she would be.

Molly headed up Ocean Avenue toward Highway One on her way to Bello Lago. It was gridlock all the way, weekenders leaving for home. The right merge onto Highway One going south was a nightmare as usual. She never could understand why drivers didn't follow the civilized rule of alternating as the one lane became two. The locals liked to blame it on the big-city tourists who brought their aggressive driving habits with them on vacation. But Molly knew that was baloney. She'd seen locals pull the same me-first routine more than once.

She was hoping to use the auction-consignment agreement as an excuse to find out whether Susan had contacted Carla. She knew Carla would be at the winery. Michelle had told Emma that her mother practically lived there, trying to cram every bit of winemaking knowledge into a mini-course. When she passed Carmel Middle School, Molly pulled over and called Randall again. She began to wonder if he ever checked his calls. And then she wondered if he was ignoring her. By the time she reached the entrance to Bello Lago, she had tried Randall once more. This time she left a message telling him where she was and what she hoped to accomplish.

Molly parked the van in the visitor's parking area. She wasn't surprised to see it empty. The tasting room wouldn't reopen for another week. But she'd hoped to see at least one car there. Maybe Susan parked in the employee's area by the office in the back. She was about to drive there when her cell phone rang. It was Randall.

"What the hell do you think you're doing? Who told you to—"

"Why didn't you call me like you promised? Did Susan rush to Carla, or what? And don't you dare yell at me!"

"I'm not yelling, for crissakes! Bad connection, okay? Yeah, she high-tailed it right for Carla. Now don't get in the middle of this, understand? Stay out of it."

Molly was staring out the window, and was about to tell Randall where to go, when she said, "There's that man again. The one with that hat? Remember I told you about him? He just drove in. He's in that old beat-up truck."

"What color is the truck?" Randall asked.

"Rusted green."

"Shit! Did he see you?"

"I don't know. I don't think so." Molly wasn't sure if Randall heard her. It sounded as if he'd put the phone to his chest. She could faintly hear him yelling to someone. She thought she heard him swearing. In fact, she was positive he'd rattled off a few choice words. "Randall? What's going on?"

"Get out of there, right now. That's an order."

"Why? What's he got to do with anything? Don't tell me you're running after illegals now," she laughed.

"Don't argue with me. Leave!"

Molly started the van and began backing out, "Okay, okay. I'm going." She snapped her cell shut and pulled away from the parking area. She could still see the truck as it drove past the small sample vineyard. She wondered if he was going to the old shack. Randall's orders to leave had made her curious, and she wanted to know why her seeing this man again had disturbed him. As she passed the offices, she noticed Carla's car wasn't there. Maybe Susan had gone to her home instead. Molly would have loved to have been a fly on the wall at that little cat fight.

Molly saw the green truck pull up to the shack. She slowed at the edge of the vineyard. She was about to turn off the engine when her cell rang.

Randall's tone was deadlier than Molly had ever heard. "I told you to leave, did I not? You're about to make me lose my cool." Each word was blistering enough to make Molly's jaw drop.

"I just wanted to—"

"I don't give a damn what you wanted. He's—"

"He's out of the truck," Molly said, "and he's got a rifle slung over his shoulder. He's gone into the shack." She began to laugh, "You should see the pants he's wearing. They're tucked into funny-looking boots with laces damn near up to his knees. He looks like one of those old-fashioned European hunters you'd see in foreign films."

"I know what's he's wearing. Get out of there, *I mean it, Molly!*"

"Where are you? Are you *here*? Randall? Answer me!"

# Chapter 31

MOLLY JERKED so violently when she heard the shot, she almost choked herself with the seat belt. Her knuckles were white as she gripped the steering wheel. It could have been several seconds, or minutes, she wasn't sure, when she saw Randall and Lieutenant Stuart roar up in an unmarked car next to her.

Randall was out of the car and at her open window. "You even try to leave this car, I'll cuff you, understand? Go home!"

Molly barely moved. She blinked twice, hoping he'd take that for her answer.

Randall turned to Stuart. He withdrew his weapon. "I'm right behind you."

When Molly heard the sound of the safety on Randall's gun being released, she winced. She started the car, then backed down the road until she could turn around. She was shaking as she pulled back into the visitor's parking lot. Her hands were ice cold as she fumbled in her tote for a cigarette. She tore one out, and had to use two hands to hold the Zippo as she lit the cigarette wobbling between her trembling lips.

A fearful silence surrounded her. It was as if the world had stopped, waiting breathlessly with her, praying another gun shot would not be heard. Finally, after a succession of rapid Hail Marys, Molly saw the car Randall and Stuart had been in drive slowly toward her.

Randall parked next to her and got out. He climbed into the passenger seat. "I knew you wouldn't go home. Damn it, Molly, why won't you listen to me?" He reached for the pack of cigarettes she'd thrown on the dash. "I'm out of cigars." He lit it, then exhaled slowly, and stared out the window.

"What happened?" she finally managed. "Who is that man?"

Randall didn't answer right away. He took another drag, then said, "Dando Osa. Mattucci's cook. He's our shooter. He killed Todd Jessop."

"Oh, my God. But, the shot I heard?"

"He blew his head off. The pact was complete."

"The *what?*"

Randall turned to look at Molly. "Mattucci and Osa had a pact. It's all laid out in a letter. It's even notarized! The old man knew he was dying. He had a month or two at the most. It wasn't the stroke. It was inoperable cancer. The family was coming apart. Carla's kid, Nicky, was on the outs with him because of Testino Giordano. Jessop was using Carla as a punching bag and threatening to ruin Bello Lago. The old man had to get things clear for his daughter, Carla. So, he and Osa worked up the plan to ace Jessop, and then Mattucci was going to kill himself and leave a confession. Osa was supposed to leave the country, but things got out of hand when Susan showed up at Mattucci's ranch."

Randall stubbed out the cigarette. He reached for the pack again, then put it back. He closed his eyes for a moment, then turned back to Molly. "Susan Jessop is dead. Mattucci shot her, then turned the gun on himself."

Molly slumped. "No! Oh, no!"

Randall reached out for her. "It's not your fault. It…it just played out that way."

Molly threw off his hand. "Don't! Don't try to…oh, God! If only I hadn't told her about Carla leaving."

"Molly, listen to me. Susan would have found out anyway. Who knows it still wouldn't have gone down that way."

Molly was having a hard time breathing. She forced herself to take in gulps of air. "How…how do you know all of this?"

"Carla was at the ranch. Susan showed up with the photos right after she left you. She confronted Carla and the old man. She accused Carla of running out on her. She threatened to give the photos to the press if Carla took off. Carla said her father offered Susan money to keep quiet, but she wasn't having any of that. She had a chance, she'd said, to be somebody on her own. Apparently, she'd already set things in motion. She had an agent and a book deal, and was ready to hit the talk shows.

"Carla said the old man went crazy. It was one thing to have a little notoriety about the murder, but that would eventually die down. But to have his daughter's picture at a lap dancing club in a gossip rag was more than he would stand for. The shame to the family would have been too much to bear. Mattucci went ballistic, Carla said, when Susan laughed in his face and said what a hypocrite he was. He didn't mind murder, but a sexy dance was shameful? That's when he shot her, then turned the gun on himself. Carla claims she tried to stop him, but it happened too fast."

"I was right about her," Molly finally managed. "Wasn't I?"

"Yeah, you nailed her pretty damn good."

"But why would that poor man, Mr. Osa, kill himself, too? Why didn't he run?"

Randall shook his head. "I guess he realized there wasn't time." Randall pulled out another cigarette, then lit it. "I think memories of jail, when he was a kid, never left him. Maybe he figured really dead was better than the living dead."

Molly thought about that. "I'd never have guessed he was the killer."

Randall gave Molly one of his lopsided grins. "Yeah? Well, that's a first. Seems like you've beaten me to the punch more than I like."

"Are you saying you knew it was Osa?"

"I had my eye on him early on. Don't ask, okay? Call it gut instinct. But you cinched it when you found the climbing gear. When Lucero's father told Dan that Osa always set up the shooting blinds on the hunting trips, I knew I was right. I just wasn't sure how to smoke him out. Stuart wanted to bring him in for questioning, but we knew the guy wouldn't cave. Hell, he'd lived through a Spanish jail. This was no amateur. By the way, his tongue was never cut out. That was baloney. And he spoke pretty good English. Dan's father told us that, too. Osa had heard the rumors. Him and the old man and a few close friends thought they were funny and played along. I knew all of this already. I had already checked with a rancher friend in Nevada. He's Basque, and knew Osa."

"What about Carla now? I mean the poison, the belladonna?"

"Osa copped to that in the letter. He claims he was the one feeding it to Jessop. They ate at the ranch most of the time."

"Do you believe that?" Molly asked.

"Not for a minute. But we can't prove it now."

"So, Mr. Mattucci got his wish. Carla is free and clear."

"Looks that way."

"And Susan—"

"Don't, Molly. Remember, she was guilty, too. You have to let it go, understand?"

Molly looked at him. "I don't think I can do that, but I'll try."

They heard the sirens before they saw the sheriff's patrol cars and an ambulance pull up the long drive. "Gotta go," Randall said. He took hold of her hand. He gave it a reassuring squeeze. "I'll see you later. Call Daria, maybe we can switch nights."

"I'm okay. Stop worrying. Go do what you need to do. I'll call her."

Molly's knees felt as if they had been glued to the floor of the Carmel Mission. She could have slipped into a pew and taken advantage of the kneeler, but she didn't feel she had the right to such comfort. At least not for Susan Jessop's rosary. She had walked up the center aisle and knelt before the altar. Her head was bowed so low it almost reached her chest. The remorse she felt in playing a role in Susan's death deserved nothing less in her mind. When it came time to offer rosaries for Domenico Mattucci and Dando Osa, she felt almost as much guilt. Her actions had accelerated their plans, and in some way, she felt she had been responsible for Osa's death as well. Others, she knew, might argue that point, but nonetheless, it was what she felt, and that was all that mattered.

Molly's legs were stiff and her knees were sore when she walked back down the aisle. She paused at the last pew, then turned back to look at the altar. Her eyes fixed on the crucifix. She knew she wasn't ready to leave. She felt compelled to stay in the quiet serenity of the church. The lingering scent of incense and burned candles offered a sense of peace she so badly needed. She took a seat and closed her eyes. She paid little attention to the sound of footsteps behind her, thinking it was a tourist or another local slipping in. When she felt, rather than heard someone moving down the empty pew toward her, she opened her eyes.

Marshall Macomber stood next to her. "I hope I'm not intruding. I passed you on Rio Road and had an idea you were headed here. When I saw you at the altar, I waited outside."

"You're not intruding. I was about to leave anyway."

Macomber sat next to her. He nodded toward the altar. "I hope I'm not the cause of your lengthy stay."

Molly's smile was weaker than she'd meant it to be. "No, not at all."

"I don't suppose you want to tell me. It's not as if we're close friends, but, well, I hope that will change. We *are* related, somewhat."

When Molly didn't answer, he said, "I was hoping to catch you before I leave. I wanted to let you know that I've made the travel plans, and I'll be flying back on Friday to fetch Emma. I've hired a car to take us to San Francisco. From there, we'll fly direct to London."

"You'll keep in touch, won't you? Not just postcards…but a call every now and then?"

"How does once a week sound? We'll set a day. Maybe Friday?"

Molly felt her throat tighten. She forced her voice to sound happy. "Friday is good. It's just that I'd want to know—"

Macomber saw how hard this was for Molly, and how much she would miss Emma. "She'll be fine. I promise. And I'll have her back to you in plenty of time for the fall semester." He reached into his jacket and pulled out a travel agent's brochure. "I thought you'd like to see our itinerary."

Somehow, Molly wasn't surprised when she saw the list of hotels. She had a feeling Marshall Macomber traveled well and that her earlier demand wasn't necessary. She had just wanted to be on record as to what she expected for Emma. He'd booked the Dorchester in London, the Crillon in Paris, in Venice the Gritti Palace, and in Rome, the Majestic. She handed the brochure back to him. Her eyes were bright, with a hint of amusement. "I think these will do."

~

Molly called Daria when she got back to the shop. She told her what had happened at Bello Lago. "I know," Daria said. "It's already on the news. I didn't know you were there. And Carla is getting away with murder? I can't believe this. Look, Molly, take a nap, read a good book, or better yet, go see a movie. Just don't dwell on what you can't change. I should know, huh?"

"You're right, as usual. It's still hard not to think about it though. But I'll try. Honest. See you tonight."

Molly left the CLOSED sign in the window. She wasn't in the mood to face people. Treasures was open seven days a week. A day or two without a sale wouldn't make a blip on Max's bottom line. Besides, he'd given her the option, from day one, to set the shop's schedule. He'd been surprised that Molly had opted to be open each day. But then, she'd been hungry when she had first landed in Carmel. Every dollar earned from her commissions and personal sales made the chance to leave and to open her own shop someday less a dream and more a reality. That was then. Now, leaving Carmel was no longer in her game plan. She knew she could stay here until she was old, creaky, and gray. Even if Emma decided to live with her father, Molly knew she would still see her. And then, of course, she had wonderful friends here. What more could she possibly want?

Molly spent the rest of the day updating her inventory database, catching up on e-mail queries from the shop's website, sending e-mail notices to out-of-town clients about new merchandise, and then, finally, an e-mail to Cleo in London. She told her about Marshall Macomber and that he and Emma would be in London next week. She gave her the hotel information and asked her to give them a call, hoping they might meet for lunch or dinner. Molly went on to tell Cleo how much she would adore Emma, and hint-hint, she might find Macomber interesting as well.

At a quarter to six, Molly left for Daria's. She walked slowly, enjoying the early evening chill. The scent of wood fires from homes, older shops with fireplaces, and new restaurants with open wood-burning ovens vied with the tangy salt air blowing up Ocean Avenue from Carmel Beach. It was June, but not yet summer for Carmel. Warm days and balmy nights would have to wait a couple of months. Molly pulled up the shawl collar of her sweater and filled her lungs with the heady perfume of Carmel.

Randall, Loomis, and Lucero were already in the back room. Daria was at the far end of the room on the telephone. Molly put her hand up, "No, don't get up, please. I insist. I can find my way."

Lucero grinned. "That's our Molly. You okay, then?"

Molly took her regular place next to Randall. She shrugged. "Sure. Why not?"

Randall eyed her. "Don't kid kidders, okay?"

"I'm okay, honest. I've had a full day to think things over. Like you always say, what happens, happens. End of story, right?"

"That pretty well sums it up," Loomis said kindly. "It's a trick we ex-cops learn early on."

Her phone call over, Daria was at Molly's side. She leaned over to hug her. "I think," Daria said, "it's not a trick most of us can handle."

Dinner was even more sumptuous than normal. There were only five of them at the table, but the platters of vitello tonnato, a salad of arugula and tomato with lemony dressing, vermicelli with clams, and veal scaloppini, were enough to feed ten. The wine on the table bore labels of a new winery Daria was thinking of adding to the restaurant's wine list. Much of the conversation centered on sports, Emma's trip, and the new wine, and the compliments to the chef were boisterous.

It was as if Todd Jessop had never entered their lives.

The closest they came to the subject was when Lucero said, "By the way, dinner tonight is on me. A little gift to my friends for all their help."

When Molly left with Daria to clear the empty platters, Randall said to Loomis, "I've got a top-priority job for you." He looked at Lucero next. "If you don't mind my stealing your top investigator for a side job?"

"For you? Hey, be my guest. What's up?"

"Missing person," Randall said. "I've got a full jacket on him for you."

Loomis's eyes lit up. "A walk in the park. Who is it?"

"Name is Derek Porter."

Randall looked at Lucero. He saw Lucero's famous wide grin, the one he usually saved for constituents, break free. He gave Randall a knowing nod. "This'll be on the house, Chief. I mean, hey, he's a fugitive, right?"

Loomis asked, "And he is?"

"Molly's errant husband. I want you to find the bastard. It's time this was settled."

Loomis gave out a soft whistle. "Like that, huh?

When Randall didn't reply, Loomis probed, "And when I find him? What then?"

Randall filled his wineglass, pulled out a cigar, and said, "You leave that up to me."

Molly heard Randall's answer when she walked in. "What's going on now? Leave what up to you?"

"Oh, just a new project Randall's working on," Loomis answered.

Molly sat down and reached for her coffee. "New case, Chief?"

"You might say that," Randall replied.

Molly laughed. "Looks like I'm on a need-to-know basis again. But you'll tell us all later, right?"

Randall smiled. "Bet on it. And then some."

ELAINE FLINN is the Barry Award-winning author of *Tagged for Murder*. Her first book in the series, *Dealing in Murder*, was nominated for the Agatha, Gumshoe, Barry, and Anthony awards. An antiques dealer for many years, Flinn peeks behind the scenes of the mystique, showing her readers how to avoid fakes and unscrupulous hucksters. Her website, which can be found at www.elaineflinn.com, emphasizes *caveat emptor*—let the buyer beware—and she can be visited and e-mailed there.

Between trips back and forth from Carmel to her new home in Eugene, Oregon, Flinn is working on the next Molly Doyle mystery.

# MORE MYSTERIES
## FROM PERSEVERANCE PRESS
### *For the New Golden Age*

JON L. BREEN
**Eye of God**
ISBN 978-1-880284-89-6

TAFFY CANNON
ROXANNE PRESCOTT SERIES
**Guns and Roses**
*Agatha and Macavity Award
nominee, Best Novel*
ISBN 978-1-880284-34-6

**Blood Matters**
ISBN 978-1-880284-86-5

**Open Season on Lawyers**
ISBN 978-1-880284-51-3

**Paradise Lost**
ISBN 978-1-880284-80-3

LAURA CRUM
GAIL MCCARTHY SERIES
**Moonblind**
ISBN 978-1-880284-90-2

JEANNE M. DAMS
HILDA JOHANSSON SERIES
**Crimson Snow**
ISBN 978-1-880284-79-7

KATHY LYNN EMERSON
LADY APPLETON SERIES
**Face Down Below
the Banqueting House**
ISBN 978-1-880284-71-1

**Face Down Beside
St. Anne's Well**
ISBN 978-1-880284-82-7

**Face Down O'er the Border**
ISBN 978-1-880284-91-9

ELAINE FLINN
MOLLY DOYLE SERIES
**Deadly Vintage**
ISBN 978-1-880284-87-2

HAL GLATZER
KATY GREEN SERIES
**Too Dead To Swing**
ISBN 978-1-880284-53-7

**A Fugue in Hell's Kitchen**
ISBN 978-1-880284-70-4

**The Last Full Measure**
ISBN 978-1-880284-84-1

PATRICIA GUIVER
DELILAH DOOLITTLE PET
DETECTIVE SERIES
**The Beastly Bloodline**
ISBN 978-1-880284-69-8

NANCY BAKER JACOBS
**Flash Point**
ISBN 978-1-880284-56-8

JANET LAPIERRE
PORT SILVA SERIES
**Baby Mine**
ISBN 978-1-880284-32-2

**Keepers**
*Shamus Award nominee,
Best Paperback Original*
ISBN 978-1-880284-44-5

**Death Duties**
ISBN 978-1-880284-74-2

**Family Business**
ISBN 978-1-880284-85-8

VALERIE S. MALMONT
TORI MIRACLE SERIES
**Death, Bones, and Stately Homes**
ISBN 978-1-880284-65-0

DENISE OSBORNE
FENG SHUI SERIES
**Evil Intentions**
ISBN 978-1-880284-77-3

LEV RAPHAEL
NICK HOFFMAN SERIES
**Tropic of Murder**
ISBN 978-1-880284-68-1

**Hot Rocks**
ISBN 978-1-880284-83-4

LORA ROBERTS
BRIDGET MONTROSE SERIES
**Another Fine Mess**
ISBN 978-1-880284-54-4

SHERLOCK HOLMES SERIES
**The Affair of the Incognito Tenant**
ISBN 978-1-880284-67-4

REBECCA ROTHENBERG
BOTANICAL SERIES
**The Tumbleweed Murders**
(completed by Taffy Cannon)
ISBN 978-1-880284-43-8

SHELLEY SINGER
JAKE SAMSON & ROSIE VICENTE SERIES
**Royal Flush**
ISBN 978-1-880284-33-9

NANCY TESLER
BIOFEEDBACK SERIES
**Slippery Slopes and Other Deadly Things**
ISBN 978-1-880284-58-2

PENNY WARNER
CONNOR WESTPHAL SERIES
**Blind Side**
ISBN 978-1-880284-42-1

**Silence Is Golden**
ISBN 978-1-880284-66-7

ERIC WRIGHT
JOE BARLEY SERIES
**The Kidnapping of Rosie Dawn**
*Barry Award, Best Paperback Original. Edgar, Ellis, and Anthony Award nominee*
ISBN 978-1-880284-40-7

*REFERENCE/ MYSTERY WRITING*

KATHY LYNN EMERSON
**How To Write Killer Historical Mysteries: The Art and Adventure of Sleuthing Through the Past**
*(forthcoming)*
ISBN 978-1-880284-92-6

CAROLYN WHEAT
**How To Write Killer Fiction: The Funhouse of Mystery & the Roller Coaster of Suspense**
ISBN 978-1-880284-62-9

**Available from your local bookstore or from Perseverance Press/John Daniel & Co. at (800) 662-8351 or www.danielpublishing.com/perseverance.**